STRANGLED INTUITION:

"An endearing cast with their own codes of conduct."
—*Mysterious Women*

"Cally is a very refreshing and likable character."
—*The Romance Readers Connection*

PRAISE FOR
BODY OF INTUITION:

"Fans of Jaqueline Girdner's Kate Jasper series will relish Claire Daniels' new Cally Lazar series. Cane-wielding Cally and the rest of the cast are a delight."
—Jan Dean, editor of *Murder Most Cozy*

"Prognosis: original, innovative and unique. Don't miss Cally Lazar's fresh approach to problem-solving. Claire Daniels creates an 'energetic' plot with captivating characters. *Body of Intuition* will open up your mind to new perspectives."
—Janet A. Rudolph, editor of *Mystery Readers Journal*

"A riveting plot. Absorbing and endlessly entertaining."
—Lynne Murray, author of *A Ton of Trouble*

"Whether your aura is serenely silver or your karma needs a tune-up, you'll enjoy following intuitive healer Cally Lazar as she uses her unusual talents to find a murderer at a Love Seminar."
—Kate Derie, editor of *The Deadly Directory*

"Daniels's portrayal of the New Age milieu is both realistic and a bit tongue in cheek."
—*The Drood Review of Mystery*

"Hilarious and outrageous . . . Murder is no laughing matter, but in Claire Daniels' capable hands, catching a murderer has never been so amusing."
—Sandie Herron, *I Love a Mystery*

"Claire Daniels has written a creative New Age psychic mystery starring a heroine that is impossible not to like."
—*Midwest Book Review*

Karma Crime Mysteries by Claire Daniels

BODY OF INTUITION
STRANGLED INTUITION
CRUEL AND UNUSUAL INTUITION

CRUEL AND UNUSUAL INTUITION

CLAIRE DANIELS

BERKLEY PRIME CRIME, NEW YORK

THE BERKLEY PUBLISHING GROUP
Published by the Penguin Group
Penguin Group (USA) Inc.
375 Hudson Street, New York, New York 10014, USA
Penguin Group (Canada), 10 Alcorn Avenue, Toronto, Ontario M4V 3B2, Canada
(a division of Pearson Penguin Canada Inc.)
Penguin Books Ltd., 80 Strand, London WC2R 0RL, England
Penguin Group Ireland, 25 St. Stephen's Green, Dublin 2, Ireland (a division of Penguin Books Ltd.)
Penguin Group (Australia), 250 Camberwell Road, Camberwell, Victoria 3124, Australia
(a division of Pearson Australia Group Pty. Ltd.)
Penguin Books India Pvt. Ltd., 11 Community Centre, Panchsheel Park, New Delhi—110 017, India
Penguin Group (NZ), Cnr. Airborne and Rosedale Roads, Albany, Auckland 1310, New Zealand
(a division of Pearson New Zealand Ltd.)
Penguin Books (South Africa) (Pty.) Ltd., 24 Sturdee Avenue, Rosebank, Johannesburg 2196,
South Africa

Penguin Books Ltd., Registered Offices: 80 Strand, London WC2R 0RL, England

This is a work of fiction. Names, characters, places, and incidents either are the product of the author's imagination or are used fictitiously, and any resemblance to actual persons, living or dead, business establishments, events, or locales is entirely coincidental.

CRUEL AND UNUSUAL INTUITION

A Berkley Prime Crime Book / published by arrangement with the author

PRINTING HISTORY
Berkley Prime Crime edition / March 2005

Copyright © 2005 by Jaqueline Girdner.
Cover illustration by One by Two.
Cover design by Lesley Worrell.

ISBN: 0-425-20158-9

BERKLEY PRIME CRIME®
Berkley Prime Crime Books are published by The Berkley Publishing Group,
a division of Penguin Group (USA) Inc.
375 Hudson Street, New York, New York 10014.
BERKLEY PRIME CRIME is a registered trademark of Penguin Group (USA) Inc.
The Berkley Prime Crime design is a trademark belonging to Penguin Group (USA) Inc.

PRINTED IN THE UNITED STATES OF AMERICA

10 9 8 7 6 5 4 3 2 1

DEDICATION

To Lynne Murray, with great affection, for all the telephonic whine and jeez parties.

ACKNOWLEDGMENT

I would like to acknowledge all the true alternative healers for their bravery, intelligence, truth-seeking, and compassion.

CAST OF CHARACTERS

PARTICIPANTS IN THE CHAKRA COMMITMENT INTENSIVE WORKSHOP:

Cally Lazar: Recovering attorney, "cane-fu" master, and intuitive energy healer whose commitment to her chakras vies with her commitment to the truth.

Dr. Aurora Hart: Leader of the Chakra Commitment movement. Her dedication to healing physical and spiritual energy centers of the human body has vastly enriched her . . . financially speaking.

Quinn Vogel: Dr. Hart's staff leader. Does he have his own ambitions?

Sara Oshima: Dr. Hart's third in command, a nursing school dropout.

Ira: Sara's boyfriend . . . for the moment.

Ed Lau: A Hawaiian chi gung practitioner. He is one of the most relaxed people Cally has ever met until Hawaii is mentioned.

Fran Marquez: A nurse who has invented an "energy wand" . . . and is sure everyone is trying to steal it.

Judd Nyman: An ex-architect who is certified in reflexology and Thai massage. He learned to be bossy on his own.

Orson Nyman: Judd's son, a thirteen-year-old expert in biochemistry.

Raleigh Hutchinson: Former lead singer for the Booi Brothers, he heals by tonal resonance. Now, if only *he* could calm down.

Dotty Booth: Aromatherapist. She can't find it in her chakras to forgive Dr. Hart's dismissal of her grief over the passing of her cat, Juniper.

Kim Welch: Psychiatrist. After all those years of school, she's decided energy work is more powerful than Freud.

Craig Zweig: Psychic reader of "entities" who have passed away but not on and out. These lingering spirits haunt his nightmares.

Taj Gemayel: Young past-life-regression worker, and Don Juan. Even *he* can't tell if his work is for real.

CALLY'S COHORTS:

Warren Kapp: Cally's octogenarian friend, billed as the Melvin Belli of Glasse County. He just wishes he could outfox Cally in cane-fu as well as he could have in court.

Dee-Dee Lee: A hypnotist and Cally's friend. She didn't sign on for the Chakra Commitment plan.

Joan Hussein: Former colleague and current pal, Joan practices law and good sense.

York, Geneva, Arnot, and Melinda Lazar: Cally's siblings. They're there to help . . . really!

Roy Beaumont: Cally's sweetie, momentarily safe in Kentucky. He worries that he causes the "darkness" engulfing Cally.

RESIDENTS OF SWANTON:

Heidi and Bob Jinnah: Nervous owners of the Swanton Hills Lodge.

Chief Phlug: Of the Swanton Police Department.

Sergeant DiMarco, Officer Diem, and Officer Jones: Also of the Swanton Police Department.

Monty English: Tour guide and guiding gossip of Swanton.

ONE

The third day of the intensive was certainly tense.

"Fran, I know you hid your energy wand in your backpack," Dr. Aurora Hart said, her tone uncharacteristically kind for the moment. She looked right into Fran's dark eyes, her own blue eyes intense. Her voice roughened. "You don't have to hide it from me. I won't steal it. Get over it, okay?"

Fran Marquez looped the strap of her backpack over the curved wooden frame of her chair and sat down at the long table set for twelve at the Best Fortune Chinese Restaurant. She didn't attempt to answer Dr. Hart. Her classic Amerind features were passive, but unyielding. Fran had been a nurse before she developed her energy wand. When she hit forty, she began her own practice, using the energy wand as its main tool. She knew how to keep her feelings away from her face, that was for sure. All I could see were her high adobe-colored cheekbones and the dark glint of her eyes under the wings of her black pageboy.

Dr. Hart turned away from Fran, shaking her long, blonde, cornrowed hair so that shiny beads flashed. It was a practiced move. Dr. Aurora Hart was a beautiful woman at fifty-something, as well as a rich and gifted one. Her full lips and wide eyes set in a perfect heart-shaped face could have made her a model or an actress. But instead, she was a medical doctor turned energy healer, leader of the Chakra Commitment movement, writer, speaker, and business-woman. I should have said businesswoman first, actually. A full chakra commitment amounted to about five thousand dollars a year for at least four years.

All of the rest of us at the table, besides her staff leader, Quinn Vogel, were here as her temporary students. We were *paying* temporary students, although I don't think any of us were going to sign up for the full program after the verbal abuse we'd taken over the last three days. Was I hav-ing a good time on that Saturday in the heart of the wine country? Was I committed to my chakras? Well, maybe my actual chakras. But I wasn't committed to Dr. Hart's vision of my chakras. Actually, I was very tired of Dr. Hart's pro-gram if the truth be told. And I knew I wasn't alone in my feelings. Dr. Hart seemed to be a real intuitive, but that was as far as her sensitivity went.

Dr. Hart's intense eyes moved toward the only remain-ing empty space at the table, the seat where Sara Oshima, her third in command, should have been sitting.   .

"She'll be here," Quinn assured his boss, lightly touching her hand. Quinn wasn't even thirty, but his long, lean hound-dog face was serious and his voice was edged with nervous-ness.

"Of course she will," Dr. Hart agreed, smiling so that her white teeth sparkled. "She works for me. If she isn't com-mitted enough to show up for lunch, she can find a new job."

I tried to think about food, looking at the menu in my hand. Food, not anger, right? I reminded myself that I was a healer. The Szechuan prawns looked interesting. Anger wasn't good for me. The moo shu might be tasty. Resent-ment wasn't good for me. Soup, I told myself, think about soup. Actually, Dr. Hart wasn't good for me. And the inten-sive wasn't over yet. Dr. Hart still had to do her speech, and then we'd be back to work with her. I closed my eyes and took a deep cleansing breath.

When I'd been invited to be one of nine special students chosen for a "limited" intensive before and after Dr. Aurora Hart's public appearance to the unchosen, I'd been truly excited. I'd already read Dr. Hart's books. I even had her audio tapes. She was a good writer, a good speaker. But I'd decided that one thing about her hadn't shown up in her books and tapes. She could be mean-spirited. In fact, she could be downright cruel. That became evident the first day we were together in the meeting room of the Swanton Hills Lodge located conveniently near the Boy Scout Hall where she was to speak this afternoon. She'd taken shots at all of us.

She began by making fun of her own staff members, Quinn Vogel and Sara Oshima. The kidding might have appeared affectionate, but it wasn't. After she was finished with her staff, she started in on the intensive-workshop students. We all had our own healing practices. Ed Lau was a chi gung master. Dr. Hart thought he was too fat. Fran Marquez worked with a Kirlian energy wand, which the good doctor found amusing. Judd Nyman was a bossy Thai massage and reflexology practitioner. Dr. Hart let him know just how bossy he was. And she dismissed the validity of Raleigh Hutchinson's resonance work, not to mention Craig Zweig's communications with invisible entities and Taj Gemayel's past-life regressions. She teased Kim Welch for having spent so many years of her life to receive accreditation as a psychiatrist, and she sniffed at Dotty Booth's brand of aromatherapy.

As for me, she told me she saw a very unhealthy darkness near me. I know, I know. My boyfriend, Roy, has been talking about the darkness for a lot longer than Dr. Hart. But she saw it, too. Luckily, Roy was in Kentucky doing good works for his family while Dr. Hart was loudly validating the inadequacy of my darkness-attracting chakras.

So we all had our quality time with Dr. Aurora Hart. She

really did seem to want to know about all our techniques, even if she verbally dismissed the majority of them. I wondered if she was going to integrate them into her own practice, which was fine with me, though not with everyone. Especially not with Fran Marquez. Aurora Hart *did* want to heal. I could feel it. Her rough handling may have even been her idea of healing.

By lunchtime that Saturday, the nine of us had worked *with* Dr. Hart for way too long, and we seemed to be expected to work *for* her, too, setting up the Swanton Boy Scout Hall for her big speech. She'd even showed us what she called her "aura maker," an electrical apparatus she was able to weave into some kind of brassiere/corset undergarment and through her cornrowed hair and bangs. As she spoke, a mist of appropriately colored light seemed to halo the approximate area of each of her chakras. It was a well-done illusion, all the better because it was so subtle, it was close to subliminal. Few people would realize that she was pushing the buttons as her apparatus lit up one light at a time from the base of her torso to the crown of her head.

Dotty Booth sighed. I opened my eyes to look at her. I liked Dotty. She was a plump, pleasant-looking woman about sixty years of age, and she had a genuine smile when she was happy. But she wasn't happy that minute. And I thought I knew why. Her aged cat had died two days before she'd come to the intensive. I would have bet she was thinking about her cat again.

"What's the matter, Dotty?" Dr. Aurora Hart demanded. This was the Aurora Hart I'd come to know and to . . . to try not to dislike. "I thought you lesbians were supposed to be tough. Why are you still grieving over a stupid cat?"

"My cat wasn't stupid!" Dotty snapped. Her shoulder-length gray and red hair seemed fuller suddenly. Or was that my imagination? "And you don't know anything about lesbians."

Spring in Swanton should have been beautiful, I thought. Rolling hills, grape arbors, the famous bulb gardens blooming. Maybe I could think about tulips. The food direction hadn't worked despite the smell of garlic wafting from the kitchen.

"Your cat wasn't stupid?" Dr. Hart persisted. "How do you know? Did you give your cat an IQ test?"

"You, you . . ." Dotty sputtered, standing, her chair pushed back.

Ed Lau reached up and put his hand on Dotty's arm. Ed wasn't tall, but he was massive, with one of the most relaxed faces I'd ever seen. When he'd told us he was seventy-five years old, I'd been surprised. His round cheeks, round jowls, and flat nose seemed filled with the same serenity that showed in his eyes, and it made him seem younger. If anyone could calm Dotty down, he could.

"So, tell me more about the house you're building," he prompted, as if Aurora Hart hadn't even spoken or Dotty stood.

Slowly, Dotty lowered herself back into her seat. "It's a big job," she finally answered, breaking eye contact with Dr. Hart and smiling back at Ed. "You know, it was completely trashed by the last people who lived there. We're doing the wiring, the plumbing, the whole gig—"

But Dr. Aurora Hart wasn't about to be upstaged.

"Better not have Ed walk around there," she threw in. "The whole place could collapse."

No one laughed. And Ed just smiled at Dr. Hart as if she were a child interrupting her elders, then turned his gaze back to Dotty.

"It must be exciting to choose paint and tile—" he tried again.

Dr. Hart tapped her finger on the table. It sounded like thunder.

"To design from the bottom up," Ed finished.

"Yeah—" Dotty began.

"Hey, Ed," Dr. Hart interrupted once more. "You're from Hawaii. Why do you do chi gung? Why not some of that Hawaiian healing, lomi-lomi or something?"

Ed Lau didn't looked relaxed any more. The roundness of his features tightened into stone. "Kuleana. I'm not Hawaiian enough," he replied curtly.

"Whaddaya mean, not—" Dr. Hart began.

Quinn grabbed the doctor's hand. I could just hear his whisper. "Come on, a little control here, okay?" he pleaded. "I know you're nervous about the speech, but don't alienate everyone, okay?"

"Too late," Dr. Hart said and laughed.

I laughed, too. I couldn't help it. At least Dr. Hart knew who she was.

Everyone at the table seemed to relax. Even Ed Lau's face returned to its round serenity.

A waiter appeared cautiously at the end of the table. He wore a crisp white shirt and held an order pad in his hand.

"I'll take care of ordering," Judd Nyman told us, waving his hand benevolently. "I'm sure most of us are vegetarian, so—"

"Hey, who made you God?" Dr. Hart cut in. "I'm not a vegetarian. I think we're each competent enough to order a dish and share."

For once, I was glad of Hart's rudeness. Judd Nyman was at least equal to her standards in the rudeness department. Judd was about Dr. Hart's age, a good-looking man with an engaging toothy smile, brushed-back graying hair, and a mouth that wouldn't stop.

"Hey, hey, hey!" he boomed. "It doesn't matter to me. Everyone can eat lousy food and feel bad. No big deal."

"Fine," Dr. Hart pronounced. "I'll take the honeyed chicken."

"Garlic scallops for me," Quinn chimed in.

And pretty soon, we'd all ordered, but not after a brief skirmish over brown or white rice, which the waiter had ended by announcing that there was no brown rice available.

"So, Cally," Dotty prompted conversationally. "How'd you hurt your leg?"

I could feel my skin flush. I'd never really *hurt* my leg. My leg had buckled when my parents had been killed in an explosion. I was fifteen at the time. And the weird thing was, my leg had buckled before I was informed of their deaths. And it had never quite healed. So I carried a cane. Some healer! I could see auras on other people. I could feel their energy and guide it. But I couldn't fix my own leg. Or the darkness that was always near me.

"It's not physical," Dr. Hart interjected for me. "It's first-chakra stuff." Her eyes looked into space. "Her family, not safe. Uncertainty over death. Still afraid after all these years."

Dack. That was what drove me crazy about Dr. Aurora Hart. I was all ready to decide that she was the one person I'd ever met who *didn't* have inherent goodness, and then she could do a reading like that.

"You're really good," I told her. She smiled and swished her gleaming cornrowed hair. I turned back to Dotty. "What Dr. Hart said," I told her. "It's all true."

"And you use that cane to defend yourself," Dr. Hart went on.

"Cane-fu," I announced, not even asking her how she knew. "My brother taught me how to use the cane as a weapon. He made a whole martial art out of it."

"I want everyone to tell us what they did before they went into healing," Dr. Hart went on, becoming a teacher once again, the one that catches you on the day you didn't do your homework. "We'll start with you, Cally."

I flushed again. "Um . . . I was an attorney," I admitted.

Dr. Aurora Hart leaned back and laughed. "And you're

ashamed of it!" she crowed. Yep. I wondered if she knew I went to a twelve-step program so I wouldn't practice law again.

"How about you, Raleigh?" she went on, her eyes lasering her next victim. Raleigh was a tall, handsome man with skin the deep color of true maple syrup, a balding head, and a compensatory moustache. His eyes lit up mischievously. He was a little older than my thirty-some years, I guessed, maybe forty.

"I was lead singer for a band called the Booi Brothers," he answered, his deep voice as resonant as his work. "And no, they weren't really my brothers. In fact, I was the only real 'brother' in the band."

Dr. Hart laughed. Were we finally having a good time?

"I was an architect," Judd Nyman threw in. "Made a fortune. My ex-wife—"

"No ex-wife stuff, please," Dotty interrupted, hand up in warning. "None of us like our exes." She took a breath. "I'm a former social worker."

"That makes sense," Dr. Hart said, shaking her head and rolling her eyes. "Taking care of everyone but yourself. It's written all over your third chakra."

"And what if Dotty takes care of others as well as herself?" Kim Welch challenged Dr. Hart. Doctor versus doctor. Kim Welch *was* a psychiatrist. Still, she was about my age, at least fifteen years younger than Dr. Hart. And Kim was such a soft-spoken women. She had broad, open features in a moon-shaped face with eyes that were as liquid and appealing as a baby seal's. But not to Dr. Hart apparently.

"So what did you do before you became a psychiatrist?" Hart demanded, a sneer in her voice when she enunciated "psychiatrist."

"Nothing worth talking about," Kim mumbled. "I was in school most of my life. I worked at my parents' during the summers."

"Craig?" Dr. Hart probed.

Craig Zweig jumped in his chair. Then he smiled, displaying snaggly teeth that gave his almost handsome face a disorganized look that matched his matted hair and wrinkled clothing. Unlike Ed Lau, I had a feeling that Craig was *younger* than he looked. Maybe he was in his sixties, but he *looked* ancient.

"I was . . . um . . ." He laughed shrilly. I had purposely kept away from uninvited peeks at anyone's auras at this intensive, but I didn't need to look to see that Craig's was as snaggly as his teeth. "I worked for the phone company," he finally offered. "Strung phone line."

"I was a science teacher," Ed Lau told us, taking the heat off Craig.

"I was a nurse, but you guys know that," Fran Marquez followed up briefly, patting the backpack strapped to her chair with one hand.

"And I . . ." Taj Gemayel paused dramatically, bending his head back as if in a caricature of thought. Taj was young. I wasn't sure if he was even near thirty yet. And he was as self-assuredly gorgeous as Aurora Hart. In fact, Taj was tall, dark, and handsome with a pointed beard, well trimmed moustache, and dark eyes rimmed by heavy black lashes. I bent forward. Was he wearing eyeliner? "I," Taj continued, "worked in the theater. Props, sets, acting . . . a bit of everything." He shrugged, sensually rippling the leather of his black jacket.

Our waiter came back with soup and appetizers. Had he been waiting in the wings for Taj's cue?

Conversation languished as we slurped vegetable wontons and crunched spring rolls. Except for Craig Zweig. He didn't seem to be eating. He was staring at Dr. Hart.

"What?" Dr. Hart demanded, catching his stare.

"You're beautiful," Craig mumbled.

That seemed to stop her for a moment. And in that moment, the rest of our dishes arrived.

I dove into my Szechuan prawns. I didn't look up for a little while. When I did, I noticed someone else who wasn't eating either, Kim Welch.

"Your energy seems so sad," Raleigh murmured to the psychiatrist and shoveled in another bite of chow mein.

"I lost a member of my family recently," she murmured back.

Raleigh frowned. "Your husband?" he asked, swallowing.

"No, my brother," she said with a painful smile on her open face. "My brother was kinder to me than my husband ever was."

"Husbands," Dotty sighed through a mouthful. "I went through two of those before I figured out who I really was."

"Hey!" Judd objected. "How come you can talk about your exes, and I can't talk about mine?"

"Because you're a bully," Dr. Hart answered helpfully. She pulled her gaze away from Craig Zweig who was still staring at her soulfully.

"It takes one to know one," Judd shot back.

"Very cool," Taj commented languidly. "When I grow up, will I be able to argue like you?"

"Hey!" Judd began again, but the door to the restaurant opened, and Sara Oshima walked in.

Sara didn't seem to be in a big hurry. Her usually sharp eyes looked unfocused in her round face. Her feet were bare, and she held a bouquet of flowers in her hand.

"Those flowers had better be for me," Dr. Hart said, her voice filled with menace.

But Sara just shrugged, unmoved by the apparent threat.

"Dammit, Sara, are you smoking dope again?" the doctor accused.

Quinn put his head in his hands, hiding the pain of his hound-dog eyes.

"Sara, this whole group is based on commitment—"

"Hey, it's cool," Sara retorted in a high voice, the voice of extended youth. Sara was thirty in years, but a lot younger in behavior. "Ira and I were just messing around, having a little fun."

"Sara, we'll talk later," Dr. Hart announced. It sounded like a prison sentence.

Quinn took his hands from his face and whispered in the doctor's ear.

"Okay, eat up, everyone," Hart ordered. "I give my speech in two hours. Four o'clock sharp. We have to set up the Boy Scout Hall. We do the chairs, the mike, the whole thing. It's going to be great. It always is." I wondered if she was trying to convince herself. Behind the doctor's abrasiveness, I could feel a pit of insecurity. Or maybe I was just projecting. "Are we ready?" she demanded.

Squeaks and uh-huhs answered her. I think she would have liked something more in the line of cheers.

So we all ate, those of us who *were* eating, and pretty soon we were leaving the restaurant for the Boy Scout Hall in a group led by Dr. Hart.

On the way out of the Best Fortune, Dr. Hart touched the side of Taj's face.

"I'm sure I've met you before," she murmured, her voice low and sultry. "Well, I'll get to know you now in any case."

Taj looked stung. I was surprised. The tight jeans and rhinestone studs in his ears made him look like a man up for anything. But still, Taj acted like a scam artist. Maybe he hadn't been at it long enough to know the potential results of his seductive poses.

We walked as directed to the hall, the doctor linking arms with Taj as we did. All of the props for the speech were there waiting, she assured us.

As she opened the front door with her key, she said,

"Time to hook up the old aura maker." Then she leaned back her head and laughed loudly.

No one else laughed with Dr. Hart. But the sound of her laughter echoed in the silence of the empty hall.

Then she stepped inside.

TWO

The rest of us didn't follow Dr. Hart into the dark hall
right away. I didn't know about anyone else, but I wasn't
feeling very comfortable about that hall. It wasn't just that
it was cold and unlit and smelled of mold. My senses told
me about those qualities without even having to step over the
threshold. But beyond the cold, moldy darkness, there was
something about the space that raised the hair on the back
of my neck. I gripped my cane a little tighter before walking through the half-opened doorway into a tiny foyer. I
could just see the glint of Dr. Hart's beaded hair swirling in
the main hall. Was she dancing in the dark?

I heard footsteps behind me and turned, raising my cane
a little. But it was just Raleigh, backlit by the slit of light
from the partially open door. He felt along the wall.

"Gotta be a light switch here somewhere," he murmured.

His fingers must have found it because lights blazed on,
one row at a time, spotlighting Dr. Aurora Hart. She *was*
dancing, whirling in the empty hall on the waxed wooden
floor with her eyes closed and her arms spread out like a
child's.

Quinn was the next to walk in. He stared at the dancing

doctor and opened his mouth to say something, then closed it again, sighing softly and shaking his head.

Finally, he turned, opened the door wide, and motioned the rest of the crew in. By the time Sara had straggled through the door at the end of the line, Dr. Hart had stopped dancing. She climbed the four carpeted stairs to a raised platform and turned to face us.

"The Chakra Commitment!" she announced evangelically, raising her eyes to the ceiling and opening her arms wide. "Are you committed?"

Raleigh muttered "amen" unenthusiastically, Craig giggled, and Taj clapped his hands.

"All right, everybody," Dr. Hart went on, her evangelical pose gone. "We've got some work to do. Quinn, give everyone their assignments. Sara, come get me dressed."

Sara moseyed on up to the platform and disappeared with the doctor into a little room off to the side.

Quinn gave the rest of us our assignments. Craig was given a broom and told to use it. Taj and Raleigh were ordered to work on setting up the stage. Ed was sent out to get bottled water for all of us. And Judd got to clean the bathrooms. I thought that was pretty funny until we women got our joint assignment.

Fran, Dotty, Kim, and I were given a task equal to our intellectual and intuitive skills. We were told to set up two hundred metal folding chairs into two sections, with aisles on the sides and in the center. Quinn even consulted a card and told us how many chairs went in each row and how much space was necessary between the rows. I lost track of what the other healers were doing as we women opened the first of the oversized drawers that were built into the walls on both sides of the hall. It was filled with folding chairs. It began to dawn on me that it wasn't going to be easy to set up two hundred folding chairs. Fran, Kim, and Dotty looked like they were realizing the same thing.

"Wow, slavery," Fran muttered. "What a healing concept."

"Two hundred?" Dotty murmured.

We decided to work in two teams. Fran and Dotty took the right side of the hall. Kim and I took the left, with Kim pulling chairs out of the monster drawers (no easy job) and handing them to me. It took me one trip to figure out that I couldn't carry more than one chair along with my cane. I told myself I probably didn't really need my cane, but then again, I rarely knew when my leg was going to buckle. So I kept my cane in hand and decided to take it slow and easy. Either I'd finish in time or I wouldn't. What was Dr. Hart going to do, dock my pay?

Kim unfolded the chairs for me, and I carried them one by one to line up in nice little rows, starting in the back. One hundred chairs, one hundred round trips. I figured I had a lot of time to think. Unfortunately, I found myself thinking about Dr. Aurora Hart and her various cruelties. Why did she pick on people? Didn't she know the hurt she caused?

After about twenty chairs, I began to wonder about something else. Why hadn't the doctor hired a normal auditorium somewhere else with built-in seats? Even my native Glasse County had a good-sized auditorium. And Quinn had told us that this afternoon's speech was sold out. Everyone who was coming had bought a ticket. I didn't think Dr. Hart had settled on the Swanton Boy Scout Hall for lack of money. Those tickets had cost eighty-five dollars apiece. And the woman drove a lavender Mercedes with tinted windows! I walked back for another chair. Was Dr. Aurora Hart afraid of an auditorium that she couldn't fill? The minute the thought grazed my neurons, I was sure of its truth. Dr. Hart wanted to be in a hall filled to the brim with her admirers. One empty seat would be an affront.

Was Dr. Hart insecure despite all her success? I picked

up another chair and carried it to my third row. Maybe no amount of success would be enough for a person like Aurora Hart. She wasn't Deepak Chopra. She wasn't Caroline Myss. She wasn't even—

"Ta-da!" a voice came from behind me.

I dropped my chair and turned around.

Dr. Hart was onstage, her microphone in hand, wearing a gauzy white pantsuit with an electric cord trailing out the cuff of one leg.

"Plug me in, Taj," she ordered.

Taj bent down and plugged the cord into the outlet at the back of the stage.

"Testing!" The doctor's voice came booming out of speakers I hadn't even noticed. "Can you hear me in the back?"

"Loud and clear!" Quinn shouted from his position by the door.

"And how about this?" she purred into the microphone, her finger touching a button on its side.

The bottom of her torso shimmered in what must have been a red light, that looked ever so softly pink through the gauze of her outfit.

"Ooooh!" Craig Zweig sang out, still holding a broom in his hand.

The doctor frowned for a moment and sought out Quinn with her eye.

"Perfect," he soothed her. "You look like Glinda, the Good Witch of the North."

Dr. Hart smiled.

"Well, some kind of witch, maybe," someone, Fran or Dotty, muttered.

I looked across the hall. But Dr. Hart didn't seem to hear. She began prancing back and forth across the stage, careful not to trip on the electric cord that tethered her, her first chakra still lit.

I turned back to the chair I'd dropped and positioned it, then headed back to Kim for the next one.

"Do we all know what the chakras are?" she called out.

"Damned straight, we do!" I heard from the bathroom. Judd Nyman was still at work.

"You are made of energy," Dr. Hart went on as I picked up another chair. "Sacred energy. And this energy is centered in seven sacred stars running up in a line from the bottom of your torso to the crown of your head."

That seemed a little simplistic to me, but I wasn't about to discuss chakra-ese with Dr. Hart during her rehearsal. Everyone in the healing community seemed to understand chakras differently. Of course, my take on them had to do with auras since that's what I tended to see, so I looked at chakras for what they said about a client in terms of color, intensity, size, shape, and rotation.

"If your chakras are muddy, they need cleaning," Dr. Hart went on.

Maybe, I thought and began moving the folding chairs faster, finding my rhythm as Dr. Hart continued speaking and pacing.

". . . up to you to heal!" she was shouting as I got to my seventh row of chairs.

By the time I'd placed my hundredth chair in place, Dr. Hart was still talking. I shook hands with Kim, and together, we sat down in the front row and looked up at the doctor. Her first chakra was still softly shining. She seemed to have forgotten about her aura maker.

"Are you truly committed?" she demanded once more.

No one in the room seemed to be paying a lot of attention to her except for Craig who'd stopped sweeping a long time ago. But she must have been listening to her own internal applause, because she bowed.

"Thank you," she said softly. "Thank you."

I looked at my watch. It was three-thirty. The ticket

holders would be arriving soon. I felt a gentle tap on my shoulder. Ed Lau held out a plastic bottle of water. I took it and drank deeply, savoring the sweet coolness in my dry mouth and throat. The hall didn't feel cold anymore after having set up a hundred chairs. Though it still smelled moldy. I looked across the aisle. Dotty put her last chair in place, and Fran joined her in their front row. I gave them a thumbs up which Dotty returned. But not Fran. Fran either didn't see me or didn't care to return my signal.

Dr. Hart turned off her microphone and spoke to Raleigh and Taj, pointing at her cord and the speakers. They each nodded. Quinn climbed the stairs and joined them. I turned to Kim.

"We won," I told her.

"What?" she asked, her face vacant, her baby-seal eyes blank.

"We got our chairs out first," I explained gently, feeling guilty. I was pretty sure it was a lot harder lifting the chairs out of the drawers than positioning them.

"Oh, right," she murmured. "I'm sorry."

"No problem," I told her, patting her hand. It felt cold to me. For a moment, I was really concerned. Could someone go into shock from lifting chairs? Kim was a psychiatrist, not a construction worker.

"Kim?" I began.

"I'm sorry," she apologized again, standing. "I have to go to the bathroom."

Dr. Hart clapped her hands together from the stage.

"Okay, people!" she called out. "Good work setting up. Now, all you have to do is enjoy the show. And I mean enjoy it! Show a little enthusiasm, okay? We want results here. If anyone asks you any questions, tell them that Quinn has the brochures for the full program. He'll be stationed at the door, taking tickets. And Sara—"

Dr. Hart stopped and looked around the hall.

"Dammit, Quinn, is she gone again?" Dr. Hart demanded.

Quinn looked around, his brown eyes round in his hound-dog face. He shrugged.

"Oh, forget it!" the doctor snapped. "Everyone grab a seat. You guys get the first row."

Enthusiasm? As everyone took their seats, Ed on one side of me and Raleigh on the other, I realized I was all out of enthusiasm.

I closed my eyes and entered my own world of meditation, breathing in earth and sky . . . and forgiveness. I didn't want to forget forgiveness. I hadn't been very forgiving of Dr. Hart lately.

I don't know how much longer it was before I heard the sound of people entering the hall. And I could have sworn I smelled a familiar aftershave.

Was that Warren Kapp? I whipped my head around and saw my friend Kapp's octogenarian bulldog face, and next to him, my friends Dee-Dee Lee and Joan Hussein, all seated near the back row. Seeing them was the best thing that had happened to me all day. Dee-Dee was a healer. But Kapp and Joan were attorneys, very unlikely to be interested in Dr. Hart for her own sake. These people were friends here to support me. I waved and blew kisses. Dee-Dee blew a kiss back, Joan laughed, and Kapp blushed. Yep, my friends were here because I was here. I wondered how they could have known how much I needed to see their friendly faces. And how come I could smell Kapp's aftershave so many rows away?

Quinn was at the door taking tickets, as far away from the stage as he could be. Once he'd taken the last ticket, the place was packed. Every one of those two hundred seats was filled, and a few people were even standing behind the last row. The only person who wasn't here was Sara Oshima. I turned my head dutifully forward.

A few minutes after four o'clock, Aurora Hart made her entrance, prancing onto the stage with her cornrowed head held high and wide-set eyes burning with intensity.

The sound of at least four hundred hands clapping erupted. Aurora Hart held out her arms as if to embrace the whole audience. And they loved it. They loved her. Maybe they'd listened to her tapes. They couldn't have known her personally.

"Tonight," she began softly, a vibrato in her voice. "Tonight, we honor our chakras." She brought her hands inward as if to pray. And she paused.

The clapping broke out once more. The doctor wasn't going to have to depend on her students for enthusiasm. Her audience was with her.

"Do you all know what your chakras are?" she began.

A resounding chorus of affirmatives filled the hall. But she explained anyway. The star bit sounded better the second time around. There was much more intensity in Dr. Hart's voice. She made her pitch.

"Each and every one of your chakras is sacred," she declaimed, flinging out her arms. "Each is your spirit, your body, your mind." She lowered her voice and looked out into the audience with a plea in her eyes. "And it is your sacred duty to keep them clean. Only you can you can do it."

She stepped back. The hall was silent.

"How?" she asked. "How can you clean them? By finding what it is that is stuck to your chakras and shaking it free. Free! Is there anyone out there who can feel something wrong in their chakras?"

People shouted back their answers.

"Do you want to know why?" she asked.

"Yes!" the room roared.

"Because you have an affinity for the negativity that is stuck to your chakras. Yes, an affinity. But you can clean it. In fact, *only you* can clean it. I can *see* it, but *you* must be committed to cleaning it." She paused, and raised her arms once more.

"Are you committed?!" she shouted.

The crowd went wild. I wondered for a moment if she

had paid shills, but I didn't think so. These people were reflecting back Dr. Hart's own intensity, her own enthusiasm, her own ego.

"Chakra number one," she announced. And the bottom of her torso shone pinkly. There were gasps in the audience. If I hadn't known the trick, I might have thought it was coming from her actual energy body myself. "Your first chakra reflects your life force, your physical being, your safety, your root. Can you stand up for yourself in your first chakra?"

"Yes!"

"Your second chakra," she went on. A pale orange color floated around her abdomen. More gasps. "Sexuality," she purred. "Sensuality. Emotions. Own them!"

"The third chakra," she whispered. A pale yellow topped the other colors around her solar plexus. "Intellect, honor, responsibility, power." She opened her arms. "Take control of your life!"

"Chakra four," she continued as the clapping quieted down. The soft light around her heart and thymus was green. "Love, compassion, hope. Can you love yourself? Love yourself now!"

"Chakra five," she offered next, her throat shining blue. "Expression. Creating your own life. Learning to speak your truth. Can you speak your truth?"

"The sixth chakra," she declared, and her cornrowed bangs radiated violet. "Clairvoyance, insight, inspiration. Truth. Are you ready for the truth?"

They were ready.

"And now, the seventh chakra," she pronounced. But no color issued from the top of her head. And no new words followed her pronouncement.

Dr. Hart's body seized. Was this part of the show? Her body stiffened and vibrated at the same time for what seemed an eternity. And then, she collapsed onto the stage.

The audience was quiet. There were no cheers. Finally, I heard Quinn yelling.

"Pull the plug!" he shouted. I felt Raleigh get up next to me. "Pull the plug!"

I could hear Quinn's footsteps running down the wooden aisle. He and Raleigh ran up the stairs at the same time. But it was Quinn who yanked the plug out of the wall socket, the plug that ran from the cuff of Dr. Hart's pants. And it was Quinn who threw himself down on her body, frantically pumping her chest with his hands.

Still, it was Raleigh who felt for her pulse after another eternity and quietly announced, "Dr. Aurora Hart is dead."

THREE

"No!" Quinn screamed, his compact body sprawled over Dr. Hart's gauze-clad one. "No!"

A low murmur came from the audience, then gasps and shouts.

"Come on, man," Raleigh prodded gently, kneeling next to Quinn. "You gotta stop this. The people, man—"

Fran went up the stairs. She bent over Dr. Hart's body. It looked like she was checking for a pulse and listening for a heartbeat, though it was hard to see around Quinn. She did a few other things I couldn't identify. When she straightened back up, she pushed a dark wing of hair from her face.

"Quinn," Fran announced softly. "Raleigh is right. The doctor's dead."

Maybe she didn't speak softly enough, because a new round of noise erupted from the audience. And from Quinn.

"No, how can you be sure?!" he cried.

Fran sighed. "Quinn," she explained. "I'm a nurse. I used to work the emergency room. I know when someone is dead."

"Aurora!" Quinn rasped.

"Quinn," Raleigh tried. His maple-colored skin had turned gray. "You gotta take charge, man."

Quinn rolled into a fetal ball.

Raleigh was right. Someone had to take charge. Quinn wasn't the only one flipping out. Shouts, screams, and shrieks were coming from the audience like bullets.

I put my head into my hands, trying to think. Dr. Hart was dead? I couldn't take it in. It had to be part of the show. But it wasn't. I lifted my head and stood up slowly, staring at the stage in front of me. Even if Dr. Hart had a dramatic agenda, she couldn't have remained still that long. And Quinn . . . Quinn, what was he to the doctor, besides an employee? Quinn had come out of his fetal ball and was flailing as Raleigh sang to him. I stopped moving. It seemed too surreal, but Raleigh was actually singing to Quinn, his resonant voice filled with a solemn, serene grief.

"Oh, Shenandoah, I long to hear you," he sang irrelevantly. But as irrelevant as the words might have been, his tone was a vessel for sorrow. "Away, you rolling river . . ."

My eyes filled with tears. Dr. Hart *was* dead. And suddenly, I could feel my own body. It was cold and shivering.

I turned around. I wasn't the only person out of my seat. A handful of people were on their feet and starting up the aisle. And another handful were heading the other way, toward the door.

Adrenaline shot through me. Raleigh was taking care of Quinn. But who was going to take care of the audience? Would they riot? Would they storm the stage? And how about the ones who were leaving? Something in the pit of my stomach told me that they might be witnesses to a murder. A murder? Was this a murder?

My eyes caught Kapp's just as he stood.

"Everyone just stay still!" he boomed.

And oddly enough, people did, at least for the moment.

"Those of you who are out of your chairs, please return

to them," my old friend ordered. "And those of you who are already sitting, please remain so."

Slowly, people obeyed his orders. At least most of them. I sat back down, but kept my head turned.

"Who are you?!" a man who'd been heading toward the door from a side aisle demanded.

"My name is Warren Kapp. Consider me an officer of the court!" Kapp shot back, his voice ringing with certain authority.

The man stood as if frozen, not heading toward the door anymore, but not heading toward his seat either.

"And my fellow officer of the court," Kapp kept on, "Ms. Joan Hussein will call the police now."

Joan rose with all the dignity of her considerable weight and walked deliberately toward the foyer to use her cell phone privately.

The man in the side aisle went back to his seat, grumbling and clenching his fists. But he went back.

And in the moment of whispers, gasps, and muffled cries, I heard Raleigh again.

"Away, I'm bound away, across the wide Missouri."

Quinn had stopped flailing at least. He lay next to Dr. Aurora Hart, his hand holding her lifeless one, his head in Raleigh's lap.

The voices from the audience began to get louder again.

"Let's get out of here now . . ."

"But what happened? . . ."

"Is she really dead? . . ."

"Who's the old guy?"

Kapp looked toward the front row, toward me. And I knew he wasn't quite as certain as he sounded.

"You! You healers from Dr. Hart's class!" he shouted. "You may lead the audience now." It was an order.

My hands shaking, I stood and walked up onto the stage. I turned toward the audience. My fellow healers looked in no better shape than Quinn. Judd was just shaking his head over and over again, his eyes closed. Kim was pale and staring. She looked as dead as Dr. Hart. Dotty cried into her hands. Craig looked at the ceiling. And Taj was slack-jawed. Only Ed seemed to have heard Kapp. He got up a step after me and joined the rest of us on the stage.

"I'm not sure what has happened here," I began quietly.

"What?" several voices called out.

I realized I was going to have to shout. I didn't have Dr. Hart's microphone. I didn't want Dr. Hart's microphone. "I said, I'm not sure what has happened here, but Dr. Hart would want us to be calm now! She'd want us to keep our chakras clean!"

I turned to Fran. She narrowed her black eyes and shrugged her shoulders. I turned to Ed. I couldn't remember what Dr. Hart had said in her speech. What would move these people? Or better yet, what would keep them still? Ed just stood: centered, calm, massive. His round face was serene. Then he spoke.

"We will lead you in some simple chi gung exercises now," Ed said in what seemed like a normal voice. But still, no one was shouting "what?" at him. He'd been a high school teacher, I remembered. He knew how to project, something I'd never learned. "First, sit as straight as you can in your chair," he began. "And breathe."

I wanted to hug Ed as he stood calmly in front of the audience, his serenity calling out theirs.

But instead, I stood exactly like him, or as exactly as I could imagine. I straightened my spine, widened my stance, tucked in my chin, relaxed my chest, and began to breathe.

"Do you know where your energy is centered?" he asked.

I saw several people in the audience point to their hearts, some to their heads, and some in the direction where Ed was going. I knew where that was. While practicing cane-fu with my brother, I'd learned where the martial arts center of energy resided, two or three finger-widths below the belly button. I placed my right hand over my lower abdomen and let my cane slide to the floor. I had a feeling I was going to need both hands for this exercise, and I already felt grounded enough that I hoped my leg wouldn't buckle.

"Your center is approximately one and a quarter inches below your navel, one third of the way into your body," Ed intoned. He placed his own right hand on his abdomen and his left hand comfortably over his right.

I saw people in the audience dropping their hands. He had them! And I saw Joan Hussein returning down the center aisle from the foyer; unnoticed by most of the audience. She nodded in my direction and winked one doe-like brown eye. I nodded ever so carefully back.

"There is a center in each of your hands as well," Ed told us. "Can you feel the centers of your hands?"

"Uh-huh," a number of voices returned.

"Good," Ed encouraged. "Now place the center of one hand over the center of your body, and place your other hand's center over the first hand's center."

I followed orders.

"Now lower your eyelids a little," he went on. "And concentrate on your center. How does it feel?"

It felt good; calm and warm. I began to sink into the feeling.

Then I heard the laugh. It was the laugh of a loon, the kind that chills people miles from the lake. Only a human was making the noise, Craig Zweig.

He was half-standing, half-kneeling on his chair, laughing.

The hall began to murmur and growl again.

"She's up there!" Craig shrilled, his unkempt features stretched into a grimace that might have been a smile. "She's there, looking down at us. Can't you see her? She's looking down at us. Look, she kept her lights!"

I couldn't help it. I looked up at the ceiling like everyone else. But all I saw was wooden rafters.

"Hi, Dr. Hart!" Craig greeted the air above him.

"Craig!" Dotty admonished from his side. "Can't you
see you're upsetting people, honey?"

Maybe it was the "honey" that did it. Craig settled back
into his chair, mumbling incoherently about "lights" and
"pretty" and "love."

Dotty put an arm around his slumped shoulders. Her
plump face held genuine concern for the man. But she
seemed to be on her own out there. Kim was still pale and
staring, Judd and Taj unmoving. Fran stepped down the
stairs to sit on Craig's other side. She took his hand in hers.
Goodness, I reminded myself. There is always goodness
present. Dotty and Fran comforting Craig. Ed by my side.
Raleigh helping Quinn. But there was still the audience to
consider.

The crowd wasn't calm anymore.

"I've had enough!" a woman declared and rose from her
chair.

"Yeah!" Agreement came from what sounded like a
hundred voices.

"Wait!" I shouted. "You came here to see Dr. Hart," I
accused.

Faces turned my way.

"She was ready to be here for you," I pushed on, not
knowing what I would say next. "For you and your
chakras."

I could hear a rumble. Was it agreement? Disagree-
ment? Both?

"So you gotta stay here for her!" Raleigh's deep voice
boomed out from behind me. "You are all observant people. Maybe you saw something the police will want to
know about."

More rumbles.

"But you're not telling us what happened!" the standing woman objected. "Was she killed?"

"We don't know," Raleigh admitted as calmly as possible. "That's why you need to stay."

"She was electrocuted!" Someone from the audience shouted.

"See, you're observant," Raleigh shot back. "That's what we need. As you sit, think back on what you saw. Be ready to tell the police."

"But—"

"It was her aura maker!" Craig Zweig yelled. He laughed. "See, it was her joke. Now she is an aura."

Now the rumble sounded like two words asked over and over again, "aura maker?"

"And we can cleanse our chakras as we wait," Raleigh went on as if Craig hadn't spoken. "I find that singing helps."

"Ladies and gentleman," Ed Lau announced from my side. "We have a world-renowned singer here, Raleigh Hutchinson of the Booi Brothers!"

Raleigh did a double take at Ed, before turning and smiling at the audience. And that man could smile. White teeth against dark skin. His smile could take your clothes off.

Some people clapped. And the words rumbling around were "Booi Brothers," instead of "aura maker." I wondered if Ed Lau had ever worked in rock promotion.

Raleigh even took a little bow. But I was close enough to see and feel the tension radiating from his body. He didn't want to be Raleigh Hutchinson of the Booi Brothers. But if that was what it would take, he'd do it.

"So, how many people out there want to sing?" he demanded, raising his arms.

A couple of people actually cheered.

"And *what* do you want to sing?" he prompted.

" 'Layla'!"

" 'She's Gone'!"

" 'Kum Ba Yah'!"

" 'Crack Hurts,' that's a Booi Brothers song!"

" 'Amazing Grace'!"

" 'Amazing Grace,' " Raleigh approved. "You all know 'Amazing Grace,' don't you?"

"Yeah!"

"A-ma-zing grace," Raleigh began, his resonant voice a pathway to the infinite light of longing.

Ed and I joined in. "How sweet the sound . . ."

Soon, the audience was with us, their voices swelling. Which was good, because I didn't know the rest of the words exactly.

And once we were through with "Amazing Grace," we did "Respect." As everyone shouted out the letters, I took a quick glance over my shoulder at Quinn. He was sitting, his eyes raised from Dr. Hart's body. And he was singing! Criminy, Raleigh was good. Even Judd and Taj were singing now.

We'd just begun "I Heard It Through the Grapevine," when the police arrived.

The first one through the door was a short, muscular man with a mean, baby face, graying short-cropped hair, and a gun in his hand.

"Everyone stay where you are!" he shouted, holding out the gun like he meant it. "And somebody tell me what the heck's going on here."

No one was singing anymore. I sure hoped this guy was a policeman. A comfortable-looking woman with brown eyes and long brown hair held back in a rubber band moved in behind him.

"Swanton Police Department," she announced, flashing a badge from beneath her blazer.

Two uniformed officers followed her, one Asian and one who looked part puppy.

"Well?" the man with the gun demanded.

"Dr. Hart died!" I shouted from the stage. That seemed to sum it up.

"She's in the rafters!" Craig piped in.

Dotty and Fran shushed him as the man with the gun squinted up at the rafters.

"Okay, you jokers," he snarled. "Who's Dr. Hart, and how did she die?"

A number of voices tried to answer at once.

"Dr. Hart was giving a speech—"

"Dr. Hart keeled over—"

"Dr. Hart did the Chakra Commitment—"

"Dr. Hart was a teacher, a healer—"

"It looked like she was electrocuted—"

"Electrocuted?" the man with the gun asked. I wondered if his arm was getting tired.

From behind me, Quinn began to speak, his voice loud and shaking.

"Dr. Hart was giving a speech tonight," he explained. "She was holding a microphone that plugged into the wall. She fell over after she pushed the button for the crown chakra. She's dead." Quinn pointed down where Dr. Hart lay and cried out, "She's right here, for God's sake!"

"Crown chakra?" the man with the gun demanded.

The woman behind him tapped his shoulder lightly.

"Shall I take it from here, sir?" she asked.

He lowered his gun and nodded her way.

"I'm Sergeant DiMarco from the Swanton Police Department," the woman introduced herself, stepping into the middle aisle and walking toward us, the puppylike officer behind her. "The man in charge is Chief Phlug. And Officers Diem and Jones are assisting. If you'll remain calm, we'll try to sort this out."

As if we'd been calm in the first place.

"Who wants to be a spokesperson?" she asked, her voice reminding me of Miss Telfer's in third grade.

I saw Kapp rising from his seat, but I waved him down. Quinn had to take care of this.

"Quinn?" I whispered, turning to him.

Raleigh held out a hand. Quinn took it and stepped up to the front of the stage.

"I'm Quinn Vogel, Dr. Hart's staff leader," Quinn said, his voice still loud, but not quite as shaky. "I'll try to answer your questions." A blue aura of grief floated around his upper chakras, so intense, I saw it without trying.

"The woman lying on the stage is Dr. Hart?" Sergeant DiMarco probed gently as she reached the foot of the stairs.

Quinn simply nodded.

"And you're sure she's dead?"

Quinn nodded again, his large expressive eyes looking incredibly sad in his long, thin face. DiMarco waved at the officer who'd followed her down the aisle and pointed to Dr. Hart. The officer loped up the stairs and bent over Dr. Hart's body.

"Is she the only victim here tonight?" DiMarco went on.

Another nod.

"Was she electrocuted?"

"I don't know," Quinn answered, his voice rising. He modulated his tone. "I don't know, but it looked like she might have been."

DiMarco looked up at the officer on the stage.

"She's dead," he announced.

"Fine, Officer Jones," the sergeant said. "Call in and cancel the paramedics. I'm surprised they're not here yet. And call in the county; I want a forensics crew and the coroner."

"It was her aura maker!" Craig shouted out.

"Who said that?" Chief Phlug demanded, running up the aisle. Officer Jones ignored his chief as he went back down the stairs to make his phone calls.

Sergeant DiMarco put up a restraining hand as Chief Phlug reached her, her warm brown eyes still on Quinn.

"Do you know what that man meant by an 'aura maker?' " she asked.

It took Quinn nearly ten minutes to explain the aura maker and another twenty to explain chakras and their relationships to auras.

"Okay," Sergeant DiMarco said finally. "Just stay with me a little longer on this. Was anyone touching the doctor when she collapsed?"

Quinn shook his head miserably.

"Who had access to her aura maker before she put it on?" she prompted.

"We . . ." Quinn tried. He swallowed and tried again. "Only myself, Dr. Hart's assistant, Sara, and the members of Dr. Hart's intensive, I suppose."

"And those would be?" she led him.

He pointed us out, one by one. I, for one, felt guilty just being pointed at. But I saw where the sergeant was heading. If Dr. Hart had been electrocuted by her aura maker, one of us who had seen it ahead of time could have tampered with it. *Was* this a murder?

"Where is Dr. Hart's assistant, Sara?" DiMarco pressed.

Quinn shrugged his shoulders.

"I think she took off before the show started," Raleigh filled in. Did Sara's leaving have to do with the doctor's death? She had put Dr. Hart into her aura maker.

"One more question for now, Mr. Vogel," the sergeant bulldozed away. "Can you see anyone in the audience who might have had access to the doctor's aura maker besides those you've pointed out?"

Quinn scanned the audience. "I see old friends, but nobody who spent the last few days with her. I—"

"Fine," she cut him off. "I want you to go help Officer Diem at the door, okay? You stand with him and point out anyone that the doctor knew while Diem takes names and addresses. Got that?"

Quinn nodded one more time and headed for his place at the door. The place where he'd been when the doctor had spoken.

Sergeant DiMarco climbed up on the stage and shouted out at the audience.

"Okay, folks, it's gonna be a long night. Anyone who wasn't in Dr. Hart's intensive group give your name and address to the officer at the door. Oh, and a thumbprint. And any of you who knew the doctor personally, tell the officer—"

"But what happened?" someone yelled out in exasperation.

"Was she murdered?" came another question.

"Yeah!" a few more people joined in.

Then the good cop took a break, and the bad cop came back on board.

Chief Phlug raised his gun and pointed it at the audience, jerking it from side to side.

"You wanna ask *me* some questions, huh?" he demanded, squinting his eyes. "Or are you gonna shut up and let *us* ask the questions?"

FOUR

The silent consensus seemed to be that Chief Phlug was going to ask the questions. No one was yelling at *him*.

DiMarco began to arrange logistics. Under her orders, Officer Jones brought in a large notebook and an electronic fingerprint device and handed it to Officer Diem. Jones began escorting the members of the audience to the doorway, beginning with those in the back rows. He stopped the people who Quinn recognized as "friends" of Dr. Hart's, and these former friends began repopulating the chairs they'd abandoned. Meanwhile, Sergeant DiMarco herded Ed, Raleigh, and me off the stage and sat us down in the front row where we'd begun.

Eventually, Chief Phlug lowered his gun.

"Where am I gonna interview them?" he asked DiMarco.

"There's a little office across from the rest rooms in the foyer that ought to do," she told him.

He marched down the aisle and took a turn into the office, muttering.

"Is the chief always like this?" I asked Sergeant DiMarco in a whisper.

"Always, honey," she answered and laughed.

I was glad someone was laughing, even if I didn't know what the joke was.

"Okay," the sergeant said. "Who wants to go first—"

But she stopped speaking, turning toward the doorway midsentence. I heard Quinn's shaky voice.

"Sara, where have you been? It's so terrible—"

I heard an unintelligible tinkle that might have been Sara's voice, some rumbles, and finally, "Dr. Hart?"

The final voice was definitely Sara Oshima's.

Sergeant Dimarco put her hand up, ordered, "Don't any of you move a muscle, including your mouths," and raced down the aisle to the door. I had a feeling Sara was going to be interviewed first.

It was weird sitting up there, silent, so near to Dr. Hart's body. I was glad when Officer Jones loped up to baby-sit us. And sure enough, I saw Sergeant DiMarco escorting Sara across the hall to the office where Chief Phlug had gone. Poor Sara.

I glanced to the left and to the right. If Dr. Hart had been killed, one of us might have been the murderer. It was too bad the doctor wasn't here herself to look into our minds and find out who. I'd been respecting aura privacy during the intensive, but I wanted a peek at people. Could I even recognize a murderer's aura? I hadn't been able to before, but that didn't stop me from trying.

I turned my head slowly and covertly scanned Ed Lau to begin with. Red dominated his aura, though it seemed well-balanced. Was he angry? And Raleigh Hutchinson: His aura was centered at his throat, an almost aqua color. I felt a sense of loss and frustration, but it was hazy, as if he was trying to mute it or deny it. Taj's colors were bleeding into each other like a messy palette. I didn't blame him. I peeked over at Craig Zweig. He seemed to have every color of the rainbow in his aura but they were jumping around as if someone was shaking him in a bottle. It made me dizzy just to look.

I turned my head the other way. Kim Welch was the opposite of Craig Zweig. I could only see white, too far above her head. It looked like a reflection of complete shock, not a connection with spirit. And I doubted that she was in her body, though the white of her skin matched her aura. Judd had a color-perfect aura, aligned with textbook accuracy around his chakras, but his auric field was huge, overblown. Fran's aura, on the other hand, was pale and shrunken, though it seemed to be growing even as I looked. And Dotty's was dominated by yellow and green, with a tendril of gold from her crown chakra. Dotty was meditating, trying to bring spirit back into her body. I would have bet on it.

I could tell Dotty was meditating, but I couldn't see anything that cried out "murderer" to me in anyone's aura. And even a murderer might meditate. Why not? A glimpse wasn't enough. The colors and positions weren't enough. To really understand an aura took one-to-one, long-term, focused concentration. Not to mention the fact that auras changed constantly. And I had no idea what a murderer's aura would look like. I imagined my aura had elements of fear and frustration as well as sadness. Or maybe it was just black. Maybe *my* aura looked like a murderer's.

I closed my eyes. I reminded myself that the electrocution might have been a simple electric malfunction. Why was I assuming murder? Because Dr. Hart seemed like the type of person one would want to kill? A malfunction? I was warming to the idea. The people who surrounded me were all good people in their own ways, healers. But then, all people had goodness somewhere in them, even murderers. *No!* I told myself, *Strike that train of thought*. We were talking about a malfunctioning aura maker here, not murder. My mind battled out the case, defense and prosecution equally represented.

I heard the sound of shuffling footsteps and a sniffle.

I opened my eyes and looked up. Sara Oshima, her previously mischievous eyes were now red-rimmed and wild. She had returned to the fold accompanied by Sergeant Di-Marco. Sara wiped her nose on her sleeve absently. And I peeked at *her* aura. Yuck! Her auric field was almost as chaotic as Craig's. Drugs? She sat down in the empty chair at the end of the row and drew her knees up to her chin. She was wearing a pair of flowered sandals that should have been fun, but looked pathetic under the circumstances.

"I want to ask you all some group questions," DiMarco began. "Just answer yes or no, okay?"

"You're the boss," Craig mumbled.

DiMarco's friendly brown eyes seemed to shrink a little. "Is that a yes?" she asked him, her voice even.

"What?" he asked back.

"He's a little confused," Dotty put in.

The sergeant sighed. She took a breath and started over. "Okay, one of you answer my questions for the group, and if anyone disagrees with the answer, raise your hand."

I nodded. "Yes" and "yeah" sounded around me. Even Craig said, "Uh-huh."

"Someone volunteer to speak for the group," DiMarco ordered.

I looked down the row. I didn't want to be the spokesperson. I could tell no one else did either. Raleigh looked at his feet. Fran looked at Judd. Judd averted his eyes. Dotty tightened her grip around Craig's shoulders protectively. Kim just stared ahead, her eyes unfocused. Taj put his arms around himself and shrunk into his chair. Ed placed his hands over his belly and breathed deeply.

"Come on," DiMarco prodded.

"All right, all right!" Judd snapped and stood. "Ask your questions."

DiMarco looked like she didn't like his tone, but I guess she didn't have a lot of choice. She started the group questions.

"You've all been together since Thursday, staying at the Swanton Hills Lodge with Dr. Hart and her staff. Is that correct?"

"Yeah," Judd spat out.

"Have you all seen the aura maker demonstrated?"

"Yeah." Judd didn't look at anyone for confirmation.

"Is there anyone among you who *knows* what happened to Dr. Hart?"

"Not me," Judd answered.

"Anyone else?" the sergeant pushed.

No one answered her. Not even Craig. His eyes were closed. Maybe he was asleep.

"Have you—" Sergeant DiMarco began.

A loud banging sounded from somewhere near the back end of the stage.

DiMarco whirled around, and I heard a gasp from our row.

I didn't know about everyone else, but I was seriously spooked. My heart was marching double-time. Was that Dr. Hart's spirit knocking from the rafters?

"There's a back door," Sara Oshima whispered.

DiMarco ran up the stairs and across the stage to the back door, which I'd never noticed was there.

"Who is it?" she demanded. She sounded a little spooked herself.

"Forensics!" a voice shouted back through the door.

DiMarco opened the door and a woman and a man stepped through. They looked at Sergeant DiMarco, and they looked at Dr. Hart's body.

"Screens," the man said.

"Yep," the woman agreed and headed back out the door.

My heartbeat got back to normal by the time the screens went up between Dr. Hart's body and the rest of the hall. DiMarco turned back to us. Judd was still standing.

"Who wants to be interviewed next?" she asked.

"I do," I answered, raising my hand. For a moment, I wondered if I'd actually spoken. Because the interviews were being done by the chief. The guy with the gun.

But I was tired. It wasn't enough to have a screen between me and Dr. Hart. I wanted to leave the hall and go back to my hotel room. Actually, I wanted to go home. For a second, I pictured my little house with its latticed deck, my cat, and my goats. And in that second, that picture seemed more real than what was happening here in the Swanton Boy Scout Hall.

DiMarco said, "Let's go," and motioned me up. The picture dissolved.

I stood and followed Sergeant DiMarco down the aisle made by the chairs we women had set up, telling myself I had nothing to be afraid of. Okay, I was wrong.

When we entered the little office across the hall from the rest rooms, the chief was already seated behind a desk stacked with files that didn't appear to be his. He didn't ask me to sit down.

"So why'd you do it?!" he demanded, pushing himself out of his chair by slamming his hands, palms first, onto the desk. His jutting face glimmered with hatred. If I were looking for a murderer, I'd bet on this man. "You killed her, Ms. Lazar. Don't try and jerk me around."

I grasped my cane. Would I need to knock a gun out of his hand soon?

"You fooled with her chakra thingie and poof, she's gone, right?"

"No, I did no such thing," I answered finally. I kept my tone down though. Chief Phlug really scared me. And he had power. I just hoped that he didn't believe what he was saying.

"What was your beef with the lady?" he pushed.

I peeked at his aura. He was afraid. He was angry and frustrated, but he was mostly afraid. Of what, losing face?

"Dr. Hart was a difficult person," I offered gently. "I'm

sure you'll hear that from all of us. And I know how hard this must be for you. As far as I know, none of us liked her much, except for Quinn Vogel and maybe Sara Oshima. But I can't imagine anyone killing the doctor either. Is it possible that her aura maker just malfunctioned?"

"D'you think I know?" he replied, but he was easing himself back down into his seat. "County forensics will have to figure it out. And they hate helping us little cities. They think we're a bunch of hicks."

"But they're working on it now," I put in hopefully.

"Yeah, they're working on it," he agreed. "They'll probably tell the papers before they tell me."

"The interview, Chief?" DiMarco's voice came from behind me. Criminy, had she become the bad cop? Was she going to throw him raw meat next?

"Yeah, yeah, the interview," he conceded. He pointed at the chair across the desk. "Have a seat."

"Thank you," I said politely.

"So explain this here deal to me," he ordered. "According to Sara what's-her-name, you're all a bunch of 'healers.' Why'd you come to spend time with this Dr. Hart anyway?"

"Dr. Hart was really good at what she did—"

"What the heck *did* she do?"

It was a good question. I thought for a heartbeat.

"Dr. Hart was a medical intuitive, a real one. She could look at a person and see the root causes of their problems, their hidden issues. If a person was depressed, she could see why. If a person had cancer, she could see why. And she used the chakra system as her own way of perceiving the client's issues."

"How?" the chief demanded. "I don't get this chakra stuff."

This was getting hard. I could barely articulate how *I* worked. And I wasn't exactly sure how Dr. Hart was able to perceive what she perceived, much less explain the process.

"Okay," I said slowly. "Let's say a person is depressed. Dr. Hart might look at the person's chakras and see that the energy in certain areas of the person's body is blocked or murky or shut down. Depending on the area, she might have an idea of what the general issue causing the depression is. And see, well, this is how come I think she was so good, she was often able to intuit the actual events and issues that led to the depression."

"Are you telling me this lady was psychic?"

"Yeah, I guess so," I admitted, "But see, she used the information she got from looking at energy fields to nudge herself into knowing." This was impossible; I couldn't explain it. But I supposed Dr. Hart had been the most psychic among us healers. No one else had been able to see like she had.

"So, she was psychic," the chief said, nodding as if he'd known all the time.

"Yeah, psychic," I agreed, realizing I could have saved myself a lot of trouble by just saying that in the first place.

"And she was better than you," he went on.

I nodded.

He raised himself back up on the desk again, squinted his eyes, and accused, "So you killed her because she was better than you!"

"No!" I yelped. "I wanted to learn from her."

It went on like that for a long time. Every once in a while, Sergeant DiMarco put in some reasonable questions about what each of us was doing during the hall setup, and whether anyone could have had access to Dr. Hart's aura maker before we got to the hall. I remembered it lying in the meeting room at the Swanton Hills Lodge in between sessions. For all I knew, it could have been there all night.

"I think anyone could have tinkered with it if they were careful not to be seen," I said finally.

"Like you, Ms. Lazar?" Chief Phlug snarled.

"Not me," I answered.

The chief was getting easier to deal with. I was just beginning to wonder if this had all been scripted, so that I would answer Sergeant DiMarco's questions without thought, when the chief and the sergeant exchanged glances.

"Anything else you'd like to tell us?" Sergeant DiMarco asked.

I shook my head.

"Then you're free to go," Chief Phlug told me.

I sat for a moment, stunned. Had I just been successfully double-teamed?

"Aw, get out of here," the chief ordered.

"Can I go back to my hotel room?" I asked.

"Fine," Chief Phlug answered, throwing up his hands. "Or go hang out with your healer friends. It doesn't matter to me."

I stood up.

"Just don't leave town," he added.

I walked back to the Swanton Hills Lodge feeling sorry for myself, *very* sorry for myself. I was homesick and heartsick. The chief had called the healers from the intensive my "friends." But they weren't real friends, just colleagues. My real friends were at home in Glasse County. I took off my glasses and wiped my eyes before walking into the lodge.

The lobby was deserted. I wondered if the owners of the lodge had heard about Dr. Hart's death yet. If they hadn't, I wasn't going to tell them. I walked softly past the wooden reception desk. The interior of the lobby was like the interior of all the rooms, rough cream-colored stucco walls with wood-timbered ceilings, copper-colored rugs, copper and wood accents, and earth-toned fabrics. Not a primary color in sight. It was nice, if you liked that kind of rustication. I just wished I did.

I walked down the hall and opened my door on the second try with my card key.

I stopped, heart jumping, as I walked into the room.

There were six people on my bed lined up like dolls. I blinked and saw who the people were: my sisters, Geneva and Melinda; my brothers, York and Arnot; and my friends, Dee-Dee and Joan. I sniffed and smelled aftershave. My friend Kapp had to be behind the door, lurking with his cane. I turned and parried his strike.

"Holy Mother, how do you always know?" he asked. I could have hugged him, but he would have blushed. So I knocked his cane sideways and poked him in the belly instead.

"Bravo!" Geneva cried and clapped.

"I taught her," York put in gruffly.

Then they were all talking at the same time.

"Criminy—"

"Are you okay?"

"Did that weird cop from Pluto—"

"Did you ever get to eat dinner?"

"I couldn't believe it when Kapp called—"

"Do you need to sit down?"

I did need to sit down. Joan pulled up a rust- and olive-green-colored chair. Despite the colors, I slumped down in it, shaking my head and smiling for the first time since Dr. Hart had collapsed. My smile muscles felt stiff and sore.

"You're all here," I whispered.

"Kapp called," Geneva explained. "And we all got in our cars and came up."

"And Dee-Dee and I were already at the speech," Joan reminded me.

"Thank you, Kapp," I said sincerely.

"Huh, poke an old man in the stomach will you?" he replied, blushing. "Anyway, I'm gonna help you investigate this murder."

"Whoa!" I stopped him. "We don't know that it was murder."

"Well, *you* may not know, but *I* sure as hell do," he told me.

"No," I tried again.

He grinned and chortled.

"How'd you find out," I asked in defeat.

"Old friend in the coroner's office," he informed me. I believed him. Kapp had old friends everywhere. "The aura maker was tampered with. Shielding removed under the armpits, electrical connection rigged to go off when she hit the seventh button. Hooboy, someone didn't like the good doctor."

"*I* didn't like her," I murmured without thinking. And I felt ashamed.

"Oh, Cally, sweetie," my friend Dee-Dee offered gently. "You don't have to like *everyone*."

"Yeah!" the room chorused.

Suddenly, they were all asking questions again.

"Wait!" I called out through the din. "Kapp, do you know if the police suspect the members of the intensive?"

"Damned straight, they do," he answered. "They figure it was either one of the doctor's two employees or one of you healers."

"Great," I muttered.

"Morons," Melinda put in.

"We'll find out—" Kapp began.

"No, not this time," I argued, putting up my hands. "I'm a healer, not an investigator."

"I've already made a reservation here," Kapp said smugly. "I'm just down the hall. So you just sit on your fanny while I investigate."

It was useless. And I was hungry. Arnot went in search of food for me, while Kapp laid out his plans.

"No," I tried again, once he'd finished.

"But you're an insider with the healers, and I'm an insider with the powers that be," he pointed out. "Holy Mother, no one can stop the two of us."

"I'm staying here, too," York threw in. "If Kapp's gonna get you involved, and I'm sure he will, someone's gotta watch your back." He glared at Kapp. Kapp glared in return.

"But—"

Arnot was back with a tuna sandwich and cookies for me before I could finish.

I ate and listened to my relatives and friends argue about my safety.

Geneva was clearly peeved with Kapp. Arnot and Melinda just wanted to be in on the fun. Joan thought the whole thing was far too dangerous. York just crossed his arms and glared. And Dee-Dee thought I needed to process my feelings about Dr. Hart's death. No one asked me what I thought.

"Dee-Dee's right," I interrupted once I'd finished my sandwich and cookies. "I need to process this thing . . . alone."

"I love you all," I whispered as I ushered my friends and family out of my room.

And finally, I was alone. Dr. Hart's seizing body played on my inner video. I breathed in. I saw Craig Zweig pointing at the rafters. I breathed out. I remembered Quinn's anguished cries. I—

The phone rang.

I approached it cautiously, picking it up as if it had teeth.

"It's me, darlin' " the voice on the phone said. It took me a moment. Roy, it was Roy, my sweetheart! But Roy was in Kentucky. "Cally," he went on gently. "There's darkness near you. I had to call to warn you."

FIVE

Too late, I thought, but I didn't say it.

I just said, "I miss you too, Roy." And I did. I could just picture his compact, muscular body and bony, freckled face. And his eyes, those golden eyes.

"No really, darlin'," he insisted. "I know I'm not there to judge. And I don't want you to fret, but it's as if something bad is hovering where you are. I'm afraid for you."

"Oh, Roy," I told him. "I'll be fine. I always am, you know. Remember, how the light—"

"Something's already happened, hasn't it?" he demanded, interrupting me suddenly.

I hesitated a little too long before answering.

"A small obstacle—" I began.

"Oh, Cally," he sighed.

"Roy, I'm *okay*," I tried. "Honestly. Everything is fine." I tried to convince myself it was true. A person could still be fine after a murder. As long as that person wasn't the victim.

"Really?" he asked softly. I felt as if I could see his face tilted to the side, wondering if I was telling him the full truth. Probably knowing I wasn't.

I breathed in. "Really," I assured him. I was thinking between words: Should I tell Roy what was going on, or was he better off not knowing? Not worrying? Not cutting his trip short? I changed the subject. "Roy, when you get back, let's go on a picnic."

"A picnic?"

"Yeah, there're some cool places near here for picnics," I went on. I'd seen them in the AAA guide anyway. "It would be fun. Especially if I could find a lake."

"Are you going to feed all of our sandwiches to the ducks like the last time?" he asked. I heard the smile in his voice.

"You were the one who started it," I countered, stretching the phone to the bed and lying down. " 'Here, duckie, duckie,' " I called, imitating his Kentucky accent.

And for a while, lying on that bedspread, staring up at the raftered ceiling, I really did feel fine. It was as if Dr. Hart hadn't died, as Roy and I let our conversation segue here and there. We laughed together, and talked, and talked some more. Then we each said, "I love you."

But just as I was going to hang up the phone, Roy added, "Cally, be careful. Promise me, darlin'?"

I promised and hung up. And I would be careful. I put on my pajamas and slid in between the white sheets underneath the earth-toned bedspread, laying my glasses next to my head on the nightstand. I would be careful, but how?

I still didn't have an answer when I woke the next morning. It was Sunday. But I had slept long and oddly well after my talk with Roy, and I was hungry. It was hard to believe that anyone had died the previous night.

The minute I stepped out of my room, I saw Heidi Jin-nah, who co-owned the Swanton Hills Lodge with her husband, Bob, coming my way. Heidi had baby-fine, shoulder-length, blonde hair, intense eyes, and a square jaw. She ran the lodge. Her husband was a poet. And Heidi was fierce in her protection of her husband's poetry, privacy, and the lodge that sustained them both.

"Ms. Lazar," she greeted me. I felt like saluting.

"Cally," I told her. "Call me Cally."

"Cally," she corrected herself. "Cally, please tell me you're staying for the rest of your intensive."

"Well, I—"

"Chief Phlug is putting a lot of pressure on us," Heidi went on. "He wants you all to stay until he figures out . . ."

". . . who killed Dr. Hart," I finished for her. All the anxiety that had fled since I'd talked to Roy reversed and tunneled back into my body through my stomach walls. I wasn't hungry anymore.

Heidi nodded. "Phlug wants you happy," she stated grimly. "And you'll be happy. First off, we have breakfast on the house." She pointed down the hall. Was that a buffet table down there in the lobby? "And tours. Wineries, gardens—"

"Is Phlug making you do all this?" I asked.

Heidi took a second to really look me in the eye. She nodded. "Phlug can make our life miserable here. Code violations, hassle our guests, hassle us. He's always hated Bob. As far as Phlug is concerned, anyone who has the nerve to come here from Canada, be of Pakistani ancestry, and write poetry should be run out of town. The chief was just easing up on us a little, getting to know Bob, when this awful thing happened. And Bob needs a serene place to write. You understand?"

I felt like saluting again, but I just nodded.

"Good." Heidi smiled. Somehow, she was as scary as Chief Phlug. "Breakfast on the house," she reminded me. "And you're due in the meeting hall at nine o'clock."

I heard a door open somewhere down the hallway. Heidi's eyes narrowed as she looked over my shoulder.

"See you later," I muttered as I made my escape.

I passed the buffet on my way outside. It looked good, loaded with pastries, cereals, fruits, and egg dishes. Once I got my stomach uncramped, I would go back in and enjoy it. Until then, I stood outside and looked past the lawns to the rolling hills of Swanton. It was a beautiful day made of blue skies, green hills, oak trees, and chirping birds. Maybe Roy and I really would find a place to picnic here. I felt my whole body unwind as I imagined our picnic.

I was smiling when I heard the sound of a car driving up behind me. I turned and saw the Swanton Police Department logo on the car that was pulling into the parking lot. I didn't wait to see who got out of the car. I went back inside and headed toward the buffet.

A fruit smoothie, a slice of vegetable frittata, and a cherry-apple scone later, I was feeling full.

Judd Nyman joined me at the buffet as I was clearing my dishes. He smiled, his strong face looking attractive.

"Always good out of bad, right?" he offered. "This place is going all out for us."

I heard raised voices from behind the reception desk.

"I can't—"

"You'd better—"

"But—"

"No buts—"

Judd just kept on talking. Maybe he was deaf.

"It's a good thing Quinn's keeping the intensive going," he went on. "You gotta stand up for yourself, ya know?"

A voice from behind us murmured, "For Dr. Hart." I turned and saw Dotty. Her eyes looked sunken, but her round features radiated kindness.

"Hey, forget the doctor," Judd advised. "She's history. But if we stick around, we can learn from each other. Everyone here has something to offer, except for that goofball, Craig."

Dotty's features hardened.

I opened my mouth to say something, anything, when I

smelled aftershave. I whipped around, lifting my cane, expecting my friend Kapp. But either I'd imagined the scent, or Kapp was keeping himself well hidden. I'd have bet on the latter. Maybe behind that huge potted plant? I moved toward it and heard the voices from behind the reception desk again.

"We'll do our best—"

"Do better than your best. Keep 'em here," came the final statement. I wasn't surprised to see Chief Phlug walk out from behind the desk. He stared at us, squinting his eyes. I turned away from the stare and found myself looking into Taj Gemayel's eyes instead.

"Was she really murdered?" he whispered. His formerly sexy voice was quiet, frightened. "Do they suspect anyone?"

With that, everyone was whispering. I felt guilty. I knew what Kapp knew. I knew the doctor had been murdered. But I couldn't say anything. I didn't want to say anything. I just wanted to be alone again. I couldn't pretend not to know.

So I went back outside, breathing in the clean air, trying to remember the fantasy of a picnic.

"Psst!" I heard from behind an oak tree. I strolled over to the tree, expecting Kapp, but it was my brother York who stood behind it. York didn't look happy. And his narrow Lazar features were not improved by his scowl.

"Cally, can you leave now?" he asked me.

"I'm not sure," I answered, thinking of the promise I'd made Heidi Jinnah. And there was something, something. *Did* I want to find Dr. Hart's killer?

"I don't like the way the doctor was killed," York pronounced. "It was rigged. It could happen again, to anyone, to you. This isn't something you can fight with your cane."

"I know," I told him seriously, remembering my promise to Roy. "But there's no reason I should be a target. As long as Kapp doesn't tell people I'm investigating."

"He won't" York assured me shortly.

I believed him. Or at least I believed that Kapp wouldn't say anything within earshot of York.

"Talk to me," York ordered.

I talked.

"And you really don't know who is dangerous?"

I shook my head.

"Cally, either Kapp or I will be watching you, but be careful. Don't fool with anything electrical. Don't challenge anyone. Don't let anyone know what you know."

I thought about what he said and nodded, resisting the urge to argue with him just because he was my brother. York looked carefully around and walked quickly toward the parking lot, disappearing among the cars.

I stayed outside a little longer. Then it was nine o'clock. I took a big breath and walked back into the lodge.

The meeting room was nearly full by the time I walked in. I knew why I was here. At least I thought I did. But why was everyone else here?

I looked around. Quinn and Sara stood where Dr. Hart had stood before, at the other end of the room across from the door. There were a few cushy chairs set out, and Judd, Dotty, Taj, Kim, and Raleigh were already seated. Fran came through the door with Craig. And Ed followed them.

Once we were all in our seats, Quinn cleared his throat.

We looked up. Quinn was not Dr. Hart. Quinn was a short man in his late twenties with a long, hound-dog face and liquid brown eyes that looked ready to spill over at any moment. He ran his hand through his short hair and stood a little straighter.

"Dr. Hart is gone but her Chakra Commitment Program lives on," he began, a small tremble in his quiet voice. "You who are here in this room are her handpicked intensive students. You have much to learn—"

"Was she murdered?" Fran asked, raising her hand.

Quinn's eyes widened. He spoke again. "The police are

in charge of finding out how Dr. Hart died. We need to keep our work moving—"

"She *was* murdered, wasn't she?" Judd challenged.

Quinn took a quick short breath. "I just can't answer that question. Even if I knew, I couldn't. Dr. Hart was . . . was—"

"Dr. Hart thought she was my mother," Sara threw in. She giggled.

Quinn swiveled his head around to look at her, his long face a mask of horror.

"What is so funny, Ms. Oshima?" Ed Lau asked from the floor. He sounded like the schoolteacher he had been.

"She didn't want me dating Ira, but we went out last night," Sara answered, her eyes dreamy. "She was always so worried about me, but she was the one who died."

"And you find that funny?" Ed pressed.

"No, I don't find it funny!" Sara shouted. "I find it hilarious!" But she wasn't giggling anymore. She was crying. "I put her in the aura maker. I didn't see anything wrong with it. I was too busy thinking about Ira. I just wanted to have some fun. I just—"

"Sara," Quinn interjected softly. The horror had left his face. "Why don't you sit down. I understand how you must feel—"

"But you don't!" Sara wailed. I looked around me. Was there a healer in the house?

I got up from my chair and walked to Sara, my hand outstretched. She took it easily, sniffling like a child as I sat her down in a chair, and murmured "there, there," at her. Her aura was less chaotic than it had been the night before, but it was still unstable.

"My mother is dead," she whispered.

I wondered if she meant Dr. Hart. "When did she die?" I asked carefully.

"Last year," she answered. "And now, Dr. Hart."

"It wasn't your fault," I whispered. The blue at her fifth

chakra separated out and grew clearer. I took her hand and imagined the chaos in her chakras all separating out and clarifying as guilt and anger and loss released. The colors began to realign. But something was still blocked. I thought of forgiveness, breathing it in and out. Sara began to breathe with me as I mentally surrounded her in a warm, womb-pink cloud of safety.

Finally, she closed her eyes and leaned back in her chair.

"I couldn't sleep," she murmured, and then her body relaxed. She was sleeping finally, curled in a fetal position in her cushy chair.

I looked up at Quinn and mouthed, "She's okay," all the while hoping I was right. Sara needed a lot of work. Whatever had helped her to sleep was just a quick fix. Maybe that's why she'd ended up working with Dr. Hart. Had she longed for a healing that would really take? A healing that would work even while she used recreational drugs? Or did she use the drugs to get past a hurt so bad that she couldn't risk mental coherence?

Quinn took a big breath, and I returned my focus to him.

"So it's up to us to continue the Chakra Commitment," he went on as if he'd never been interrupted. "I know, under the circumstances some of you would rather leave. There is a part of *me* that would rather leave. But I think there are some very good reasons for you not to leave. I have at least four—"

"Dr. Hart is still here," Craig put in. I didn't think that was one of Quinn's reasons. But at least Quinn gave it a hearing.

"I can understand why you might feel that," he told Craig. "Emotionally, spiritually, energetically, Dr. Hart is here—"

"She's here, but she's hiding," Craig expanded. He smiled knowingly, exposing his snaggly teeth.

Quinn nodded as if he understood. That was a kind gesture . . . or maybe he did understand.

"So give us your reasons," Judd prodded impatiently.

"Oh, right," Quinn murmured, refocusing. He straightened his shoulders again. "The first reason has to do with being a good citizen—"

"You mean Chief Phlug," Fran corrected him.

"Well, um . . . yes, Chief Phlug," Quinn floundered. It was painful just to watch him.

"He's going to suspect anyone who leaves now," Ed asserted quietly.

"Of what?" Fran argued, her hands flapping in the air. "We're all acting as if Dr. Hart was murdered. We don't know that."

"Don't we?" Kim whispered.

"What?" Taj asked her. "Have they told you anything?"

But it was Raleigh who answered. "Chief Phlug thinks she was murdered until proven otherwise. And he thinks each and every one of us might have been in on it."

"Did he tell you that?" Taj demanded, his voice growing more shrill. Taj's sensuous eyes looked more frightened than compelling today.

"No," Raleigh answered. Even the one word was resonant when he used it. "I've just got a deep-down feeling. I watch people. When you're black, you've gotta watch people like the police. And Phlug is afraid. He's afraid of us. We're too weird for him. He wants to get this thing settled fast. I think we should let the man do his work. If the doctor was murdered, we want to know who killed her. We can't just leave."

"Thank you," Quinn offered sincerely. "That's what I was trying to say. The police need us to stay. And I, for one, want to know who killed Aurora . . . the doctor, if anyone did kill her."

"Me, too," Dotty threw in.

"Okay," Quinn said softly. "May I go on to my next point?"

"Go for it," I encouraged him.

"Yeah," Raleigh and Judd agreed.

"You came here to learn," he told us. "And you can learn from each other. And maybe help each other heal. And you'll get your certificates—"

"Hell, we'd better," Judd piped up.

But people were nodding, at least some of us.

"Point three," Quinn forged ahead. "The Jinnahs who own this lodge have offered to add even more to our stay. They are planning special events right now, tours and food. They are trying really hard—"

"Because they're afraid of Chief Phlug," I put in. I couldn't help myself. "And maybe for good reason."

"Right," Quinn agreed amiably enough. "We can help them as well as ourselves."

That was a good appeal to a group of healers. I was convinced.

"And one final thing," Quinn uttered softly. I bent forward to hear him better. "We have to live with ourselves. We have to find closure. We need to be able to sleep at night."

"Sleep," Sara muttered beside me.

I felt instantly guilty for my good sleep the night before. I looked at the deep circles under Quinn's eyes. He probably hadn't slept any better than Sara had. I looked around me. Taj's face was a casebook illustration of panic. Kim was still pale with shock . . . or maybe depression. Craig was jerking his shoulders and staring at a spot on the ceiling. I had a feeling he'd stepped over a line of sanity he'd managed to keep himself behind before. Fran was clenching and unclenching her fists. Frustration? Ed and Raleigh seemed to be consciously reining in their emotions. Dotty's eyes were wet with tears. Judd was the only one who looked like he was enjoying himself.

"So, will you all stay and finish the intensive?" Quinn asked. "Please raise your hand if you're willing."

Everyone's hand went up but Fran's and Taj's.

"What?" Judd demanded of the two holdouts.

"What if the doctor was killed?" Taj shot back. "How do we know we're safe?"

"Give it a break, kid," Judd advised. "You could get killed driving home in your car. Nobody's got any reason to go after you, do they?"

"No . . ." he faltered.

"Well, just forget it," Judd said cheerfully.

"Oh, all right," Fran announced sullenly from Judd's other side.

"Taj?" Quinn probed gently.

"Okay, okay!" Taj snapped. He threw his arms open theatrically. "I'm cool."

"Thank you," Quinn breathed. He steepled his hands together and bowed low. "Thank you."

"So what are we gonna do?" Judd pressed.

"One-on-one sessions in the morning," Quinn answered. He'd obviously prepared for this part. He could barely get the words out fast enough. "Each of you pick a partner and decide who goes first. The first person can practice his or her unique healing skills on the second. After half an hour, you switch and the second person can demonstrate their skills. And please, try not to pick any issues you can't resolve in that time. We'll discuss what we've learned in the afternoon."

I was busy wondering if Dr. Hart's death came under the category of an issue that couldn't be resolved in a half hour when I saw Raleigh walking toward me.

I felt a little tingle. Was it fear? No, not fear. Then I recognized the tingle. It was that tingle I felt with Roy. It was lust.

SIX

Lust! Everyone reacts differently to stress. Especially someone who talked to her sweetie all night long and didn't get to touch him. Especially when a man as attractive and comforting as Raleigh Hutchinson was heading that someone's way. Especially—criminy, did I have enough excuses?

The thing was not to act upon it. Right? I loved Roy.

"So, Raleigh," I greeted him when he reached my chair, my tone businesslike. At least I hoped it was businesslike. "Do you want to pair up for the first exercise?"

I felt my skin flush. Why did I have to use those particular words?

"I'd love to, Cally," he purred, smiling that sexy smile at me. "But I suppose we ought to do energy work instead." He slapped the side of his leg.

He was making a joke. But I couldn't figure it out for an instant. When I did, I blushed. He was saying he'd heard me say I'd like to "pair up" with him. Son of a lizard! Were pheromones at work here? I stretched my face into a tight smile and tried to laugh. It came out more like a cough, or maybe a death rattle.

Raleigh's smile disappeared. "Are you all right, Cally?" he asked seriously.

"Fine," I squeaked. "Just fine."

He peered into my eyes. He looked worried.

I took a big breath. "I really am fine, Raleigh," I told him, my voice back to something near normal. "Just a little spooked."

"Yeah," He murmured. "Me, too." He bent close and whispered. "That's why I wanted to work with you first. You have a calming way about you, um—"

"Usually?" I supplied.

The light came back into his eyes. "Yeah, usually," he agreed and chuckled. This time, I was with him. I did love Roy. And Raleigh was cool. I was beginning to realize that it was his assurance that I found attractive right then, not his body. Raleigh was not just a handsome man, he was a big, confident man, a man who'd taken charge along with Ed Lau last night. And for all of my meditations, I was scared. What a relief! I wasn't suffering from lust, just mind-numbing terror that I'd been busy denying. I wanted to giggle, but held it in. I couldn't explain all of this to Raleigh.

"I could use a little calming about now," he said, breaking into my thoughts. So much for my presumption of Raleigh's unfailing confidence. Still, he was honest.

"Do you want me to go first?" I asked, starting to get out of my chair.

"No, no," he answered, motioning me back. "Let me do my thing on you first. Doing my work always calms me down."

So I sat in my chair and let Raleigh do his thing. He pulled a chair around to face me and lowered himself into it.

"I heard you sing last night," he told me. My skin flushed again. My singing wasn't for anyone's ears but my cat's and goats'.

"You sound about like this," and Raleigh let out a high, almost shrill note. It didn't sound right coming from his mouth. Was *that* what I sounded like?

"Dack!" I muttered.

"Did you say, 'dack'?" he demanded.

"Um, yeah," I told him.

He just laughed. "I gotta add that to my list. People never realize what they sound like."

I smiled. I wasn't alone.

"Now, sing it with me," he ordered.

I wanted to argue, but I just closed my eyes and obeyed.

We hummed together for a while. He lowered his voice a notch. I lowered mine with his. That was nice. It didn't just sound better, it felt better. His voice reached deeper into his chest. My voice did the same, into my own chest, of course. His voice went even deeper into his body. I could almost see it through my closed eyes, a crystalline pointer. I followed it, singing the note from the center of my body. I forgot that I was in a room full of people. I just felt the note. I was the note. And I was almost where my meditations took me. Sensations and images floated deliciously through my mind at random: the flight of a bird, the sweet scent of narcissus, the release of making love—

My eyes popped open, and I stopped humming.

Raleigh stopped a second after me.

"What?" he asked gently.

I couldn't tell him where his voice had taken me.

"I was overwhelmed," I told him instead. It was true in its own way.

"Ah," he replied. "Can you just go with it?"

Could I?

Before I could answer, I heard Judd across the room, haranguing Craig. I had forgotten Craig. I had forgotten Judd.

"Chill out, man!" Judd snapped. "Are you trying for the insanity defense or what?"

Craig just laughed, staring at the ceiling.

Raleigh frowned. His smile was sweet, but his frown was scary.

"Believe it or not," I whispered. "I think Judd is trying to help Craig. But still, I'm an optimist."

Raleigh turned back to me and sighed.

"I wish I was an optimist," Raleigh murmured. "I've watched you. You see good in everyone. Even now."

"Well, not exactly—" I began.

"More than me, anyway," he cut back in. "And it isn't just the people. It's the cruelty of life that bothers me. I can't seem to get past it, except for my singing. And my work. Damn. Dr. Hart was nasty. And her death was even nastier. How does it get this way? We all want to do the right things, and then somehow—"

"Time to switch roles with your partners!" Quinn yelled out. Ed Lau stood with Quinn, apparently his partner for the exercise.

Sara shifted in her seat where she was still dozing next to me. I reached out and patted her hand. She needed her sleep.

"I guess we've already switched," Raleigh said ruefully. "I was supposed to be working on you, and I was busy bending your ear."

"That wasn't part of the treatment?" I asked, opening my eyes wide.

He laughed. It was a good laugh. I resisted patting *his* hand.

"Listen, Raleigh," I ventured. "That singing deal was amazing. I want to do more sometime."

His eyes brightened. "I hope so," he volunteered. "Lots of times, I worry I'm just thinking it helps because it feels good to me."

"It helps," I assured him.

"Thanks," he offered. "So, do you want to work your magic now?"

"I'll try," I told him, "but half an hour isn't enough to do much more than peek. I don't want to open up any issues I can't resolve."

He held out his hands as if to open his heart to me. "Go ahead, peek away," he invited.

Could Raleigh be a murderer? I looked at his face and saw the sadness underlying the show-business smile. I sat for a moment, getting a feel for his energy. There it was! Strong, but suffering. Good-intentioned, but ambivalent. His aura wasn't hidden. It was as open as he was. I couldn't see any anger there, not even much fear. What I saw was grief, overwhelming grief in the form of a gray-green mass overpowering everything else. That was a surprise. Raleigh who seemed so good at expressing himself was helpless against the onslaught of the suffering of others. It was all there. I reached out and touched his thumbs and first fingers to begin with, inviting the grief to release energetically.

"You can let it go," I told Raleigh's body. "It isn't yours."

Raleigh's face became serious.

"You can't take it all on yourself—" I tried.

Judd's voice rang out again.

"You're psychotic!" he blared at Craig. "There are no ghosts in this room."

"I'm sorry," Craig answered. "But they're not sorry, especially Aurora. She's here. I know where—"

"Stop it, you nutcase!" Judd shouted.

The red of anger flowed into Raleigh's aura so quickly, it startled me. I dropped his hands.

He jumped from his seat.

In three or four long strides, he went to where Judd and Craig stood. He grabbed Judd's shoulder, none too gently.

"No, *you* stop it!" he demanded. "Right now. This man needs help, not bullying. What kind of healer did you claim to be?"

"But—"

"No buts, man—" Raleigh interrupted him. "Are you here to help this man or to abuse him?"

Craig giggled.

"But look at him," Judd insisted. "He's nuts."

"Why?" Raleigh challenged.

"Whaddaya mean, why?" Judd shot back.

"Why is he 'nuts'?" Raleigh bulldozed on. "What can you do to help his suffering? He's human . . ."

Sara woke up next to me.

"Dr. Hart?" she murmured.

"Dr. Hart isn't here, honey," I told her gently. But my mind was still on Raleigh. How had he changed from grief and suffering to rage in seconds? Could he have killed Dr. Hart? He might have done it instantly, I decided, in anger. But could he have planned it ahead of time? I shook my head. Raleigh was angry in defense of someone he saw as helpless. That made sense of the twinned feelings he held in his aura of rage and suffering for others. But could he have killed to help someone else?

"Cally," Sara whispered. "Why are they fighting?"

"I'm human, too," Judd was arguing. "How come I don't get any of your sympathy? You think I'm not whacked out over this thing, huh? I'm handling myself my way. I just hate to see someone like Craig disintegrate right in front of me."

"And you think that bullying him is helping?" Raleigh demanded.

"Yeah, I do!"

"Cally," Sara prodded me, her voice a little louder now. I turned toward her. Sara's red-rimmed eyes were wide in her oval face. "Do I have to stay for this? I don't like to see people fighting. It's scary."

I looked up at Quinn who was watching Judd and Raleigh along with the rest of the intensive members. Except for Craig, who was staring at the ceiling again.

"I don't see why you have to stay here," I told Sara cautiously. "But I need to ask Quinn."

"I want to go to my room," she insisted, shrillness entering her tone.

Craig waved his hand. "Hi, Aurora!" he called out. "Hi, Buckley. Hi, Jessica."

Great. It looked like Dr. Hart wasn't alone anymore. She had invisible friends.

"Does he really see Dr. Hart?" Sara demanded. "Is she really still here?" Then she shouted out, "Dr. Hart, do you see me?"

Uh-oh. I looked up at the ceiling myself. I didn't see anything but ceiling, not even a telltale wisp of aura.

"Dr. Hart!" Sara tried again. She stood up from her chair and waved her hands. "It's me, Sara."

Kim and Taj were looking at the ceiling, too. And they both looked frightened.

"Sara," I asked as calmly as I could. "Do you really see the doctor up there?"

"No," Sara admitted, and she began to cry.

"Sara," I instructed. "It's okay. You have your memories of Dr. Hart in your mind and body and spirit. You don't need to see a ghost."

"But I miss her!" she wailed. "I thought I hated her, but I miss her."

I looked over at Quinn. He was walking our way fast.

"Can I take Sara back to her room?" I asked, standing up next to his stricken next-in-command.

"Oh, yes, please," Quinn whispered urgently. "I need some control here."

At least Judd and Raleigh didn't seem to be arguing anymore. Judd was watching *us*. And Raleigh was humming at Craig.

"Sara, do you want me to walk you to your room?" I asked.

Sara fell against me, practically knocking me over. I

grasped my cane with one hand and wrapped my other hand around Sara's waist.

"Help me," I whispered in her ear. "Walk with me. I can't carry you."

"Okay, Cally," Sara replied drowsily. And she straightened her small but heavy body, standing next to me like a sleepwalker. Together, we walked out the door into the hall.

"Need any help, ma'am?" a loud voice asked from behind me.

It was lucky Sara wasn't still leaning on me, because I jumped straight into the air like a kangaroo on amphetamines.

When I landed, I turned, cane poised.

"Officer Jones," I said, recognizing the officer that reminded me of a puppy from the night before. I couldn't say anything more until my heart settled down. I lowered my cane. Had he been spying on our group? Of course, he had.

"Just keeping an eye on things," he told me, blushing.

"Thanks," I spit out. Actually, once I knew he'd been there all the time, I felt a little safer. "I'm just taking Ms. Oshima to her room," I added. "She's pretty upset by everything."

"Right, right," he muttered, nodding and blushing some more. As I hustled Sara away, I wondered if he blushed when he gave out traffic tickets, too.

Sara's room was upstairs. She pulled a card key from her pocket and inserted it when we reached her door. I entered the room with her and saw a mirror image of my room downstairs. Except that my room didn't have clothes strewn on the floor. Or food containers, or papers, or makeup devices, or jewelry.

"Sara?" I probed gently. "Did your room look like this when you left it?"

She looked around absently. "I guess so," she answered, "but someone made the bed."

I laughed. I couldn't help it.

"What?" she asked.

"It looks like someone searched your room," I explained.

She smiled. "Oh that. Hey, it's cool. Dr. Hart used to get on my case about it. I told her, the messier the room, the cleaner the mind."

The smile left her face.

"I almost forgot she was gone," she murmured.

"Are you going to be all right alone?" I asked.

"I think so," she answered slowly. "I think I just need to be alone and cry for a while. It's all so weird now, with the doctor gone and all."

"Sara, you won't take any drugs, will you?" I prodded. I knew it was none of my business, but without Dr. Hart, I was afraid Sara might go under.

"Not today," she told me. "I promised myself. Not today, you know, for Dr. Hart."

I squeezed her shoulder.

"Thanks," I breathed.

"Thank you, Cally," she said back. She even tried a smile. She lay down on her bed and closed her eyes.

I shut her door quietly behind me and walked downstairs, worrying. Sara needed help. And beyond that, I wondered if she might actually be the murderer. She *had* put Dr. Hart into her aura maker. Maybe Sara's current breakdown was merely all-too-appropriate remorse.

By the time I got back to the meeting room, nobody was acting out anymore. Craig sat in a chair across from Raleigh, humming with him cheerfully. Judd was working with Kim. It looked like he was massaging her feet. She didn't seem to notice. Fran and Dotty were sharing something in intense whispers. Taj stood with Quinn. Only Ed Lau was alone.

He walked my way. I was relieved to find that I didn't feel any tingle of lust with his approach, even though Ed Lau had been dependable last night, too. His round face was relaxed, almost serene.

"I'm your partner for the hour," he announced, his quiet voice deep and raspy with age. "Would you like to do some chi gung with me?"

"Absolutely," I told him.

"Energy or calm?" he asked. "Which do you need the most?"

"Calm," I answered without thinking. I laid down my cane.

"You know how to stand?" he asked.

I nodded, assuming his stance. My martial arts background was kicking in. I stood straight, the crown of my head suspended as if by a thread, my legs spread shoulder-width apart and rooted to the ground beneath me, my arms curved downwards. I breathed in relaxation.

Ed Lau smiled his approval.

"What kind of martial art do you practice?" he asked.

"Cane-fu."

He laughed.

"No, really?" he prompted.

"Really," I assured him. "My brother teaches martial arts. He taught me how to use my body and cane as weapons."

"Does he teach aikido, tai chi—"

"Everything," I cut in. "Honestly. My brother excels in just about every martial art you've ever heard of. Years ago, he made up his own brand of defense, Zartent. It uses all the arts and has to do with intent. He specializes in martial arts for the disabled. He developed cane-fu for me."

"I'd like to meet your brother some day."

I opened my mouth to say that he was staying here right now and closed it again. Wasn't that supposed to be a secret? I was too shell-shocked to even remember.

"Some day," I offered instead. "York's very interested in chi gung."

"Right," Ed replied seriously, the playfulness on his face receding. "Chi gung. I don't have to tell you how to stand. You're already doing it, supported by heaven and grounded by the earth."

I nodded, feeling the support and grounding. I took a breath in and let it out slowly, allowing my body to hold vitality and stillness at the same time.

"I don't even have to tell you how to breathe," he murmured. "Check your body now. Are you holding tension anywhere?"

"My shoulders," I told him.

"Do you know how to release it?"

I rolled my shoulders in a slow circle: front, up, back, and down.

"Can you feel the tension melting?"

I nodded.

"Let your arms get a little longer," he advised, his voice hypnotic.

I took in a breath and let the muscles loosen.

"And your leg—" he began.

He'd found it easily enough. My weak leg was tingling. The energy never quite flowed through that leg correctly. I just hoped it wouldn't buckle.

I breathed in again, erasing the negative thought. Or trying to.

"This is very interesting, Cally," Ed told me. "Have you specifically practiced a form of chi gung?"

"No, just some exercises—"

"—that your brother taught you," he cut in. "I would seriously like to meet your brother. Is he of Chinese ancestry?"

I shook my head. At least I didn't think we had any Chinese heritage. My family's ancestry was a hodgepodge, but nobody had ever mentioned China. Just France. My mother had loved the French side of her heredity—

"You're tensing up your leg, Cally," Ed told me.

I flinched. It happened whenever I thought of my mother.

I took in another deep breath.

"Better," Ed encouraged me. "I think—"

"Hey!" a young voice shouted somewhere in the room. Who was that?

Ed looked over my shoulder. I swiveled my head to follow his gaze. So much for chi gung.

There was a gangly boy in the doorway. He might have been in his early teens. He had a strong-featured face with dark brows under badly bleached and spiked hair.

"What's going on?" he demanded. "Is this Dr. Hart's class?"

"Who—" Quinn began.

"I'm Orson," the boy introduced himself. "My mom dropped me off. It's Dad's weekend. And this class is supposed to be really cool—"

"Orson," Quinn interrupted in a long-suffering voice. "You are not a part of this intensive. You are not registered. You are not—"

"He's my son," Judd Nyman interrupted. "He's with me."

SEVEN

What do you mean, he's 'with you'?" Quinn snapped.

"I mean my boy is here to hang out while we work," Judd explained easily. "He can watch and learn, maybe teach the rest of you a few things."

Quinn bent his head down and massaged his temples with his fingertips. When he brought his head back up, his voice was restrained.

"Mr. Nyman," he pronounced carefully. "Only registered members of this intensive may participate. You know that. We are all sensitive to the recent events here, but that doesn't mean we're throwing out the rule book."

"Well, hell, just register him," Judd offered genially. "I'll even pay his fee, prorated, of course."

Quinn shook his head violently. "No," he forced out. "No. This is an intensive for trained healers. Your son is not a trained healer—"

"Hey, hey!" Judd cut him off. "My kid, Orson, didn't just fall off the tofu truck. He's a smart kid. Anyway, it's my weekend, like he said. Where do you want him to go?"

"To your room?" Quinn managed.

"Nah, he wants to hang out here like everyone else."

Judd turned to his son where he still stood in the doorway. "Don't you, kid?"

"Yeah," Orson agreed enthusiastically. "I know a lot about alternative healing anyway. And I read a couple of books about chakras. It's cool stuff, interesting—"

"Did you okay this with Dr. Hart?" Quinn asked Judd.

Judd shook his head. "Hey, I didn't have to." He threw up his hands. "I figured the doctor would go for it. Just for the last few days after her big show."

"No," Quinn insisted, his voice a little stronger. "No."

"What's the matter with all of you?" Orson asked as Quinn and Judd glared at each other. "Everyone's metabolic cascades are completely skewed. Has something, like, happened?"

"See, I told you my kid was smart," Judd argued, side-stepping Orson's question.

Now Quinn really looked at Orson.

"What do you mean by 'metabolic cascades'?" he asked.

"You know, chemicals being converted from one form to another by enzymes, the way they should be," Orson answered easily.

I was pretty sure I knew what he meant. When the body was working correctly, the metabolic cascades had standard paths. But a shock could throw them off. I wondered if Quinn knew what the boy was talking about.

"And where did you learn about metabolic cascades?" Quinn moved on.

"At this class Dad went to last year," Orson answered cheerfully. "It was just part of the class, but I thought it was pretty cool. I can actually see the disruptions in normal metabolic cascade patterns. It's one way of learning about a person. Everyone here in this room, for instance. It looks like something blew the whole group away, some of you worse than others." He pointed at Quinn. "Like you. Whoa, dude! Most of your cascades are in shut-down. Did you know that? Especially your digestive system. Have you had anything to eat today?"

Quinn opened his mouth to answer and closed it again.

"Come on in," Judd invited his boy, motioning with his arm.

Orson wiggled his shoulders, then shambled into the room, looking uncomfortable. His uncertain gait went with his youth, even if his words didn't. Orson was way too smart for his age. But as he sucked on his upper lip, I realized that only his intellect was ahead. Socially, he was as nerdy as any other young teenage boy. I even felt a little sorry for him.

"Anyone want their metabolic cascades read?" he asked hopefully.

On the other hand, there was something about Orson that reminded me of Judd.

"No!" Quinn yelped, holding up his hand. "Look, you can stay for this morning's session, but that's all I'm promising. And I don't want you bothering any of the other participants, understood?"

Orson nodded, blowing air into his cheeks as he did. He lifted one leg and curled it around his other, standing like a stork.

"Okay," Quinn said. "Now, everyone—"

"Want me to get you something to eat?" Orson asked him.

"No!" Quinn shouted. He bent his head to massage his temples again. "No, thank you," he said more quietly. "Mr. Nyman, if you'll please take charge of your son?"

"Can I ask one question?" Orson asked.

Quinn took a big breath and answered, "Yes, one."

"What happened here?" Orson charged ahead. "Why are you all so weirded out?"

Quinn looked at Judd. Judd looked at his son.

"Listen, kid," he began gently. "Remember how I told you Dr. Hart was leading this group?"

Orson nodded.

"Well, she was killed last night."

"Really?" Orson whispered, his observant eyes widening. "What happened?"

"We don't know," Quinn interjected quickly.

"But it was probably murder," Judd added.

"Murder?" Orson swiveled his head around, looking at all of us. Could he see who the murderer was by their metabolic cascades? It was worth a shot.

"Orson—" I began.

"We don't know that Dr. Hart was murdered!" Quinn hissed. "And it is highly irresponsible to spread rumors—"

"Whoa, whoa!" Judd objected, holding up his palm. "You can think whatever you like, but it's pretty obvious to me that she was murdered. And I say it's irresponsible to hide it from people. Let people know the truth. We gotta stand up for ourselves here."

"Are you sure she was killed?" asked Taj, looking as young as Orson for a moment.

"No," Quinn replied.

"But it looks that way," Fran threw in.

"How?" Orson asked.

No one answered him right away.

"How'd the doctor get killed?" he asked again.

"She was electrocuted," Quinn admitted. "Okay, she was electrocuted by a stage prop. Is that enough for you?"

"Sure, man," Orson agreed. "What kind of stage prop?"

Quinn ran his hand through his short hair, pointedly ignoring Orson. "We are here to practice healing," he announced quietly. "That's what Dr. Hart would have wanted. It's no use second-guessing the police. They'll tell us more when they know—"

"The police?" Orson asked.

Quinn continued to ignore him. "So, now, please, everyone get back to what you were doing. In fact . . ." He looked down at his watch. "It's past time for you to switch roles with your partner, so please do so now."

I turned back to Ed Lau, but I could hear voices whispering, rumbling. Orson had brought a breath of death back into our little group.

"Dad, that woman you're working with is really whacked out," Orson offered from behind me. "Do you want me to work with her?"

"No, thank you," Kim answered quietly for herself. "I think I'll rest a little now."

"Judd is right," Fran whispered loud enough for the whole room to hear. "We have a right to know what's going on. The police aren't going to tell us—"

"But what can we do?" Dotty put in, her voice trembling.

I willed myself not to listen anymore.

"Ed, do you want to have me work on you now?" I asked

He paused for a moment, his usually serene features tightening a little. "I suppose so," he finally answered.

"You don't have to," I assured him, surprised by the obvious vote of no-confidence in his voice.

"I'm sorry, Cally," he apologized. "I'm a very private man. These 'sharing' exercises bother me sometimes."

"How about if you can stop the process any time you want to?" I offered.

"Okay," he agreed, with all the enthusiasm of a man agreeing to a dental extraction.

I sat first and motioned Ed to sit across from me. He lowered his solid body gracefully into his chair and brought his eyes up to meet mine. And I saw that there was something besides serenity in his eyes.

And there was something besides serenity in his aura. I could see a sparkling of crystalline light that usually signified spiritual certainty, but below that I saw a murk of sadness and something else. Guilt? I looked more closely.

"What do you see?" Ed asked abruptly.

"Nothing for certain," I began cautiously. "A spiritual grounding—"

"And . . ." he prodded.

"Guilt?" I asked him.

"Yes, guilt," he told me. "Now you know why I don't like 'sharing.'"

Was this 'guilt' as in guilty of committing a crime? No. Not Ed Lau. I just couldn't believe he'd killed Dr. Hart. But—

"Have you ever had a healing that went wrong, Cally?" he asked.

It took me a moment to reply. "Not everyone responds to my work—"

"No," he interjected. "I don't just mean the people who are no better or no worse for your work. I mean a person who dies because you took responsibility for their health . . . and you failed."

The murk in his aura thickened.

"I don't think so," I answered carefully.

"Kuleana," he muttered, lowering his eyelids.

"What?" I asked.

"Duty, responsibility, honesty," he answered. "When you take responsibility for another's life, you must be honest in your ability. You have a duty. You must not fail."

I just nodded. I didn't think he was speaking of Dr. Hart's life. But I wasn't sure yet. Ed Lau was guilty, but I wondered if he was only guilty in his own self-perception.

"Ed," I put in tentatively.

"Yes?" He raised his eyelids.

"Would you like some help with your pain?"

"No," he told me, shaking his head. "I want to keep any pain I have. Pain serves a purpose. In my life, it keeps me honest. I don't attempt anything I can't really handle. Chi gung is safe. It cannot harm. It doesn't claim to save lives."

I was trying to understand what he was saying, but I wasn't succeeding.

"Isn't chi gung a healing practice?" I asked gently.

He shrugged his shoulders. "It helps people a little. I don't claim anything more."

"How long have you done chi gung?"

"Probably forty years," he answered. "I should have stuck with it."

"You worked with another healing modality?" I asked. I wasn't sure if we were really conversing, or if I was just a bit player in Ed Lau's internal conflict.

Ed looked up at me as if suddenly remembering I was there.

"You don't have to talk to me anymore, Cally," he said. "I'm just confusing you."

"Well—"

"No, really," he insisted, a little serenity sliding back into place. "I have pain. I know it. I also know where I am in the world. I'm fine."

"But—"

"Let's just breathe for a while," he suggested.

So we sat in our chairs and breathed. I felt better for it. And I wasn't about to peek at Ed's aura anymore. At least I'd learned one thing by working with him. He really didn't like to share.

"Time to switch partners," Quinn called out after Ed and I had breathed for the rest of our time together.

Ed muttered, "thanks," as we both stood, looking for new partners.

I thanked him back and wondered if maybe I was wrong. Maybe Ed really did like to share. Maybe he just had.

Dotty Booth caught my eye. She smiled. I smiled back. It would be a relief to work with Dotty. Her plump-cheeked face radiated goodness and nurturing. She walked my way, taking her time. Dotty had said she was sixty, but she looked younger, her ample body huggable in a bright turquoise silk shirt, her red hair graying but not gray, freckles across the bridge of her nose.

"Cally," she caroled when she reached me. "I've been wanting to work with you. You see auras. I do aromatherapy. We can be next to each other in the encyclopedia of healing arts."

I laughed. Yes, working with Dotty should be a pleasure.

"Shall I work on you first?" I suggested.

"No," she replied. "Let me do you first. You're going to love these oils. You have animals, right?"

"A cat and three goats," I told her, wondering what that had to do with her oils. And wondering why no one wanted me to work on them first.

"Do you miss them?" she asked.

"Yes," I said slowly. I did miss them. I remembered that Dotty's beloved cat had died right before the intensive.

"Oh, Dotty," I whispered. "I forgot about your cat. You must be so sad."

"It's getting a little better," she reassured me, unrolling a long piece of felt with more than forty pockets, each with its own little bottle of oil. "I'm realizing now how lucky I was to have had Juniper for so many years."

I studied her face. Dotty really did look better than she had the first day of the intensive, unlike the rest of us.

"People who love animals tend to like a different set of oils," she explained belatedly. "But your own unconscious will pick the oils you need. I like to test my 'pet' theory and see if you choose the oils that animal-people usually do."

"How does my unconscious choose?" I asked.

"I'll show you," she offered, laying the pocketed felt across two chairs. "Close your eyes now and let your hand search for the right oil. It's different for everyone. An oil may call out to one person, or you may feel a vibration when your hand passes it, or you might even see it with your eyes closed. Take your time."

I closed my eyes and bent over, touching the felt cloth with my fingertips. My hand grazed the first bottle. Nothing. I skimmed the row, lightly touching each of the bottles. I was on the forth row when I felt one. It didn't exactly vibrate, but it felt warmer than the others to my hand.

"This one?" I questioned uncertainly.

"Yes," Dotty answered. "Keep going, there may be another one."

By the time my hand had skimmed all the pockets, I had chosen two bottles. I opened my eyes.

"Animal person!" Dotty crowed.

"Why?" I asked. "What did I pick?"

Dotty pulled the stopper out of the first bottle. "Smell," she invited.

I did. Whoa! My mind filled with memories of my sister Geneva. She'd worn that oil. I was sure of it.

"Patchouli oil," Dotty told me. "You did a good job."

She had me smell the second bottle. It was sandalwood, another scent that Geneva had worn.

I looked at Dotty with more respect. There was no way she could have known to guide me to these two fragrances. My unconscious *had* chosen them. But why?

"I usually use these oils in conjunction with massage," Dotty told me. "But half an hour isn't really long enough. It's interesting that you chose these two. I use them a lot for people with poor circulation in their legs."

"My leg doesn't have poor circulation," I informed her defensively. I'd been to doctors. There was nothing really physically wrong with my leg.

"I know," she replied, putting up a hand as if to fend off my reaction. "Medically, your leg doesn't have a circulation problem. But does it have a circulation problem energetically, emotionally?"

"Well, yeah," I admitted.

"If I had you in my massage room, I'd give you a whole body massage with these oils," she went on. "But since we've only got a little while longer, maybe you'd like a little of the oil on your face?"

"I guess so," I agreed, belatedly realizing I was showing

about as much enthusiasm for Dotty's work as Ed had shown for mine. "That would be fun," I amended.

I lay my head back on the top of the cushy chair and took off my glasses. Dotty put oil on her fingertips.

"Ready?" she asked.

"Ready," I replied.

I closed my eyes. The scent of patchouli and sandalwood was overpowering as I felt Dotty put her fingers on either side of the bottom of my face and pulled outward toward my ears.

"How's that?" she asked quietly.

"Nice," I told her. I felt sleepy.

She continued to draw her fingers across my face.

"Mmmm," I murmured.

"Now, I'm going to give you these two bottles to take with you," Dotty said. "You might want to massage some oil into your leg. Or get a friend to do your whole body." She giggled. I opened my eyes.

I could see a blurry benign face smiling down at me. Dotty withdrew her fingertips.

That wasn't so bad.

"Look who's working with Quinn," Dotty whispered.

I put on my glasses and followed Dotty's gaze. Quinn was sitting in a chair and Orson was giving him a foot massage. And talking. "You gotta get some food in you first," Orson insisted.

"You're right," Quinn agreed softly. "After the practitioners switch."

"I'll get you some," Orson proposed. "That way, you can still run the group."

Quinn thought for a moment, looking around the room.

"Okay," he finally conceded. "Maybe a sandwich."

"From the mouths of babes," Dotty whispered and giggled again.

Orson loped out of the room, a boy on a mission.

"Okay folks," Quinn began, standing. "Time to—"

But before Quinn could finish, someone new came through the door, walking as if in a dream, slowly, murmuring to himself and writing in a notebook, his mild, brown-skinned face oblivious, his soft dark eyes half closed under wire-rimmed glassed.

"Mr. Jinnah?" Quinn prompted.

But the man just continued to wander through the room, writing in his notebook. At least he looked happy.

"Is that Bob Jinnah?" I asked Dotty in a whisper.

"Yeah," she answered. "I met him the other day. Heidi was hustling him out of the lobby."

It was my turn to giggle. "Do you think Quinn will let him stay for free, like he did Orson?" I joked.

"I guess Quinn has to," Dotty threw back. "Bob owns the room we're standing in."

I don't know why it seemed so funny, but it did. As I laughed, I wondered what kind of happy juice might be in Dotty's oils.

"Hey, Bob!" Judd greeted the lodge owner as he floated by. "Out for a morning stroll?"

"Oh!" Bob Jinnah yelped, his eyes focusing on Judd, and then on each and every one of us. "Oh, dear, I hope I haven't interrupted anything."

"Just a little energy work," Raleigh replied to the startled man. "Not to worry, okay?"

"Oh, my," Bob murmured. He tried a smile. "Well, as Blake would say, 'Energy is eternal delight!' "

"Sounds right to me," Raleigh assured him, and gently took him by his elbow out of the room.

"Blake?" Judd questioned. There was sarcasm in his voice.

"William Blake," Ed Lau answered without sarcasm. "British poet and visionary. Also, if I remember correctly, an artist and engraver—"

"Fine," Quinn interrupted. "Just fine. Bob Jinnah and

William Blake." He took a big breath. "It's time for you partners to switch roles now."

Pretty soon, I had Dotty Booth across from me in the hot seat.

Dotty began by telling me about her cat Juniper who had died so recently.

"She was a lovely little girl, a silver tabby," Dotty recounted quietly. "She sat in my lap when I worked. I had her nineteen years. People say I'm too emotional, but I loved my Juniper. Why not?"

"Um-hm," I murmured, seeing the blue sadness in Dotty's energy field. It might as well have been a black mourning band around her heart. I reached out to clasp her hand.

"I don't know how come Dr. Hart was so mean about my Juniper," Dotty went on. Red joined the blue. Anger. "She was a cruel women. I care about animals. I care about people." I loosened my grip on Dotty's hand. The red field felt more like rage than sadness.

Dotty bent forward and looked into my eyes, her voice still quiet as her aura burned.

"Sara told me that once Dr. Hart hit a dog with her car and kept on driving. Can you imagine?"

I shook my head, feeling uncomfortable with the intensity of Dotty's anger. What had happened to her good nature?

"Juniper didn't deserve to die," she went on, her voice as soft as a lullaby. "But maybe Dr. Hart did."

EIGHT

"You don't really mean that, do you?" slipped right out of my mouth.

Great therapeutic technique . . . or interrogative technique for that matter.

"Oh, but I do," Dotty answered earnestly. "Dr. Hart was so cruel. Who knows what harm she's done? A cat is innocent by nature. Humans should be responsible for their actions."

Orson came loping back into the room with a sandwich for Quinn. But Orson's and Quinn's new relationship didn't seem amusing anymore.

"Did you do it, Dotty?" I asked quietly, looking into her hazel eyes.

"Do what?" she asked back, crinkling her forehead.

My hands were shaking. But I had to finish.

"Did you kill Dr. Hart?"

Dotty stared at me, her rosy cheeks going pale till the freckles all over her face stood out.

"Me?" she whispered. Then louder, "Me?"

I just held her gaze, willing her to speak the truth.

"No!" she yelped suddenly, halfway rising from her chair. "Oh, you can't believe that." Dotty's usually quiet voice rose with each word. "I just said what I said 'cause I care. Dr. Hart was mean. But I wouldn't kill anyone, not Dr. Hart. Not anyone!"

All around the room, people turned to look at us.

"Of course not," I said in what I hoped was a soothing tone. But the tremor in my voice must have betrayed me.

Dotty stood all the way up. "You don't believe me!" she accused. And she began to cry.

Son of a lizard! What had I been thinking? *Did* I believe Dotty?

"Dotty, I know you're a good person," I began, hoping that would help. I didn't tell her that I believed *all* people were good at their center. "I'm not sure why I asked you if you killed the doctor. It was just—"

"Just because of what I said," she interrupted and lowered her body back into her seat. She wiped tears from her eyes, pulling a tissue from her pocket. "I shouldn't have said Dr. Hart deserved to die. I was just thinking of Juniper, and how the doctor made fun of my grief. I don't know who deserves to live or die. I just meant that—I don't know what I meant. I was angry. I'm sorry."

She blew her nose loudly and a piece of tissue drifted to the floor.

"I'm sorry, too," I told her.

Her tear-stained face lit up. She grabbed my hands. "Oh, Cally, I'm so glad. I really like you. This has all been so overwhelming . . ."

And pretty soon, I was helping her to ease out some of her overwhelming feelings. Anger emerged first, then grief, and finally fear. I just hoped I wasn't working on a murderer.

"Thank you, Cally," Dotty murmured. I could still smell the patchouli and sandalwood scents on my face. I had a feeling I wouldn't be smelling much of anything else for a while. Was Dotty a murderer? I couldn't believe that. But that was the problem with my presumption of goodness. I never seemed to be able to properly sense whatever it was that made a murderer a murderer until it was too late. I squeezed Dotty's soft hand and mentally wished her well even if she was a murderer.

I looked around the room, searching for an auric clue. Was there something—

"It's time for lunch," Quinn announced. "So take a little time to finish up with your partner."

Dotty and I smiled at each other. We were done.

I looked around the room again as people finished up what they were doing. All I saw was a group of well-intentioned people doing as good a job as they could. Healers. Could the police have been wrong about Dr. Hart's aura maker? Maybe it had just been an accident. Or suicide? My neck stiffened. Could—

"What?" Dotty asked. She must have been watching me.

"I just wondered," I whispered. "Could Dr. Hart have committed suicide with that contraption?"

Dotty's body stiffened. "Suicide," she murmured. "I never thought of that."

"She could have rigged the aura maker herself—"

I stopped myself mid-theory. I wasn't even supposed to know about the rigged aura maker.

But Dotty was still thinking.

"She doesn't seem the type," Dotty began slowly. "All that anger, all that cruelty."

"But what if she turned it inward?"

"No," Dotty argued. "She would never hurt herself, just others."

"But—"

"Okay, time for lunch," Quinn intervened. "The hotel has made a nice little buffet for us in the lobby. And I want you back here in exactly an hour. We'll have a short afternoon session, then we're having a real treat." Quinn forced a smile onto his face that was as phony as his cheerful tone.

"We're going on a winery tour, compliments of the Swanton Hills Lodge."

There was a short silence in the room. A winery tour?

"Quinn," Raleigh began slowly. "Some of us don't drink—"

"And some of us shouldn't," Judd finished up for him.

Fran laughed. No one else did.

"Oh," Quinn said. He rubbed his face, looking lost.

"A lot of the wineries make non-alcoholic wines," Orson jumped in. "Dad and I went on a tour last year. They make all kinds of nonalcoholic versions of stuff. It's sweeter than Coke."

"Would that be okay for everyone?" Quinn asked hopefully. "I should have been more sensitive on this. But if everyone has nonalcoholic choices—"

"That would be fine," Ed Lau pronounced.

And for some reason, no one argued with his voice of authority. I looked at Ed. What was it about him? His age, his outward calm, his massive body? When Ed spoke, people listened.

"And I'll call the tour guide and make sure he knows what we want," Quinn promised. He ran his hand through his short hair. Poor Quinn. He was trying so hard to keep this going.

"I'll help," Orson offered. "I remember the good varieties."

"Thanks," Quinn offered softly. I smiled. Quinn had a new assistant. Or maybe Quinn had a new boss.

Pretty soon, Quinn and Orson had herded us all into the lobby. The buffet table was piled with an assortment of sandwiches, wraps, fresh fruit, juices, soft drinks, and cookies. I wondered how long the Jinnahs could do this without going broke.

I started toward the buffet table and found Raleigh by my side.

"You sure smell good," he told me.

"It's just the oils that Dotty put on me," I mumbled, blushing all the way down to my toenails.

"I'm looking forward to her treatment," he went on. "But I bet I won't smell as good as you."

Was he flirting with me? I wasn't sure. I opened my mouth to ask. But I wasn't fast enough.

"*I'll* probably pick out some oil that smells like swamp water or something," he followed up.

I laughed nervously. I tried to think of a way to bring Roy into the conversation.

"The food looks great," he commented, looking over my shoulder. Maybe he really wasn't flirting.

Ed walked up next to us.

"Ed," Raleigh greeted him, his face breaking out into that sexy smile.

"Raleigh," Ed greeted him back brusquely.

I seized the chance to move up to the buffet, leaving the two men behind. Maybe Raleigh just didn't know how sexy his smile was. I was pretty sure he wasn't flirting with Ed.

I found myself a tuna sandwich, a peach, and a bottle of apple juice, wrapped them all in a large paper napkin, and went toward the exit. I needed some quiet time to think. But Raleigh was standing at the door as I tried to leave.

"Cally, he whispered. "I just needed to apologize about my behavior toward Judd. Anger doesn't overcome anger. I ought to know that. And you were right. He was trying to help Craig in his own way."

"Don't worry," I advised. "Judd's here to push our buttons. I think he likes to."

"Yeah, but I've been working this plan, you know, to always meet anger with love. And I really blew it."

"Listen, Raleigh," I said, smiling. "That's my plan, too, but I blow it all the time."

"Really?" he asked. "I haven't seen you blow it yet."

"You haven't seen me with my family," I told him.

He laughed. His laugh was deep and contagious.

"Or Roy, my boy—" I began.

"Raleigh, were you really the lead singer for the Booi Brothers?" a voice interrupted. It was Taj, his young face and tone both radiating adulation.

Raleigh laughed again, turning to the younger man.

"I was indeed," he answered.

"I was in theater," Taj murmured.

Well, I'd tried to get Roy into the conversation.

I sighed internally as the two men talked. And I took a quick look around the lobby. Judd and Fran were standing, each waving their hands as words left their mouths. I would have suspected they were arguing, but they were both grinning. They hadn't even approached the buffet yet. Orson and Quinn were at the buffet together, Orson piling up enough food for the whole group on his plate, while Quinn picked at things and put them back. Dotty was helping Craig to choose his lunch. Watching her in compassionate action, I felt guilty about my earlier suspicions. Ed sat at a little table, alone with a sandwich and a soft drink. And Kim hadn't even bothered to pick up any food before she exited the lobby.

I hoped she wouldn't go hungry. But leaving the lobby was the right direction. I followed her example.

Outside, I lost sight of Kim, but gained a renewed sight of Swanton. It really was a beautiful place. The rolling green hills were soft and sensual, the oak trees grand, and the sky as blue as only the air far away from heavy industry can be. I sat down carefully on a grassy slope and listened to warbling birds and buzzing insects for a while before unwrapping my sandwich. I closed my eyes and happily breathed in scented air. Patchouli and sandalwood, right. Still, I could smell tuna and earth and things that would probably make me sneeze later mixing in with the aromatic oils. Heaven.

I was chewing my sandwich and wishing I'd picked

something more original than tuna on white when I heard voices. I looked up. Two people stood behind a nearby oak tree. I focused on the tree, seeing flashes of arms and legs and the occasional torso and head as they disappeared behind the trunk and reappeared in their animation. Then I recognized Sara Oshima, her black hair swirling as she threw up her arms. But who was the other one? I caught a flash of long hair and a bushy beard.

"Listen, babe," the voice was insisting. "You don't have to stay here. Just screw the whole thing and take off. You could drive the doc's Mercedes. I'll bet I could even find someone to buy it, no questions asked. That'd be a nice chunk of change, more than you've been getting for sure."

I took another bite of my sandwich, barely noticing the bland flavors.

"No, Ira!" Sara protested, her voice panicky. "You don't get it. Someone killed Dr. Hart. I don't want to get in trouble with her car. I have to be careful. They probably think I'm the one who killed her. Hey, I may have been skimming a little of the profits, but I don't deserve to get railroaded for murder. I don't deserve any of this crap."

"Oh, screw it," Ira told her. "You were the only one who ever drove that car anyway. It wouldn't hurt to just take it for a ride and get away—"

"Ira," Sara interrupted. "You've got enough in your stash to keep you high for a month. Isn't that enough? I can't leave now. Maybe in a couple of days, when people aren't so uptight. Maybe then I'll drive over to your place and pick you up. But I have to act cool now."

"But I'm bored," Ira whined. I was beginning not to like Ira, and I hadn't even met him. "This was supposed to be fun."

"Well, why don't you just check into the lodge and get interrogated by Chief Phlug?" Sara snapped. "I'm not having any fun here either. And I shouldn't be fooling around. Dr. Hart is dead—"

"But you hated Dr. Hart."

"Maybe, maybe not," Sara muttered so softly I could barely hear her. "I don't know anymore. All I know is that I could be in trouble. Real trouble."

The front door of the lodge opened, and Dotty Booth came out, carrying her own plate of food. A calico cat slithered up to her. She laughed and bent down to pet the cat, murmuring feline endearments.

"You'd better get out of here, Ira!" Sara whispered urgently.

"Fine," Ira hissed back. "But I'm not going to wait for you much longer."

They both exited from behind the oak tree, Ira slouching off into the distance, and Sara running lightly to the back of the lodge. She didn't look like a woman in distress anymore. Who was she really?

"Yes, you're a good kitty," Dotty purred. "Do you like tofu?"

The cat looked up at her, a sneer on its little feline face. Had it already learned the word "tofu?"

"I don't blame you," Dotty assured the animal. "Cats and soybeans don't mix. I could go get you a tuna sandwich."

The cat's eyes widened. It tilted its head winningly.

The door to the lobby opened once again, and Orson came out, his full plate almost empty now. But not quite. The calico cat's ears went up.

"Hey, Quinn said to tell you guys out here—" he began.

The calico cat trotted toward the boy.

"Hey, scat!" Orson shouted. The cat kept on moving.

Orson bent down and grabbed a handful of ornamental pebbles. He took aim to throw them at the oncoming cat.

But Dotty was on Orson before he could carry out his attack.

She grabbed his throwing arm and yanked . . . hard.

"What's the matter with you?" she spat out. "You should know better than to hurt an animal."

"But—" the boy tried, squirming to loosen his arm.

"Don't you think you can live in peace with one small innocent cat?" Dotty demanded.

"No!" he shouted back. "I'm allergic. I've had tests and everything. I sneeze, and swell up, and all kinds of gross things."

"Allergic?" Dotty questioned, dropping his arm.

Orson nodded miserably.

"Just throw him some food," she suggested.

Orson broke off a piece of his wrap and tossed it to the cat. The cat sniffed it suspiciously, and dragged it off behind the tree where Sara and Ira had been.

"Quinn said to eat up," Orson tried again. "It's almost time for the afternoon session."

I bit into my peach as Orson reentered the lodge. It wasn't a supermarket peach, but one of those real ones with flavor and juice that ran down onto my chin. It made up for the bland sandwich. But it wasn't a picnic with Roy by a duck-filled lake.

I tried not to think of Dotty's violent display as I slurped my peach. I tried to listen to the birds and insects instead. But I couldn't seem to hear them anymore.

Once I'd finished my peach and juice, I shuffled back into the lobby. Orson was there, rounding up the strays. Dotty and Kim came in seconds after I did.

"Let's go, you guys," he urged. "It's time for the afternoon session."

We allowed ourselves to be shepherded into the meeting room again.

Quinn stood up front and cleared his throat.

"The morning sessions are for experiencing the healing techniques of your fellow intensive members," he announced. "And the afternoon is reserved to talk about that experience. What did you learn? What feelings came up for you?"

"I learned that some people really care," Craig piped up

in a voice that sounded almost normal. "Working with entities all the time, sometimes I get a little agitated." He flicked something invisible from the air. "Like that one, a mean one. But some people here were really nice to me. Dr. Hart appreciates all you're doing—"

"Thank you," Quinn interrupted. He clearly didn't want to go where Craig was headed.

"Well, we do care," Dotty put in. "Just remember that you're not alone. And your perceptions are okay. They may be different than other people's, but that's okay, too."

"Well, I don't know that Craig's perceptions are strictly okay," Judd argued. "To us, maybe. But he's gotta chill out or he's gonna end up institutionalized—"

"But—" Dotty tried.

"Do you eat three meals a day?" Judd asked Craig.

"Eat?" Craig repeated.

"See!" Judd barked, flinging out his arms.

"Let him answer in his own time," Raleigh told Judd. "He's just gotta think it out." He turned to Craig. "Do you remember breakfast?" he asked gently.

"Toast," Craig replied. "Eggs."

"It's just what happened to the doctor that's got you upset, isn't it?" Raleigh led Craig further.

Craig smiled, showing his snaggly teeth, and nodded.

"Do you live with someone?" Kim jumped in, her scratchy, unused voice barely recognizable.

"Yeah, my wife," Craig assured her.

Raleigh and Kim exchanged a look of relief.

"I think she's alive," he added. "But I'm not sure."

"Awesome," Orson whispered. "Kinda like my mom."

Judd guffawed.

"Craig," I leaped in. "Do you think you could give us your phone number so we could call your wife?"

He nodded. But he didn't hand me a phone number.

Orson found a pad of paper and a pen and cautiously passed it to Craig.

Craig wrote on the pad and handed it back to Orson.

"Look's like a Mill Valley phone number," Orson told us.

"How do you know?" Quinn asked.

"The prefix."

"Hey, kid," Judd called out to his son. "Run down to the Jinnahs and call that number."

"Cool, Dad," Orson agreed and jogged out of the room.

"Do you think that your son is old enough to handle the responsibility?" Dotty asked once Orson had left the room.

"He's thirteen," Judd answered dismissively. He smiled. "He's a smart kid. He'll do good."

"So," Quinn broke in. "Let's hear from some of the rest of you. "What did you get from this morning's session."

No one answered.

Quinn's hound-dog eyes took on a frantic look.

"I got a lot of validation for my resonance work," Raleigh put in. I could tell he was talking for Quinn's sake. "My clients enjoy the work, but when healers tell me it's good, it means a lot."

"Thank you," Quinn said. "And who else has something to say?"

No one spoke.

"Ed?" Quinn prompted.

Ed just shrugged his shoulders.

"Fran?" Quinn tried next.

"You can't have my wand," Fran answered clearly.

Quinn's head jerked back as if he'd been slapped.

"What?" he asked.

"I said, you can't have my wand. I know what's going on here."

"But I—"

"No buts," Fran plowed on. "That's why Dr. Hart invited me. She wanted to steal the design for my wand. Well, I told her she couldn't have it. And you can't have it either."

The silence in the room was louder than a scream.

Orson came trotting back in.

"I called Mrs. Zweig," he told us. "She said she's coming down as soon as she can. She wanted to know if Mr. Zweig had gotten violent yet."

NINE

"Violent?" Judd demanded, turning to Craig. Craig sat quietly smiling. "What did I tell ya—"

"Excuse me," Kim put in softly before Judd could get going. She may have been petite and distressed, but there was something firm about Kim even in her distraction. "There are many types of violence. Did Mrs. Zweig happen to mention the type of violence she was concerned about?"

"Yeah!" Orson replied eagerly. He wiggled his shoulders. "It's real interesting. He breaks stuff. Not, like, important stuff, but, like, old bottles and eggs and stuff. Carlotta said it was how he let off steam."

"Carlotta?" Quinn asked weakly.

"Mrs. Zweig said I could call her Carlotta," Orson explained.

"Oh, of course," Quinn murmured and lowered himself into a chair.

"And I still say you can't have my wand," Fran threw at Quinn.

Craig nodded as if *he* understood Fran. Maybe he did.

"I don't want your wand, Ms. Marquez," Quinn insisted

after a deep breath. If eyes can flinch, Quinn's large eyes did. "I promise you I'm not interested in your wand—"

"What kind of wand do you have?" Orson asked Fran.

"An energy wand," she answered absently. "It measures fluctuations in life force."

"Like Kirlian or something?" Orson hazarded.

Fran looked more closely at Orson. A smile gentled her classic Amerind features, and suddenly I saw the healer within her. "Yeah, where'd you learn about Kirlian energy?" she asked.

"Oh, Dad took me to this lecture. The Russians were really into that stuff. I know a lot about the photography, but I've never heard about a wand."

"That's because I invented it," Fran said proudly.

"Cool."

"Take my advice, kid," Fran offered. "Follow your dream and don't let anyone, I mean anyone, get in your way." She glared at Quinn menacingly, then looked back at Orson. "You're one bright kid."

"That's what I've been telling you guys all along!" Judd boomed. His son blushed and squirmed. "My kid's the best."

"Ah, Dad—" Orson began.

But a new voice interrupted him from the doorway.

"Whoa, people!" the voice shouted. "Are you ready for the tour?"

I turned and saw a well-built, balding man with a large nose, smiling eyes, and a luxurious moustache.

"I'm Monty English," he introduced himself, "and I'll be your tour guide for what's left of this lovely afternoon."

"The winery tour?" Quinn asked.

"Anything you guys want," Monty answered enthusiastically. He threw his arms out from his body. "Swanton's got it all, right? Wineries, *nonalcoholic* wineries, gardens, massage, hoochie-coochie shows, you name it. We may be in the hills, but our hills are wild!"

"Wild?" I asked, taking the bait.

"With flowers," he came back and slapped the side of his leg.

"Wildflowers," Ed Lau said slowly. He wasn't laughing.

"You got it, buddy," Monty went on. "So they tell me you want the nonalcoholic winery tour. Guess you hear enough whines being in the healing business." He slapped his leg again.

I was surprised by my own snort of laughter. But I was tired of angst. And Monty might be the antidote. At least for me. Somehow, I didn't think he was ever going to make Ed laugh.

"Well, walk this way," Monty ordered, swaying his hips like a cigarette girl from an old B movie. "The carriage awaits."

So we followed him all the way out the lobby doors.

The carriage, as it turned out, was a fifteen-passenger van.

"Stretch van," Monty announced gleefully. He bowed. "And I am your chauffeur."

"I heard these can be dangerous," Orson commented.

"Heard from who?" Monty asked, unruffled.

"Ralph Nader."

"That Ralph's a real kidder, isn't he?" Monty commented briefly. "Everyone on board."

Fran and Judd were the first to board, then Ed, and then Dotty guiding Craig. Taj motioned me forward. I lifted my foot to step up when I felt a gentle tug on my arm. I turned and saw Sara Oshima, looking rested and possibly stoned.

"Go ahead," I told Taj, motioning him ahead of me onto the van.

Sara looked behind us where Quinn still stood with Raleigh, Kim, Monty, and Orson.

"Did you know that Quinn was sleeping with Dr. Hart?" she asked me, loudly enough to be heard outside the van, maybe even inside. Her words were clearly meant more as an announcement than a real question.

I looked at Quinn, who was walking toward us, Quinn, short and muscular with a long face and expressive eyes that expressed anger at the moment. Quinn, who couldn't have been out of his twenties. How old had Aurora Hart been? Mid-fifties and beautiful. And in those few moments, I told myself not to judge. If they had actually slept together, hopefully they had liked or even loved each other.

"Sara!" Quinn hissed. "I've put up with a lot from you. Aurora put up with a lot from you. You think I don't know what you and Ira were up to. You think Aurora didn't know, but she did. She let you steal money from her because she cared about you. She thought you'd stop after a while. Aurora tried to help you. She wanted the best for you. And now she's dead. I won't even try to say what that means to me. It's something you can't understand, you or your Ira. But I will say this: You will not slander her memory. You will not hurt her like this."

Sara stepped back, paling slightly. Finally, she balled up her fists and stuck her face forward.

"I cared for her, too, damn you!" she cried. "Don't you act like you're the only one who's lost someone. I lost my mother. And I've lost Aurora. She didn't just belong to you because you were sleeping with her."

"Sara," Quinn said, his voice dangerously low. "You want me to react. This is your form of a tantrum. Well, I won't be engaged in your little drama. If you really cared for Aurora, you'd stop this, right now. Think about it. What is it you've lost with Dr. Hart's death? Are you going to memorialize it with petty hatred?"

"I'll do whatever I want!" Sara shrieked in Quinn's face.

Quinn didn't even blink. I'd never seen this side of him before. Still, he'd been dealing with Sara a lot longer than I had.

"I hate you," she added more softly, and she turned on her heel and ran through the lobby doors.

"So, let's get the show on the road," Monty suggested as if Sara had never been there.

"Yes," Quinn agreed, his back stiff, unshed tears moistening his eyes.

Dack. He had cared for Dr. Aurora Hart. And he had cared for her in a way probably *no one* else would understand, much less Sara. I wanted to hold him, to say something comforting, but I was afraid to touch him. Love and hatred were so close sometimes.

"Yes," he repeated in a zombielike voice. "Everyone on the bus."

"Van," Monty corrected softly.

Quinn didn't seem to hear him as he stepped into the van.

Kim was next, looking tearful herself, followed by Raleigh and Orson. I entered the van and sat down next to Ed Lau, in the first row behind the driver's seat. At least Ed would be restful . . . I hoped. No one sat on my other side. They were already seated behind us.

Monty took his place in the driver's seat.

"This here's Swanton," he announced. He didn't need a microphone. His voice was loud enough on its own for a stadium. "Now the Swanton Hills Lodge is a very nice place, but you folks haven't seen the rest. You've probably barely been out of the lodge except to go to restaurants. And to meet my cousin."

I couldn't help it. I had to ask, "Who's your cousin?"

"Chief Web Phlug," he answered. He didn't slap his leg this time, but I could tell he was grinning. Maybe it was the set of his shoulders, maybe it was psychic ability on my part, or maybe just inference. But I would have bet my little house in Glasse County that the man was grinning like the Cheshire cat.

And I would have bet something a little less valuable that no one else in the bus was grinning. We were all trapped in a dangerous van with Chief Phlug's cousin?

"You've all met him, of course," he carried on. "Pure case of testosterone poisoning, right?"

"Right on," a voice from behind me agreed. I was pretty sure it was Fran.

"If you look to the left, you'll see the major voting bloc of Swanton," he told us.

I looked through a window and saw a herd of cows. Maybe angst was preferable to leg-slapping after all.

And if you look you the right . . ." He paused as our heads swiveled. ". . . you'll probably just see hills. We've got lots of hills in Swanton."

Now he was chortling aloud. Was he trying to jolt us out of our communal funk? Did he hate us? Or was he just being Monty English, a man who probably would have had us laughing by that time if we hadn't had murder on our minds?

I turned to Ed Lau. Maybe a little conversation? "So, you live in Hawaii?" I tried.

"Yes," he answered, his usually relaxed face like rock. Well-grounded rock, but rock nonetheless.

So much for conversation, though I could hear a few whispered ones from behind us.

"So, Monty," Judd finally ventured. "What do you do for a living besides taking murder suspects on winery tours?"

I snickered. Judd had made me snicker! I must have been desperate.

"Oh," Monty answered nonchalantly. "I own a bike shop and a couple of restaurants."

"Really?" Dotty asked incredulously. I could tell the word had just slipped out.

Monty laughed. "It's better than milking cows," he answered.

"Did you grow up with . . . um . . . Chief Phlug?" I asked.

"I sure did," he replied. He bent his head back. "Whooee!" he sang out.

"Right here in Swanton?" I prompted, hoping for something to give me a grasp on the chief's belligerent psyche.

"Right here in Swanton," Monty conceded cheerfully. "Milking cows can do a lot of weird things to a man's mind, let me tell you."

"Like . . ." I prodded.

"Like . . ." He paused tantalizingly, then went on. "That tale will have to wait. We're here at the Hillsock Winery. Emily and Scott Penderson will be your hosts."

And with that, he cut the wheel, and we were parked among a scattering of other cars in front of an adobe building surrounded by California poppies and lupine. Staked grapevines stretched out behind the building as far as I could see.

We all exited the van like good tourists/suspects and followed Monty's lead into the adobe building. The place smelled of wine and grapes, and of course, patchouli and sandalwood for me.

Emily and Scott were a couple who had retired early to devote themselves to making wine, they told us earnestly. *Nonalcoholic* wines, they quickly added.

They passed around wineglasses with tablespoon samples of their nonalcoholic white zinfandel. It was sweet, but I couldn't pin any other adjectives onto it. Though the Pendersons could. Many, many adjectives.

We tried a little of their recent chardonnay which was less sweet and deserving of more adjectives.

After a few more rounds of non-wines whose names and adjectives I couldn't remember, we reboarded the van. I was glad that Judd and Raleigh had bought a few bottles. I had been tempted, not so much by the flavors but by the obvious longing for sales on the Pendersons' faces.

"So, tell me about the chief," I ordered Monty once the van was rolling again.

"Boy, oh boy, he really hates you guys," Monty complied. "But—"

"Sergeant Dimarco doesn't seem to hate you though, even though she's married to him."

"Wait a minute," Raleigh objected from behind me. "The sergeant is married to the chief of police?"

"Yep," Monty plowed on merrily. "It's a hoot. Whooee! Sergeant DiMarco is a better policeman than Web any day of the week. Everyone in Swanton knows that. She went to police school and everything once her last kid left home. She was married to Don DiMarco real young, but he passed when the kids were real little. She used to work as a dispatcher for the police department. So once her kids had flown the coop, she became a policewoman. Nobody can figure out why she married Web, except to keep him out of trouble. And he's always threatening to fire her, but he doesn't dare 'cause he's afraid the people of Swanton would just make sure she replaced him as chief. They would, too."

My head was spinning with grape juice and information.

"So who really holds the power?" Ed Lau asked from next to me.

"Sergeant Laura Dimarco," Monty answered. "That's why I always use her full title. We're all proud of Sergeant DiMarco here in Swanton."

"If she holds the power, how come she lets him harass the Jinnahs?" Dotty asked.

Monty laughed. "She lets Web do all the dirty work when she thinks it needs doing," he answered. "She's not stupid."

"But—" Dotty began.

"Next stop, Grapeland," Monty interrupted.

Dack. How did he make these places appear just when the conversation was getting interesting?

Grapeland was a very different animal than Hillsock. Located in a dark purple building that might have also been adobe underneath the paint, they stocked nonalcoholic wines, purple "Grapeland" T-shirts, wineglasses, grape key rings, pens, posters, wine stoppers. And then there were the cow-themed gifts. We tasted a few of their nonalcoholic varietals and did some shopping. The young woman who rang up my cow pens showed me the cow tattoo on her shoulder by pulling down her shirt.

"Wow!" I blurted, impressed not just by her tattoo, but by the absence of underwear beneath her "Grapeland" T-shirt. At thirty-five, I was just beginning to understand that youth was relative.

Soon, we were back in the van. And back to the conversation about the Swanton Police Department.

"So here's the deal," Monty was explaining. "Sergeant DiMarco's the better cop, but Web scares people. Sometimes that's a good thing. He can break up a bar fight faster than a bull's belch."

"But why does he hate us?" Taj asked, a whine in his voice vibrating with the movement of the van.

"Oh, man! Web hates the yuppies who've moved up here to do their winery things bad enough. But then the New Agers started coming. Now we've got Rolfers, 'faerie' guides, rebirthers, colonic irrigators, you name it. He says it 'ain't Christian.' Every once in a while, when I'm feeling kinda suicidal, I ask him if waving his gun around in a crowded room is Christian. Heh—heh."

"Are you really feeling suicidal?" Dotty asked.

"No, ma'am!" Monty shouted. He hooted with laughter. "I always start running before I even ask Web a question."

I shook my head, smiling in spite of myself as I looked out the window of the van. We were passing a lake now. I squinted my eyes as we moved along. Those were ducks in the lake! Maybe Roy and I would have a picnic after all.

"Web was always a goofbag, even when we were kids. But the sergeant likes him, so he can't be all bad . . . I guess," Monty finished up.

"Are they really investigating Dr. Hart's death?" Ed enquired.

"Well, I'm not really privy to that information. In fact, I'm supposed to grill *you* folks some. But what the hell." He paused. I waited eagerly for his next words. He announced, "Next stop, the Bears."

"Bears?" three voices, including my own, demanded.

"I thought you just had cows," Orson added.

"Heh-heh, gotcha!" Monty crowed. "The only Bears in these parts are Gerda and Tom Bear. They work their own little fruit farm. They have for over fifty years."

He pulled his van toward a roadside stand next to an orchard, rattling our seats on the uneven road. "Treat these folks nice," Monty ordered, turning toward us once he'd parked. He looked serious for the first time since we'd met him. "They've been here longer than God, done a lot of good in Swanton, and they're facing hard times now."

Gerda Bear had white hair cropped close to the scalp. Tom Bear had no hair on his head at all. They were both elderly round people who could have doubled for the Clauses if Santa and his wife had been darker skinned and hazel-eyed.

The stand was made of sturdy wood that stretched at least twenty or thirty feet, overhung by a striped awning. Bottles and fresh fruit and boxes were lined up in even rows all the way down the stand, with a cash register at the center, one of those black cash registers you don't see anymore where the keys go *kachunk* when you bang them.

"Please, do come in," Gerda Bear offered, and I felt as if I were stepping into her parlor, despite the cool wind on my sun-warmed face.

Maybe it was the tea. Because the first thing that we were offered was an apricot and almond tea that knocked the socks off all the grape juice we'd had.

"We blend each tea ourselves," Gerda confided. "This one has peach, almond, a little lemon peel, cinnamon, hibiscus and rose hips, of course, and nutmeg. So many herbal teas depend heavily on cinnamon, but I like a little nutmeg."

"It's wonderful," I told her honestly. I wished I could have remembered some of those wine adjectives.

"Grow all our own fruit," Tom put in diffidently, shrugging to the trees that surrounded them. "And vegetables."

"Vegetables?" Judd asked, looking down the table.

"We have a lovely line of vegetable pâtés we're trying out. Would you all like to taste some?"

Murmurs of assent rippled on the afternoon breeze.

Zucchini never tasted so good. Or carrots. Or tomatoes.

I thought of my brother York. I was going to spend money at the Bears'. It was fated.

Then they had us try their fresh conserves of fruit.

The pear-peach medley was to die for. I thought I tasted nutmeg there, too. I was in love.

"Can I buy cases and have them shipped?" I asked.

"Oh, certainly, dear," Mrs. Bear answered, patting my hand with her rough one. "Of course we wouldn't charge any shipping—"

"Gerda," Monty's voice warned. "Don't you go giving away—"

"I'd be happy to pay shipping," I told her, buying a case of the pâtés for my brother York, and another case of conserves for myself and a few friends, and a case of teas for my guests.

Gerda even had a credit card machine. When she touched my hand again, I smelled peaches. But maybe it was just the trees. I wished the Bears lived in Glasse County. I drank in the beauty of their orchard under the hydrangea-blue sky as I stepped back and watched the other members of the intensive step up and make their purchases. Even Craig bought some conserves.

Monty was grinning as we got back into the van. For a moment, I wondered if he was on commission for the

Bears. But no, he was just happy for his friends. He waved as we left to return to the lodge.

"Thanks, folks," he boomed once the van was rolling.

"The Bears don't hate us, do they?" Orson asked quietly. The boy was so smart, it was too easy to forget he was just thirteen, with all the hurt that age could entail.

"Whoa!" Monty exclaimed. "No way. I don't think the Bears know how to hate anyone. Not them. And no one really has it in for you guys personally. There are just some people in Swanton who are never going to accept outsiders. I don't hate you either," he added, his voice surprisingly gentle. "Web is just, well, wishing it was like it used to be."

"How did it used to be?" Orson prodded.

"People mostly had dairy farms, a little ranching, orchards, chicken farms, that kind of thing. People knew each other. Small general store. Merchants. But after a while, the real world found us. It's a paradise to people from the cities. But the more of them who come, the less of a paradise it is."

"Like Hawaii," Ed Lau put in quietly.

"But Hawaii has always lived off of tourist money," Judd stated. "It's just spreading to the—"

"You know nothing of Hawaii!" Ed shouted, rising from his seat in the still-rolling van, and turning toward the rear in one fluid movement. He didn't waver as the van rounded a curve, his feet glued to the floor. "Hawaii was raped by people like you!"

TEN

"Hey, hey, hey!" Judd shouted back as my own heart thudded with the tires of the van. What had happened to Ed?

"I haven't done anything to you or Hawaii," Judd continued his protest. "Don't try and lay your trip on me."

"I think he means people like us, Dad," Orson tried to interpret. "Not us personally. You know, like missionaries and governments and stuff. They trashed the Hawaiian culture. It was really cool a long time ago—"

"But *I* didn't do anything," Judd objected, still obviously stung.

Ed remained on his feet, swaying slightly with the van's movement. His face was a portrait of grief. No wonder he didn't like to share. My heart's thudding quieted, but it hurt for the man who stood next to me.

"Not you personally," Orson explained to his father once more. "It was just what you said about Hawaii *always* being a tourist place. It was really cool before there were tourists."

"So was Mexico before it was conquered," Fran put in softly. "Ed, I have some idea of what you mean. I don't claim identical experience, but I get angry, too."

"Yes," Ed replied quietly. I wasn't sure if he was answering Fran or Orson or maybe even Judd. "Yes," he repeated again and sat back down. "I apologize."

He sat for a while with his eyes closed, clearly breathing in calm. And his face relaxed as he did. Ed had to work hard for his serenity. I could see that finally.

When he opened his eyes again, I put my hand gently on his.

"Thank you," he murmured. "I've behaved badly. This tour business has raised too many ghosts. I hope Judd will accept my apology."

"You haven't said anything Judd can't handle," I whispered back. "I'd guess that his *ego* is plenty well-centered and balanced. It's certainly big enough for the whole group."

Ed actually smiled. I decided not to press him on his memories. But I wondered . . .

Monty began to talk again.

"Maybe next time, you folks would like to see one of our garden tours," he suggested, his voice ever so slightly lower than it had been. "We've got some beautiful gardens here in Swanton."

"Gardens would be great," I chimed in, glad for the change of topic.

A slew of voices began to chatter about plants. Dotty bred dahlias, prize-winning dahlias. Raleigh had a sensory garden that provided the delights of fragrance and texture as well as visual pleasure. Fran had just begun to cultivate daisies and roses. And Judd was extolling the virtues of his watering system when Craig broke in.

"Did you know that butterflies are the spirits of fallen flowers?" he asked.

"Ah, come on," Judd chided him.

Craig went on, undeterred. "But people don't look for the butterflies anymore. They're still here. People just don't see them."

And just as I was sighing internally and feeling sorry for

this poor delusional man, a classic monarch butterfly whizzed past the van window, its reddish-brown wings veined with black.

"Whoa!" Monty exclaimed. He swiveled his head for an instant and met my eye before swiveling his head back to the road just as quickly.

In turn, I peeked over my shoulder at Craig. He smiled, and his snaggly teeth looked sweet to me, innocent. Was he right about the butterflies after all? And was he right about Aurora Hart's spirit as well?

Maybe we were all wondering about Craig when the van arrived back at the Swanton Hills Lodge. Because the group had gone very quiet again after the butterfly drive-by.

"Enjoy!" Monty ordered after we'd all filed out of the van. Then he spun off into the distance.

As we entered the lobby doors, small groups began to congregate, but I went straight to my room. I had too much to integrate. My mind was full. Maybe if I thought long and hard about each individual's behavior, I might be able to guess the murderer's identity. Or maybe I'd just take a nap. But I wanted to be alone.

I opened the door, deep in thought. A figure stepped out from the shadows of the room.

My cane came up in a flash. I executed a forward leap and thrust my cane at the intruder's solar plexus in less than a breath.

"Very good," my intruder complimented me, turning so quickly that my cane was still where his solar plexus should have been before I even recognized him.

The intruder was my brother York. Of course. Anyone else would have been pinned and struggling ineffectually against the pressure of the cane's point. Anyone else would have been frightened. York was smiling, genuinely pleased with my move. Of course, he had taught me the move.

"York!" I objected.

"What's that smell?" he countered. "Have you been using Geneva's smelly glop?"

"Patchouli and sandalwood," I answered brusquely, remembering. I didn't add that I was also into post cane-fu sweating, and that probably added to the mix of fragrances, too. "And no, it isn't Geneva's. *Geneva* went home. I thought you all went home."

I walked to the bathroom to wash my face. York followed me. I didn't even try to shut the door. He was my big brother. Shutting him out hadn't worked when I was a kid, and it wouldn't work now, decades later.

"I came here to take you to dinner," he told me. "You must be tired after your sessions and your touring."

"Who told you what I was doing?" I demanded, washcloth halfway to my face.

"Guess."

"How should I know?" I sputtered. "Santa Claus, butterflies . . . oh, Kapp."

"Bingo," he confirmed.

I ran the cool, wet washcloth over my skin. It felt good on my overheated face.

"I'm not even going to ask how he knows," I muttered after I'd cleaned the last remnants of oil from my skin. "So why are you still here?"

"I'm rooming with Kapp. You need protection."

"York!" I objected again. "I'm an adult, okay. Criminy, you can't keep an eye on me every moment."

"You'd be surprised," he murmured.

Sometimes York could be scary. Maybe he'd hidden out in the luggage compartment of the van.

"Look," he said softly. "I got the rest of the family off your case. They agreed I should stay. And I'd feel better if I stayed here in your room—"

"No," I stated firmly.

York just stared at me.

"*You* look," I went on angrily. "I haven't told anybody I'm investigating. And I'm not. Maybe Dr. Hart committed suicide with that thing. Did you ever think of that?

York thought. Then he said, "Naah, no way."

"Fine," I shot back. "But *I'm* not in any danger. Whoever killed Dr. Hart had their reasons. Those reasons don't extend to me. And I'm not asking questions. No one's going to think I'm looking to find a murderer—"

"Unless someone told them you were," York interrupted.

"But no one would . . ." I faltered. "Not Kapp?"

"Who else?" York returned.

"But why?" I asked, my voice cracking. "Why would Kapp talk to anyone about me like that?"

"Kapp thinks you two are a private-eye team, Cally. He's a loose cannon. He was talking to Quinn Vogel early this morning—"

I shivered. Quinn? Quinn was a suspect. If Sara had been telling the truth, he'd been Dr. Hart's lover.

"What?" York asked.

"Quinn, bad choice," I tried. I couldn't talk. My pulse was sounding in my ears.

"Cally," York murmured softly. "Work with me. Don't lose it. Why is Quinn a bad choice?"

I told my brother what Sara had said about Quinn's relationship with the late doctor. "And Quinn may gain financially. What was Kapp thinking?"

"Do you think Sara was telling the truth?" York asked.

I thought for a while, picturing her distraught face in my mind.

"Maybe," I concluded. "She wouldn't be above lying, but Quinn's reaction . . . I just don't know."

"Cally," York ordered. "We're going to dinner now. You need some food. You're too shook up to think clearly."

But I was on a roll.

"Ed Lau freaked out today," I informed York.

"What about?"

"I'm not sure," I answered slowly. "It was something about Hawaii. I think he felt that Judd insulted his home. But he was really upset."

York thought for a moment before speaking.

"Did Dr. Hart ever go to Hawaii?" he tried.

That was a good question. It was too bad I didn't know the answer. I just shrugged my shoulders.

"What else?" York prodded.

"Craig Zweig is completely flipped out, or at least I thought he was—" I began.

"I thought you always said everyone's emotional processes were equally valid," York reminded me, his voice smug.

"Don't interrupt me!" I shouted.

Now it was York's turn to shrug.

"I was going to say that I *thought* Craig was flipped out, but he started talking about butterflies, and I saw one."

"And?" York prompted, his head slanted back as if he thought that position might help him understand me better.

"He could really know stuff," I struggled to explain. "You know, one of those people who acts really weird, but is actually on a higher spiritual plane?"

"And Craig Zweig is on a higher plane?"

"No, yes, maybe." I threw up my hands and realized I was still holding the washcloth. I set it back on the bar.

"Fran accused Quinn of trying to steal her energy wand," I added as I shoved past York to get out of the bathroom. Except, of course, I didn't shove him. He moved a split instant before I could actually connect with him.

"An energy wand? Does she really have an energy wand?"

"She has some Kirlian contraption she uses to diagnose energy disruptions. Sort of a biofeedback thing. After she uses it, she works with people to get their energy into a better state." I reflected for a moment. "I think that's what it is anyway."

"And did Quinn really try to steal it?" York demanded.

"I can't imagine Quinn stealing anything, much less Fran's wand."

York sighed. "Let's go eat," he suggested again.

"Oh," I plowed on, remembering. "And Dotty thinks some cats deserve to live longer than some people."

"People like Dr. Hart?"

I was back to shrugging. At least it was good for my tight shoulders. And I felt like crying.

"What?" York asked again, more gently this time.

"York," I mumbled. "How do I make any sense out of all this? Everyone's stressed. Everyone's acting out. Any one of them could have killed Dr. Hart."

"Just keep talking to me, little sister," he advised. "I'm here for you, okay? Now let me get you to some food."

So we left my room to drive to Yams, the only vegetarian restaurant in town. That evening, York's brotherly affection did not extend to eating in a place where animal products were served.

We had only gone a few blocks when York peered into his rearview mirror.

"What are you looking at?" I demanded.

"We have a tail," he told me.

"A tail?" It took me a moment to figure out what he was talking about. "You mean there's someone following us?"

"That's what I said, a tail."

"But who?" I asked, turning around.

There was a car behind us, but I didn't recognize it. And I couldn't glimpse the driver's face through the windshield.

"Do you think the murderer is following us?" I whispered, frightened suddenly.

"No, it's the police."

"The police!"

"Kapp told me they would," York replied shortly.

"But why?"

"You're a suspect, Cally. What do you expect? They're going to keep tabs on you."

I don't know what I expected, but once I calmed down, I was glad the car following us was driven by a police officer, not a murderer. Assuming York was right.

Yams had a brightly colored sign featuring a six-foot-long yam on the outside and oversized paintings of other vegetables inside the doors. And the fragrance of curry, onion, and garlic wafted gently through the room.

A young man with green hair, matching earrings, and a Yams T-shirt showed us to our table. A large eggplant watercolor hung to my right and an even larger carrot to my left. Ethereal flute music poured from a speaker.

"How come a ranching town like Swanton offers vegetarian food?" I asked, putting on a concerned face. "Do you think Chief Phlug knows?"

But York wasn't laughing at my attempt at humor.

"I think part of the reason Chief Phlug is so angry is because there *is* a vegetarian restaurant in town, not to mention a New Age bookstore, a gay bar, and some alternative healers."

I nodded, remembering what Monty had said.

A young woman strolled to our table. She wore the Yams T-shirt, but her hair was brown, not green. Still, I suppose both the young man and woman did have hair the color of vegetables.

"Our two soups tonight are a cream of carrot and a mushroom-almond," she announced and handed us our menus. "Please let me know if you have any questions or allergies." She smiled. Her smile was as sudden and bright as Raleigh's, but somehow it didn't have the same effect on me.

I smiled back though. It was nice to share a smile with someone who wasn't from the intensive. I had almost forgotten the pleasure of simple humanity. Simple humanity without suspicion of murder. Something in me loosened.

York was immersed in his menu. Young women held no special appeal for him. He was as gay as he was vegetarian.

Once the young woman had left, I looked through the menu and told myself to choose quickly. As hungry as I might have been, I was more interested in talking suspects than food. Still, the garden vegetable crepes with mushroom sauce would certainly do. And the avocado-almond salad with the honeyed tahini dressing to start. Okay, so maybe food was more important than I'd thought. My stomach seemed to agree, awakened by the artful descriptions of the dishes, ". . . sprinkled with parsley, thyme, marjoram and gently tossed with . . ." Oh, yum. I shut the menu, sniffing the air again. Spice and citrus floated off a nearby plate.

York shut his menu, too. "So tell me about the suspects."

"You wouldn't believe it, York," I said, shaking my head. Whatever had loosened in me tightened again. "It's hard to know what's important."

York sighed. "Ed Lau?" he prompted.

"He does chi gung. He's usually incredibly centered, but he lost it today."

"Did he know the doctor before?"

"I don't know."

"Who *did* know the doctor before?"

"Well, Quinn and Sara—"

The waitress was back before I could get any further.

I ordered the avocado salad and crepes. York asked for the nutloaf and carrot soup.

"Good choice," our waitress commended York, beaming his way. But York was oblivious. I wondered if mine had been bad choices.

"Okay, Cally," York started in again after she left with our orders. "Is there anyone who *doesn't* seem to have issues with Dr. Hart?"

I thought for a moment.

"Well," I started tentatively. "There's Taj. He seemed all

right with her. And Kim. And Judd's son, Orson. He arrived after she died."

"Which ones are Kim and Taj?"

"Kim's a psychiatrist who dabbles in energy work. At least, that's the impression I got. She's a little younger than me—"

"Short?" York guessed. "Sad face?"

"Yeah, that's her. She seems very quiet. I think she's totally freaked out by what happened."

"And Taj?"

"He does past-life regressions."

"He's the one that looks like some kind of actor, right?" York hazarded. "Tall, dark, and handsome, with a trimmed beard."

I nodded.

"He also looks like a scam artist to me," York pronounced.

"Hey," I reminded him. "Lot's of people would think *I'm* a scam artist." But I wondered. Was Taj just doing an act? He wouldn't be the first.

"How about the good-looking black guy?" York pressed on.

I felt my skin heat up.

"What?" York said, eyes widening.

"I . . . I just agree that he's good looking," I compromised. "He sings, does tonal resonance. No big deal."

York grinned.

"You have a crush on him," he whispered in a singsong voice.

"I do not!" I hissed back.

"Do, too."

"York, you cut that out!"

"You gonna make me?"

I was tempted, but York was too fast for me. I knew that. And he knew that. It wasn't fair. I was about to threaten to sic Geneva on him when our soup and salad arrived.

I bit into the avocado salad. And it was good, the honey-tahini dressing tangy and not too rich. But as I took my second mouthful and crunched almonds, Sara and Taj walked in, giggling together.

"Whoa," I said, keeping my voice soft as I elbowed York.

He swallowed his mouthful of soup and lifted his eyes casually.

It didn't really matter. Sara and Taj were completely involved with each other, oblivious to the other diners. Taj threw his head back and laughed, patting Sara's arm as they were seated.

"Sara Oshima," I whispered.

"Dr. Hart's third in command?" York asked quietly.

I nodded. "And she's not with her boyfriend, Ira."

"What boyfriend, Ira?" York pushed, never raising his voice. "You didn't tell me about her boyfriend."

"I saw them today," I specified. "They were arguing. They'd been skimming money from Dr. Hart. But Quinn said Dr. Hart knew."

"Explain," York commanded.

I told him everything I could remember in hushed tones. The skin around his eyes tightened as I did. I knew that look. It was his warrior look.

Taj turned to survey the restaurant. I shoveled in avocado salad, my head bent low. I could barely taste it.

By the time our entrees came, York was eyeing the pair as if waiting for an attack. But all we got was nutloaf and crepes.

The crepes were good, though. Even in my nervous state, I could taste the well-sauced mixture of portabella mushrooms, broccoli, zucchini, and onions, rich with herbs and sunflower seeds, wrapped in warm whole wheat jackets.

York and I ate in reverent silence for a while.

Then someone new came through the door and stood,

looking around the room with a sneer on his face. Chief Phlug. I coughed up a sunflower seed.

The chief shook his head as if he couldn't believe how disgusting the room was. Or maybe it was my sunflower seed trick.

The room went silent just like an old Western when the gunslinger walks in. Which actually made some sense, I realized. Chief Phlug was carrying his gun.

"Um," the young man with the green hair ventured. "May I seat you, sir?"

Chief Phlug scanned the young man from head to toe. He shook his head again.

An older woman came in from the kitchen.

"Hey!" she greeted the chief. "Want some tea, Web?"

"Sure thing, Terry," he replied, a smile replacing his sneer. "Just make sure it has some caffeine in it."

Once the chief was seated with his tea in hand, people began to talk again.

"Is he here to watch us?" I whispered to York.

"Maybe to watch them," York whispered, jerking a shoulder toward Taj and Sara.

York and I finished our meals quickly and efficiently.

Our waitress brought us our bill. She wasn't smiling anymore.

"What was that all about?" I asked, once York and I were out of Yams and back in York's Subaru.

"I think Sara killed Dr. Hart," York answered, or didn't answer.

"But why?" I demanded. "Dr. Hart was a mother figure to her—"

"Not everyone loves their mother," he reminded me.

And our mouths were off and running. We never even got to the question of Chief Phlug's presence at Yams before we were back at the lodge, disagreeing about all the suspects.

I hugged York good night in the lobby. He started to follow me to my room anyway.

"Thanks for caring, big brother," I said softly. "But I need to sleep now."

"Cally—" he began.

I put my hand on his arm.

"I'm safe, York," I insisted.

He sighed and whispered, "I'm in room thirty-two if you need me."

And finally, I was back in my room alone. I had changed into my flannel pajamas and was just snuggling under the covers when my phone rang.

I picked it up, expecting my brother or Kapp. But it was my sweetie's voice that came through the speaker.

"Cally," Roy breathed. "I still see darkness near you. You wouldn't be keeping anything from me, would you, darlin'?"

ELEVEN

"Me!" I squeaked. I lowered my voice. "I wouldn't keep anything important from you," I lied. I told myself it wasn't a real lie. In the cosmic scheme of things, maybe Dr. Hart's murder wasn't important. Not to Roy anyway. He didn't know her.

There was silence on the line from Kentucky. I wasn't convincing Roy. I wasn't even convincing myself.

"Nothing I can't handle, anyway," I amended, getting a little closer to the truth.

The silence continued.

"Roy, I'll be okay," I told him.

"Someone's passed away where you are, haven't they?" Roy asked.

"Kind of," I answered cautiously.

"Oh, Cally," Roy murmured. "I was sure of it. Another murder?"

And this time, my sweetie was not diverted by my efforts to change the conversation. I could almost hear the gears of intelligence and ethics creaking in his brain as he pressed me for the truth. Finally, I told him everything. Well, almost everything. I didn't tell him that Kapp was putting me in danger with his claims again. I didn't tell him that I was attracted to Raleigh Hutchinson. And I didn't tell him how afraid I was. I did tell him I loved him.

"I love you, too, darlin'" Roy soothed me. "I want you to be well and safe. And *you* want to take care of everything and not worry me. But Cally, I do fret. You are too important to me. My mama can do without me for the time being—"

"No, Roy," I said. "You're where you should be. Remember how you got hurt the last time you tried to protect me—"

"Oh, darlin', I'd take a hundred bumps on the head if I could really protect you," he insisted. "I just hope that my presence *will* protect you. What if it harms you?"

Now, we were arguing backwards. I thought I had convinced Roy that the darkness he saw near me had nothing to do with him. But it sounded as if he was having an attitudinal relapse. Even from Kentucky, he was blaming himself for my current predicament. I never could explain it, or explain it away.

"Roy, it isn't your fault," I enunciated carefully. Why do the people we love make us want to shout? "You aren't even here. How could Dr. Hart's death be your fault?"

"I'm not sure, darlin'," he said quietly. "I'm not sure."

"Oh, Roy," I sighed. "Think of light. Think of us. Think of—"

"You are so good, Cally," he interrupted. "You really can't see the evil, can you?"

"Not evil, Roy. Someone was very upset. Not evil."

"I'll try and think of light, Cally. I'll try," he promised. "But you stay safe till I see you."

"I will," I assured him. Or at least, I would try.

Later, after a few more volleys back and forth of attempted comfort, I hung up the phone. I put the receiver in the cradle very gently. Roy.

I got into bed and snuggled under the covers again. I was in between clean white sheets. They smelled of chlorine and felt crisp against my skin. And soon, I was dreaming. But I didn't dream about Roy. I dreamed about butterflies.

I was in a field of dying flowers, and butterflies were floating up everywhere, their brightly colored wings flapping around me. Too many butterflies . . .

A passing butterfly rang. I turned my body, my arms outstretched into the swarm of flapping wings, and it rang again—

I was awake, reaching for the phone.

"Hey, Lazar," Kapp greeted me. I looked at my clock. It was five-thirty in the morning. I asked myself why Joan and Dee-Dee couldn't have stayed with me at the lodge. Why did it have to be Kapp?

"Kapp!" I whined.

"Rise and shine, Lazar," he ordered. "It's Monday morning, and we have investigating to do."

"You sneaking son of a lizard," I mumbled. I wanted to yell, but I was too sleepy.

"What did you say?" Kapp fired back genially.

"Kapp, you've been telling people I investigate murder," I accused. "Stop it, right now." Someone once told me that the secret to men was to treat them like dogs.

"Hooboy, did you get out of bed on the wrong side this morning or what?" Kapp demanded. The dog thing clearly wasn't working.

"I'm not out of bed," I told him with what I felt was admirable restraint. "And you could get me killed telling people stories about me investigating."

"Not you, Cally, you're too fast with your cane to be killed."

Something in me was pleased by that one. Still, I remembered the main focus. Death.

"Kapp, seriously." I deepened my voice. "There is probably a murderer in my intensive group, and if you tell people that I'm investigating, they may feel threatened and react by killing me." Was that clear enough?

"Ah, come on, Lazar. Where's your sense of adventure? You're more likely to be killed by a grocery truck than by

this murderer. Anyway, I've only talked to a few people."
Nope, not clear enough. And I was wondering about the alleged grocery truck. "Come and meet me for an early breakfast and we'll hash it out."

"No," I replied firmly.

"Ah, come on," he cajoled. "That's why I called so early. No one else will be up to see us. Holy Mother, if you're so worried about people seeing us together—"

"No."

"There's a place that starts breakfast at six—"

"No."

"Lunch," he countered.

I hesitated. This is always a big mistake when dealing with Kapp.

"We have to talk, Lazar. We have to compare our findings."

"I don't have any findings," I told him.

He laughed, the sound booming over the phone line.

"Okay," he conceded. "I'll be Nero Wolfe and you be Archie Goodwin. You tell me what you know, and I'll tell you what it means."

"Fine." I yawned, just wanting to go back to sleep. "Lunch. I'm sure you can use your deductive skills to find me."

He was still laughing when I hung up and rolled over to go back to sleep.

I slept, but I never got my butterfly dream back. Then my alarm clock rang.

After I'd showered, meditated extra long due to distraction, and cursed Kapp for my lack of good sleep, I wandered down into the lobby. Once again, there was a buffet set up, though it looked as if I was one of the last to visit it. Trays were emptied. Used paper plates filled the garbage. Still, I grabbed a pear and some muffins and balanced them on a remaining paper plate. I reached toward a half-filled tray of yogurt containers for good measure.

"Hey there, Cally," Raleigh greeted me as I was reaching.

I turned and looked at him. After talking to Roy the night before, Raleigh no longer seemed quite so attractive. But he was still *too* attractive.

"Hi, Raleigh," I answered belatedly. I took in a big breath and forged on. "So, Raleigh, are you married or are you—"

"Hey, Cally," a younger voice interrupted me.

Raleigh looked over my shoulder, and I swiveled my head around.

Orson stood on one leg next to me, his observant eyes excited. "I heard that you're a private eye," he blurted out. "That's awesome."

"I'm not a private eye," I stated firmly. "You probably heard that from Warren Kapp—"

"No, from my dad. He says you've solved a bunch of murders—"

"Your father heard that from Warren Kapp," I cut back in. "Warren Kapp is a friend of mine. He doesn't exactly lie, but he gets carried away when he tells stories. He's staying here at the hotel." I sniffed the air for Kapp's after-shave and found it over the smells of the food buffet. Kapp was probably hiding somewhere nearby.

"You mean . . . it isn't true?" Orson asked, rubbing the side of his face.

"No, Orson," I repeated. "I'm not a private eye. I'm a healer."

"Oh," he mumbled. "I've got a friend who tells stories like that. I think he does it to get attention."

Someone harrumphed from behind a giant potted plant. Hah! Kapp. And suddenly, I remembered that York had promised to keep Kapp from talking about my investigative skills. But even York couldn't keep Kapp from talking. Kapp *did* want attention. I should have guessed that.

"You're a smart kid," I told Orson. "I think you've got it in one."

"Thanks, Cally," he said, blushing.

"Can you do me a favor, Orson?" I asked.

"Sure," he shot back.

"If anyone tries to tell you that I'm a private eye or anything like that, explain to them about Warren Kapp. Okay?"

"Cool," he agreed. "Maybe someone should work on this Kapp guy. Sounds like he has a problem."

The potted plant looked ready to explode as I nodded somberly.

"Thanks, Orson," I murmured.

He saluted and ambled off down the hall, leaving me alone with Raleigh . . . and the potted plant.

I turned my head back to Raleigh. He was smiling, and somehow, I thought he was laughing, too, quietly, like a cat.

"I've met your friend Warren Kapp," he told me. "He never said you were a private eye, just that you and he had uncovered a couple of murderers together."

"Well, that isn't strictly true—"

"That man was on the cover of *Newsweek*," Raleigh rolled on. "As I remember, he was called the Melvin Belli of Glasse County. Gotta give it to the man. He's good. You'd think that would be enough attention for him."

"You would," I agreed loudly. "Wouldn't you? But his imagination just doesn't quit!"

Raleigh laughed out loud.

He reached out and patted my shoulder.

"Don't worry," he whispered. "I won't say anything about your friend's 'stories.'" He turned to walk away. Abruptly, he turned back. "Oh, and I'm not married," he added. Then he turned away from me again and walked down the hall where Orson had gone before.

"Kapp!" I hissed. I put my plate on the buffet table, pulled my cane up at the ready, and strode toward the potted plant.

But there was no one behind the greenery when I got

there. Kapp was good. I never saw him go. Or else, he was never there in the first place.

I took my breakfast outside and found a spot behind an oak tree where I could eat alone, enjoying the cool morning air and trying to forget Warren Kapp and Raleigh Hutchinson. Not to mention Aurora Hart. The muffins were good. I could taste peanut butter in them as well as chunks of raspberry. And the pear was crisp and sweet. But I never did get to the yogurt. As I reached to pull off the lid, I glimpsed my watch. It was after nine. I was late for the morning session.

By the time I got to the meeting room, everyone else was already there. Sara and Quinn stood at the front of the room, side by side, with strained smiles on their faces. If I hadn't heard them arguing the day before, I would have thought they were true partners today. Only they weren't looking at each other. Fran, Judd, and Orson stood in a little knot, heads bent together and whispering. I wondered what they were saying. Dotty was talking to Craig. I could hear her. She was talking about butterflies she had seen. Raleigh and Taj sat next to each other quietly in a couple of cushy chairs. Only Ed and Kim were by themselves: Ed standing near the front of the room with his eyes closed, and Kim sitting in a chair in the back.

As I walked into the room, Quinn clapped his hands. It was the clap of the school bell. I was tardy.

"It's time to do some more one-on-one work this morning," Quinn announced. "Pick someone you haven't worked with before. That way, you'll be able to learn more about their unique healing skills. And please, try not to raise issues that can't be solved in a short session. Half an hour, then switch roles." Quinn paused and added, "Sara, you can work with Orson." Maybe they weren't partners, after all.

I approached Kim Welch cautiously. She still looked spooked: her skin pale white, her large eyes vacant. She was as small and sad as York had described.

"Kim," I said quietly.

She flinched and bunched up her hands as if to control her reaction.

"Cally," she replied, focusing her eyes. "Do you want to work together?"

"If you do," I answered, feeling shy suddenly. This woman was an actual psychiatrist. Even small and sad, she seemed aloof.

"Oh, of course," she murmured. "I don't suppose you'll be real impressed with my energy work. I've spent most of my life in school to be a psychiatrist. I've just recently begun a little work with guided meditations, hypnotism, light work, things like that. Mostly to let my patients relax. I don't like to use drugs unless I have to. But their issues can be overwhelming if they're not relaxed. I'm sorry I don't do anything more exotic."

"Relaxation sounds good to me," I assured her. And it did. I was tired of anxiety.

So Kim asked me to sit in the chair in front of her. I wouldn't be able to see her from there. I supposed this was part of her technique. I lowered myself into the chair, resisting the urge to ask if she usually used a couch for her patients. A number of psychiatrist jokes rolled through my mind unbidden. *A hundred dollars an hour to talk to some guy . . . you must be crazy. A parrot walks into a psychiatrist's office—*

"So, Cally," Kim murmured, "is there anything troubling you now?"

"Uh-huh," I mumbled.

"Would you like to keep the anxiety over whatever it is that's troubling you? Or would you like to let it go?"

I paused. There were so many things troubling me. Dr. Hart's murder. Kapp's behavior. Roy. My parents' death. Criminy, that was weird. Why was I thinking of my parents' death?

"Let it go," I answered finally. I'd allow my subconscious to decide what to let go. I trusted my subconscious.

"Close your eyes," Kim instructed.

I closed them. And Kim led me with her quiet voice down a long path, bordered by flowers. I followed her in my mind, seeing the path, smelling the flowers. Her voice seemed less real than the flowers after I'd traveled into her woods.

"Can you see a body of water in front of you?" she enquired finally.

"A lake," I murmured. I yawned. I was sleepy. "A big blue lake . . . with ducks."

"Good, good," she praised.

The lake filled my mind. I could hear the ducks now.

"And your trouble." She paused. "What could carry the anxiety caused by your trouble?"

"A grocery truck?"

"Yes," she chirped, as if I'd given her the right answer. "A grocery truck is very big, but smaller than a lake."

"Smaller than a lake," I repeated.

"And its doors are very tight."

"Tight," I agreed.

"Can you push the back of your grocery truck with your hand now?" she asked me.

I found that I could. I pushed the anxiety-laden grocery truck and it rolled toward the lake. "Yes," I whispered.

And the truck went into the lake with a big splash.

"That felt good," I said.

"Is the truck in the lake now?" Kim asked.

"Underwater," I told her. I was surprised she hadn't seen it go.

"Do you remember what your trouble is?" she prodded.

"Yes." My parents' death.

"But you don't feel as anxious about it any more?"

"No, just curious." And it was true. What had caused the

explosion that had killed them? Something fluttered in my brain. My father had been a careful man. No one had ever really known what had caused the explosion. Certainly, I hadn't at fifteen years of age.

"Look back at the lake," Kim ordered. "Do you see a light rising out of the lake?"

I did. The light was beautiful: crystalline, tipped with gold and silver.

"Do you want to be in the light?" she beckoned.

"Yes."

"Let it surround you."

I don't know how long I basked in the light, but it felt like it might have been forever. Even my curiosity left me. I was the light. I swelled and flowed—

"Is Bob here?" a voice interrupted my mind. Who was that in my light?

"Bob, my husband," the voice continued incessantly. "I can't find him anywhere."

I opened my eyes and saw the meeting room, filled with pairs of healers: humming, crying, talking.

"I haven't seen him," Kim murmured behind me. "I'm sorry."

I turned my head and looked into Heidi Jinnah's concerned eyes. Her jaw was square and tight with tension.

"How long has he been missing?" I asked.

"All morning," she said. "But he does this."

She pulled back her shoulders and stretched her mouth into a smile.

"I'm very sorry to have bothered you," she apologized, and turned and left the room, her blonde hair swinging with her determined footsteps.

"Cally, are you all right?" Kim prodded, walking around my chair so that she could sit across from me instead of behind me. "I'm sorry. I put you under, and then you were jerked out again."

"I'm fine," I told her as she took her new seat. "You do great work. I can still feel the light, even with my eyes open."

"Really?" Kim said, smiling gently for the first time that I could remember since Dr. Hart had died.

"Really," I told her. An insecure psychiatrist?

"Neither of the Jinnahs were at the Boy Scout Hall that night, were they?" I asked, not realizing that I'd voiced the thought aloud until I saw Kim's face fall.

"I don't think so," she whispered.

"Oh, Kim," I whispered back. "I'm sorry. You got me so relaxed, my mouth was flapping."

But Kim didn't smile again. Maybe we were both realizing that the Jinnahs might have had reason to dislike Dr. Aurora Hart. And the aura maker had been left overnight in the meeting room. And—

"Switch!" Quinn shouted out. "Begin winding down, and switch roles with your partner."

I looked at Kim automatically, really looked. Maybe it was the beauty of the light I had just seen in my mind, but Kim's aura looked strange to me. It wasn't so much *of* her body as *around* it, mostly white, tinged with the primary colors of grief at its edges. I drew in a breath and felt my way toward her. The grief was vast, but disconnected. Maybe it had to be. Maybe she had pushed too many of her own grocery trucks into lakes.

"Cally?" Kim ventured.

"Yes," I answered automatically.

"You don't think the Jinnahs had anything to do with Dr. Hart's murder, do you?"

"Well," I began slowly. "I don't know. It just occurred to me that they might have had access to the doctor's aura maker here at the lodge. I'd thought only the people at the Boy Scout Hall could have been involved."

"Oh, but I'm sure they couldn't have done anything,"

Kim insisted. "And they'd have caused themselves so much trouble. I worry that the chief will blame them. That wouldn't be fair."

I looked at Kim. She was really upset. Even I could see that.

"Kim, would you like to get rid of your anxiety on this one?" I asked.

"No, no," she said, visibly shrinking into her chair. So much for that approach. I'd hoped she would laugh. Maybe after all her years of schooling, the laughter had been squeezed out of her.

"Seriously," I pressed. "Would you like me to work on you? That's what I'm supposed to be doing."

"You don't have to," she insisted. "You need time to integrate your own work. Time to remember the light."

"The light was beautiful," I remembered aloud. "I was the light."

"Yes?"

"My parents died when I was a teenager," I began. I stopped myself. "Wait a minute, I had my turn. This is supposed to be your turn."

"But you were interrupted in your process," she explained. "Now you're remembering your parents' death. And you can do so without as much anxiety. You see, that's just what I was trying for."

"Well, it worked," I conceded.

Kim told me a little more about her practice, how after all her years in school, she hadn't really learned how to let her patients work with their issues in relative relaxation until she took some courses from a friend of hers.

We were still talking when Quinn yelled out, "Next! New partners, everyone!"

I paired up with Craig Zweig.

"I like to stand," he told me.

So we stood in the corner of the meeting room, face to

face. His snaggly teeth weren't as innocent-looking up close. There was something feral about them.

"So you work with unconscious entities?" I prompted.

"Uh-huh. They interfere with your life energies. I try to get them to leave. They're dead, but sometimes they don't know it."

"Right," I said, smiling with an effort. "Do you see any entities interfering with me?"

Craig smiled, too, exposing his snaggly teeth like a wolf.

"Do you really want to know?" he stage-whispered.

"Sure," I invited him.

"You've taken on Dr. Hart's spirit!" Craig shouted, and then he threw his arms around me.

TWELVE

Craig pulled me to his chest so tightly that my face was smothered. And his chest didn't smell good. It smelled of unwashed flesh and insanity and antidepressants.

"Cra—" I tried.

He just squeezed me tighter. I couldn't even move my lips to speak. Or to scream. My neck was bent back so hard, I was afraid it would snap.

Still, I was holding my cane. And even if my upper arms were immobilized, I could use my forearms, especially the one connected to that cane. Not breathing, I grasped it with my hand and whacked at the back of Craig's ankles.

But Craig didn't so much as move his feet. He kept his grip on me, and my face was still imprisoned against his chest. I couldn't get enough leverage for a good swing. I breathed in with difficulty, wondering if I really could smother here or if it was just the smell that made me sure of it, and tried to think strategically. I could probably hit his head with a good wrist move, but I didn't want to really damage him . . . or myself for that matter. I took another labored breath, and my cane hand took over. My forearm came up and went down again, smashing the metal tip of the cane into his toes.

He loosened his grip for a second. That was all I needed.

I went limp and slid out from Craig Zweig's arms, stepping back quickly the moment I was free, and raising my cane as I stepped.

Craig lunged forward again, but he was stopped by the tip of my cane at his chest. I was breathing in huge volumes of air, clean air. The colors in the room seemed acutely bright, even the empty space glistened. I resisted hitting Craig hard, but kept him at bay in a long-distance mirror dance, moving as he moved, keeping the cane between us.

The butterfly dream flashed through my mind, and I wondered if it had been a warning. Had Kapp's five-thirty phone call kept me from smothering in butterflies? *No*, I told myself impatiently. The dream had nothing to do with this. And I needed my focus.

I heard concerned voices, some coming toward us. How long had it been since Craig had first embraced me. A minute? Or less? Had anyone even seen what had happened?

Raleigh was there first, striding up behind Craig. He looked at me. He looked at Craig. He put his arms around Craig from the back in a bear hug. Good choice. I lowered my cane to half mast.

"Aurora!" Craig cried out. "Aurora, don't you recognize me?"

"I'm Cally Lazar, Mr. Zweig," I stated, keeping my voice as even as my heartbeat was unsteady. "I'm not Aurora Hart."

"But you have her spirit!" he insisted. "You know you do."

"No," I told him. "I don't know what you see or feel, but I don't have any sense of Dr. Hart's spirit near me or in me."

Raleigh continued to hold Craig as Craig begged me to give him Dr. Hart's spirit. Raleigh began to hum softly.

"I love Aurora," Craig mumbled. "Don't you see?"

Raleigh hummed a little louder. It was a soothing sound. Even my heart seemed to find its natural rhythm again. And Craig's eyelids began to droop.

"I didn't mean to hurt anyone," Craig explained, his voice soft. "But Aurora was taking refuge in Cally's body. I just wanted to hold her."

"Do you see her there now?" Raleigh asked cautiously.

Craig looked at me in confusion.

"Aurora?" he whispered. He shook his head. "She's gone. I scared her. I'm so sorry."

One tear beaded up and descended his cheek.

I took a few more steps backward just the same. As another tear followed the first down Craig's face, I realized I was wet with my own perspiration. And I was cold. Craig had embraced me with the unnatural strength of the insane. I'd seen that strength demonstrated before, but I'd never felt it used against my own body. I realized that it was easier to treat the insane as people whose vision was not wrong, only different than ours, when they were under someone else's supervision. For all I knew, Craig *had* seen Dr. Hart. For all I knew, he'd killed her, too. For all I knew—

"Raleigh, you'll work with Craig now," Quinn ordered. As if Raleigh wasn't already working with Craig. For a moment, I disliked Quinn. I turned and took a good look at Dr. Hart's successor. His narrow face looked even more morose than usual. He massaged his temple with a shaking hand. Dack. Quinn had seen what had happened. I was sure of it.

"And Cally and Taj?" he tried more softly. "Would you like to work together now?"

What I really wanted to do was leave and take a shower. But before I could say anything, Taj had stepped up to me. He bowed theatrically.

"Madam?" he offered. "Would you like a quick past-life regression?"

"Sure," I accepted, breathing in and trying to smile. "As long as I can sit down for it."

"It's a deal," he told me, smiling back. But his smile was as pasted-on as mine was. I looked into his dark eyes. Taj was a handsome young man, but somehow he wasn't attractive, despite the eyes and sensual lips and trimmed beard. I wondered why.

"Would you like to close your eyes?" he asked.

"No," I said. I was surprised I'd actually spoken aloud. "Sorry," I added.

"You're still freaked out?" Taj asked, his smile gone, his face looking better to me suddenly, less phony.

I just nodded. Closing my eyes around strangers didn't appeal to me at the moment. And that bothered me. I tried to see the light in everything, but I couldn't even keep my mind on what had just happened with Craig. Had I lost my trust?

"Maybe a trip to the little healer's room?" Taj suggested.

I laughed. I liked the designation "little healer's room." And it was a good idea.

"Thanks, Taj," I said sincerely. I stood up. "I'll be back in five minutes, okay?"

I wandered out into the hall, my mind a mass of conflicting ideas. Craig's sudden attack had really frightened me. I told myself I should have seen it coming. But I hadn't. And yet, I was fine. My cane hadn't failed me. And Raleigh, and even Taj, were actually concerned about me. *There* was the light of goodness I sought. But my mind kept replaying Craig Zweig's actions, not Raleigh's, not Taj's, not all the people's who cared about me.

I had just reached the public rest room, when I saw Bob Jinnah walking past me. Hadn't his wife been looking for him earlier?

"Bob," I greeted him.

He turned toward me at the sound of my voice and blinked liquid brown eyes under his glasses. But he didn't speak.

"Bob, have you connected up with your wife yet?" I asked him gently.

"Connected?" he asked.

"With your wife," I repeated.

Bob continued to blink.

"Your wife, Heidi," I expanded.

"Oh, dear me, Heidi," he muttered. "Heidi, my wife."

"That's the one," I told him. "She's looking for you."

"I'm supposed to be at the front desk?" he tried, massaging his chin.

"Sounds like a plan," I offered.

"Oh, thank you so much," he burbled. "That's it! I *am* supposed to be at the front desk. I was lost in thought." He laughed lightly. "Shelley might say, 'like a poet hidden in thought,' though I'm sure Shelley wasn't as absentminded as I am. He was speaking of the—"

"The front desk?" I reminded him.

"Oh, yes, the front desk," he replied. He turned to walk down the hall, then swiveled his head back around for a moment. "Enjoy your stay here at the Swanton Hills Lodge," he recited and finally walked briskly away.

I entered the rest room and took the quickest sponge bath I'd ever taken, and the coldest. And it felt good. By the time I'd rushed back to the meeting room, I was beginning to feel like myself again, though I was still uneasy about Craig Zweig. Would a murderer be so obvious? Should I call Chief Phlug? Or would Quinn take care of that? I felt guilty about Craig. If he was actually Dr. Hart's murderer, the police should be notified of his assault on me. But what if he wasn't? I just didn't know. I saw Craig sitting with his back to me, humming along with Raleigh Hutchinson.

"Hey, Cally!" Taj called out. I told myself to forget Craig Zweig for the time being. Taj was waiting for me right where I'd left him.

I sat down in my seat, said, "I'm ready," closed my eyes,

and prepared myself for whatever Taj had to offer, grateful that I trusted enough to close my eyes again.

"We don't have a lot of time," he began. "So I'm going for some highlights."

I grunted my approval.

I waited in the silence until he began.

"You've lived many lives in many places." Taj's voice had changed. He'd sounded businesslike before, but abruptly his voice seemed softer and slower, dreamlike, as if he were in trance. "But there are common threads. Religious institutions, for instance. Many of your lives have been spent in various religious institutions. You have been a nun, a priest, a shaman, a priestess, a monk, a hermit, so many roles. And many times, you have challenged authority. And many times, you have died for your challenge."

I rolled my shoulders, trying to shake off the shiver that had reached them. I saw a fire in my mind, a stake at the center.

"Yes," Taj replied, as if to my unspoken vision. "In medieval times, you refused to give up your own views. And in China . . ."

I was taking poison, knowing that it would be better than the alternative. I had dissolved the poison in tea in a cup that had no handle. I felt at peace.

". . . once again, you held to your views. You were to be executed, but you took your own way out."

"This is spooky," I told him. Where was I getting these memory flashes? They might be real past-life experiences, or they might be from Taj himself. Was there a way he could induce them?

"But there is another thread, not so exotic. You've been a farmer in more lives than any."

I saw neatly planted rows of what might have been wheat. I sighed with pleasure at a job well done.

"Your lives as a farmer were the happiest. So you try to replicate them with your gardening."

He could have gotten that piece from our discussion in the van the previous day, I reminded myself. I wondered why I was so resistant to Taj. For all of what I was feeling and seeing, I had sensed the trickster in him earlier. But now?

"Another thread, it's harder to see," he went on, his voice even slower. "You have lived many lives with the same soul under many circumstances."

"Roy?" I asked. But Taj didn't seem to hear.

Even with my eyes closed, I could feel his frown. "There's a sort of darkness between the two of you, and yet, you can't be parted."

"A darkness?" I demanded, my eyes flying open.

Taj was indeed frowning, his eyes shut tight in apparent concentration.

"The darkness," he went on. "Is it yours or is it his?"

I opened my mouth to answer, as if I could, but Taj kept on speaking. "It is yours jointly, something you have shared through many lifetimes, a pain that one or the other of you cannot bear or even see, so you swathe it in darkness. That is how you have each protected one another so many times in so many lives. But the strategy of darkness is no longer working. You need to see what it swathes in this lifetime—"

"Switch!" Quinn shouted. "Time to switch roles with your partner."

I flew out of my chair with Quinn's shout. And Taj's eyes popped open.

"What?" I demanded, standing over Taj. "What is the darkness swathing?"

"Huh?" he asked.

"You were talking about the darkness between me and Roy—"

"Was I?" he said, looking dazed.

Was it using Roy's name that was throwing him?

"The darkness," I repeated. "You were telling me about a darkness swathing the pain. And you said—"

"I don't exactly remember what I say when I'm in a trance," he told me.

I was stunned into a silence for a moment, but for no longer than a moment.

"You really don't remember what you said?" I demanded.

"No." He shook his head. "I usually tell people ahead of time, but we didn't have much time, so I didn't warn you. I'm sorry. Did I open some issues that need resolving?"

I kept my lips pressed together. I wanted to force Taj to go back to where he had been before Quinn had shouted. But it was my turn to work on Taj. Maybe I could make an appointment with Taj for later. I scrutinized him. Was he faking all this stuff? Dr. Hart had spoken of an unhealthy darkness near me. Maybe he'd taken his cue from that. Dack! I was completely confused. The images in my mind had been so real. And yet, there was something about Taj that seemed off.

I closed my eyes for a minute and breathed from my center. My intuition would find the answers I needed about whatever the darkness was "swathing." I didn't need to squeeze information from Taj . . . I hoped. For all the strength of the voice that was telling me I would find my own answers, there were the voices telling me it was hopeless. I breathed in again and focused on strength.

When I opened my eyes, Taj asked me if I needed more time with him.

"Yes," I answered honestly.

"When I'm interrupted, I don't always go back to the same place that I left off," he warned me. "But it might be worth a try."

I sat back down, closed my eyes, and waited.

"South America," Taj intoned finally. "You are in South America. A church is standing before you, but you refuse to go in."

I saw the church. I knew it might take my life. Still, I couldn't accept this church. But my children. What of them?

I opened my eyes again. Where was this stuff coming from?

"Darkness," I prompted Taj. "Do you see the darkness between Roy and me?"

He didn't answer.

"You must hide," he went on instead. "You and your children will be fine if you can hide."

"The darkness—"

"The fields are dark enough for you to hide. The fields you have planted yourself. You will be safe."

"No, not that darkness—"

"You are in Africa now," he started up again.

"Taj!" I blurted out. The sound of his name rang through the meeting room. I didn't want to hear about another life where I'd farmed and bucked established religion. "What about the darkness, you know, between me and Roy."

But Taj's eyes were open again.

"Are we finished?" he asked me.

"Yes," I answered, keeping my sigh internal. There was no way I was going to get him back on track in the time allotted to the exercise. I was already running over my share.

"Did I answer your questions?"

"I . . ." I hesitated. "You gave me a direction to pursue."

"Oh," he murmured and looked at the floor.

It was clearly my turn to work on Taj. I reached out to him energetically and felt and saw humiliation. Humiliation? Oh, dear.

"Taj, are you happy doing past-life regressions?" I asked him.

"I guess so," he answered. Frustration and anger flared along with the humiliation.

"How did you start?" I asked gently.

"I wanted to be an actor," he told me. "But I wasn't really good enough. I did a little small theater and a couple of ads, but that was it. Then I was at this party, and this guy said I could read past lives. I don't even know why he said it. But he kept talking about it. He told me to close my eyes and tell him about his past lives. And the next thing I knew, everyone was sitting around, looking impressed. I'd gone into a trance and done it."

"Wow," I murmured.

"But I'd wanted to be an actor. It was really weird. I look the part for a swami. It isn't as if I don't know what I look like. My mother was Pakistani. I'm the picture-perfect swarthy mystic. And I'm a lousy actor. But this channeling stuff just happens. So I do it. I make money doing it. But I don't know if it really helps people."

I studied Taj more closely. I saw the anger flare near his liver.

"I know what you're seeing," he hissed.

"What am I seeing?" I asked him.

"You're seeing a scam artist!" he snapped. "A man who is good looking, but not talented enough to act. So he pretends to be psychic. You think I'm a con man."

"No," I said softly. "But *you* think you're a con man."

"Me?"

"Taj, I don't think you're faking anything. I don't know if what you see is real or metaphorical, but it's powerful. I can feel it. I can see what you're seeing. I don't understand it. But I don't think you're faking it."

"Really?"

"Really."

"Dr. Hart thought I was a fake," he muttered. "When she first let me in the program, I thought, that's cool, someone really believes in me."

"Maybe she did."

"So why did she want to sleep with me?" he asked, humiliation bubbling up again. "She didn't respect me. She just wanted to sleep with me."

I was surprised, but I kept my surprise to myself. Taj needed help.

"Is it possible that Dr. Hart could have both believed in your work *and* wanted to sleep with you?" I asked, clearing an energetic path for his humiliation to leave his body as I spoke. "Couldn't both be true?"

"Yeah," he conceded tentatively. And I saw the humiliation beginning to clear. "I suppose so."

I imagined confidence growing in him. I saw spiritual certainty unfold in violet light.

"Taj," I assured him once more. "You are for real. If you don't want to pursue this path, you can always step away, but you have the gift. I felt it. I saw it."

"I really am doing this," he stated. Healing colors filled his body.

I smiled at Taj.

We sat for a while in silence as he absorbed the possibility that he didn't have to doubt himself anymore, and I guided his energy field to support his new belief. I just hoped his new belief in himself would last beyond the intensive, or even beyond the hour. And I had one more question to ask. The question wasn't an easy one.

"Taj," I led in. "Did Quinn know that Dr. Hart—"

"Time's up!" Quinn shouted.

THIRTEEN

I turned to look at Quinn, wondering if he'd heard the question I'd been about to ask Taj. *Did* Quinn know that Dr. Hart had propositioned Taj?

"It's lunchtime," Quinn announced, not meeting my eyes. He surveyed the whole room with studied neutrality instead. "There should be sandwiches and snacks in the lobby. But please, be back in an hour. We'll have a short afternoon discussion session, and we'll go on another tour—"

Someone groaned behind me. I looked around, but I couldn't tell who it had been. I looked back as Quinn glared. I followed his glare. Sara, of course.

"A garden tour," Quinn bulldozed on, groan or no groan. "Monty assures me it'll be fun." Quinn didn't smile as he said this. His morose face might have been better used as a deterrent than a sales pitch for the tour. "Fun," he repeated.

I couldn't stand it. "It sounds like fun," I tried.

Quinn met my eyes. He looked like an abused dog who'd finally received a friendly pat.

"I love gardens," Dotty put in.

"Oh, good, then," Quinn murmured. He straightened his shoulders. "So, let's all be back in an hour."

"Will do," Raleigh replied.

"Fine," Ed agreed.

People started toward the door. I stared at Quinn. Did he know Dr. Hart had wanted to sleep with Taj? Of course, I was assuming that Taj had told the truth. And I was still assuming that Sara's accusations of intimacy between the doctor and Quinn were true. I wanted to ask Quinn about all of it, but I just couldn't. I shook my head. If Quinn had loved the deceased doctor and didn't know about her behavior toward Taj, it could only hurt him to find out.

I turned around, hoping to find Taj nearby. But he had left with the rest of the intensive group.

I turned back to Quinn, and he stared at me intently.

"Do you want me to report the incident with Craig Zweig to the police?" he asked quietly.

That wasn't what I'd been expecting to hear from his mouth, but of course it should have been. I rubbed my arms. I was too cold.

"I . . ." I faltered. Did I want the police to jump all over Craig?

I looked around the room a second time. Craig was gone. *Everyone* had left, except for Quinn. And me.

"I don't know," I finished up. "I don't want to get him in trouble, but I—"

"I understand," Quinn told me, eagerness lightening his long-suffering voice. "I don't know whether I should report him either. If he was just acting out, and it had nothing to do with Aurora's death, I would leave it alone. There's enough misery in his life already. But if it shows some kind of pathology . . ." Quinn faltered.

"Let's wait and watch," I suggested, speaking like an adult even if I didn't feel like one.

"Thank you, Cally." Quinn curved his mouth into a wistful half-smile and I saw the potentially attractive young man that hid behind the gloom and unwanted authority. "This is a sensitive situation all around. We're dealing with feelings and spirit . . . and Dr. Hart died. I'm a little out of my depth."

"Anyone would be, Quinn," I assured him. "You're doing really well under the circumstances."

"I hope so," he whispered, the half-smile leaving his face. "I just hope so."

I didn't know what else to say, so I just said, "See you later," and walked out of the meeting room, going toward the lobby.

I was halfway down the corridor when I smelled familiar aftershave behind me. I'd forgotten my lunch date with Kapp. I turned on my good leg, meeting his uplifted cane with my own and blocking it.

"Oh hell, Lazar," he complained. "I don't even know why I try. How do you always know I'm there?"

I shrugged my shoulders, looking inscrutable. If Kapp ever forgot his aftershave, I was in big trouble.

"Would you actually hit me with your cane if I didn't stop you?" I asked, truly curious.

"Holy Mother, hit a woman?" Kapp reared back, feigning horror. He grinned. "Just a little tap, that's all. Just one little tap. Is that so much for an old man to ask for?"

"Yep," I replied, twirling the tip of his cane with mine.

"I'll get you someday, Lazar," he hissed and yanked his cane back.

I laughed. It was good to be around someone who was only pretending to terrorize me.

"I've got one hour for lunch, Kapp," I informed him, tapping my watch. "One hour, then I have to be back."

"I know just the place," he said, hustling me out one of the lodge's back doors that I didn't even know existed.

Minutes later, we were figuring out how to approach our wooden stools in a little onion and garlic–scented deli right across the street from the Boy Scout Hall where Dr. Aurora

Hart had done her last show. I had tuna, Swiss, and pickles on multigrain bread with a water chaser. Kapp had ham on rye and a beer. We set our plates and glasses down, slid our stools closer to the tall, scarred, wooden table, and climbed on the high seats.

I stared out the window as I took my first bite. From my perch, I could see the hall looming and Dr. Hart's lavender Mercedes still parked in front of the building, as opaque as ever with its tinted windows.

"Good food, fast service, bad location," I mumbled through a mouthful of sandwich. And the sandwich was good. Lots of pickles. Yum.

"Hey, scene of the crime, Lazar," Kapp mumbled back, looking smug. "Maybe you'll be inspired. By the way, Joan and Dee-Dee said to say hi. And to tell you that your animals are well fed."

My cat, Leona, and my goats, Ohio, Moscow, and Persia popped into my mind. I felt a wave of homesickness.

"You talked to them?" I asked wistfully.

"Of course, I talked to them. They can't get ahold of you. You're never in your room. What are they supposed to do, channel you up?"

"I've had enough channeling for the day, thank you," I grumbled.

"Really?" Kapp leaned forward, almost losing his stool in the process. "Are you guys really doing all that weird stuff?"

"You tell me, one-who-knows-all," I requested. "I've got forty-five minutes left. Tell me what you've found out."

Kapp leaned back precariously, setting his sandwich on its plate. "Okay." He stuck one finger in the air. "Raleigh Hutchinson used to be a drug addict."

I shrugged my shoulders and took another bite of my sandwich.

"Not impressed? Fine. How about this? Kim Welch's

parents owned an electrical repair shop. Bet you didn't know that."

"I didn't," I said slowly. Kim had mentioned something about working for her parents, but she'd never mentioned electricity. Could she have rigged the aura maker? Did a person even remember electrical skills after going to medical school? Assuming she had actually learned about electrical repair in the first place. "Maybe she was just a receptionist or something," I added.

"Maybe," Kapp agreed amiably, tearing into his ham on rye. He swallowed about half his sandwich, blotted his face with a napkin, and went on. "My source just said he knew her in school, and that she'd worked at her parents' shop part-time to support herself. He didn't know what she actually did there."

Kim Welch? As I chewed, I tried to picture her small hands wielding a soldering iron, her soulful eyes intent on . . . on whatever electrical repair people do.

Kapp picked up the other half of his sandwich and went on.

"And there's Craig Zweig," he whispered and paused.

"What about Craig Zweig?" I demanded, suddenly feeling a weird tingling that I realized was my pulse.

"Zweig did electrical wiring for the phone company," Kapp announced.

I put my sandwich down. I wasn't hungry anymore.

"What's wrong?" Kapp asked. "Too many pickles?"

"No, it's Craig Zweig," I answered honestly. "He kinda attacked me today."

"He what?!" Kapp roared.

"Shush!" I hissed. Other people were turning on their stools to look at us.

Kapp lowered his voice. "Tell me," he commanded.

"Well, we were doing this exercise," I explained, trying for some sort of coherence. My brain was dancing with my pulse. "And Craig thought that I'd taken on Dr. Hart's spirit—"

"What kind of nutcase—"

"It's what he does," I cut in, suddenly wanting to defend Craig. "He looks to see if dead people's energies are interfering with yours. It's not so strange. Lots of times people are still enmeshed with the issues of people who've passed on. There're plenty of practitioners who believe that those issues are actually remnants of the dead people, entities—"

"But why did he attack you?"

"He didn't hit me or anything," I assured Kapp. "He just lunged at me and, well, squeezed me, like he was hugging me really hard or something. I thought I was going to suffocate." I could hear my own voice rise. I lowered it. "I think he was just trying to embrace Dr. Hart."

"Why didn't you hit him with your cane?" Kapp demanded.

"I did, eventually," I muttered, starting to perspire all over again. Post-embrace stress. "But not right away. See, that's what scared me," I confessed. "I didn't see it coming. I wasn't vigilant. If he'd had a real weapon, I'd be dead."

"Hey, Lazar," Kapp interjected gently. "You were in healing mode, right?"

"Well, yeah," I agreed tentatively.

"That's all," he told me. "You weren't expecting an attack. You're probably a different person in healing mode."

"Thanks, Kapp," I said, touched by his kindness.

"But don't let it happen again," he warned, his voice rough once more. "Even in those silly exercises, be on your guard."

"But—"

"Listen, Lazar," he insisted. "You're working with a bunch of lunatics—"

"Kapp!" I objected.

"Hooboy, Lazar, I've been researching your group. Take

it from me, they're a bunch of loonies, present company excepted . . . maybe."

"So how do I go into healing mode and martial mode at the same time?" I asked. "And how do I open up to others when they do their healing without endangering myself?"

"Focus," he answered. He tapped his forehead. "It's like playing poker. You just gotta focus on a lot of things at once. Don't you ever get real goofballs on your table?"

"Well, yeah," I admitted.

"So, what do you do then?"

I closed my eyes for a second, remembering guiding a sometimes violent schizophrenic with one part of my mind while another part watched for danger. "You're right, I focus on both aspects at once."

"See, case closed," Kapp announced, taking another bite of his sandwich. "You wanna hear more dirt?"

"Sure," I answered, keeping my smile hidden. Kapp's kind streak was not something he was proud of.

"Taj Gemayel," he went on. "That's not his real name by the way. His real name's Doug Gruber."

"Can't blame him for changing it," I argued before tearing into my own sandwich again. It seemed that my appetite was back. "Taj Gemayel has a certain ring."

"So this Taj guy was the Don Juan of the small theater set. That's what he did before he became a medium or whatever he's calling himself."

"Hmmm," I replied through my sandwich. I wanted to tell Kapp how ironic it was that Taj had been insulted by Dr. Hart putting the moves on him when he was a Don Juan himself, but that felt like privileged information to me.

"So, do you think this Taj guy's for real, Lazar?" Kapp asked me.

I just nodded. It was too hard to explain.

"And you don't believe you're working with lunatics?!" Kapp boomed. "This guy tells you about your past lives and gets paid for it. Your other little friend tells you about dead people floating around. And this Raleigh character sings to people or something."

"Hey, it works for me," I mumbled back. It was fun to play with Kapp.

"Lazar, if I could figure out how you always know I'm there, I wouldn't believe in *you* either."

"Well, you'll just have to wait until that happens, won't you?" I teased. And Kapp let me tease. If I ever accused him of letting me rile him so I could let off steam, I'd really rile him. So I just smiled at him like a maniac.

"Someday, Lazar . . ." he threatened. It would have been more impressive if his mouth hadn't been full of ham and rye as he shook his fist.

He swallowed, took a sip of beer, and went back to the information parade.

"Okay, you'll like this one," he told me. "It's legal. Fran Marquez can't get a patent on her so-called 'energy wand.' There are a few zillion other people who have inventions that are too close conceptually. She's going absolutely nuts. Fred Westbrook, her attorney told me—"

"Isn't that supposed to be confidential if he's her attorney?" I asked. It was a question I might have asked seriously at one time. But over the years, I'd realized that Kapp worked in a world I'd never been privy to, even when I was an attorney.

"Not since Fran became a royal pain in the butt," Kapp answered, guffawing.

"Oh, of course, the 'royal pain in the butt' exception," I exclaimed, slapping my forehead. "How could I have forgotten?"

This was actually getting fun.

Kapp frowned and swallowed the last bite of his sandwich.

The hair went up on my arms. I was afraid of what he was going to tell me next.

"So this Craig Zweig," he growled. "Man went crazy after his daughter died."

"Craig's daughter?" I whispered.

Kapp nodded. "Drug overdose. It was messy."

"Criminy," I whispered. "No wonder he looks for entities on the other side. Do you think he did it, Kapp?"

"I don't know," Kapp admitted. He shook his head.

"Should I tell the police that he attacked me?"

"Oh, they know already," Kapp answered.

"They what?!" I yelped.

"Holy Mother, Lazar!" Kapp defended himself. "I heard it down at the police station right before I came to get you, just that Zweig had attacked someone in the class. I didn't know it was you."

"But who told them?"

"They got a phone call." Kapp shrugged. "If I hadn't been there when it came in, I wouldn't have heard the buzz. But someone called it in."

Who? Someone more responsible than I was? Someone wanting Craig to take the blame for Aurora Hart's murder? Someone—

"Now for the interesting stuff," Kapp announced.

My obsessing screeched to a halt.

"You mean you haven't told me everything yet?" I asked incredulously. This man had more connections than the Internet.

Kapp leaned forward and whispered. "Dr. Hart had a son at an early age. She gave up custody of that son to her husband when the boy was five. She left and never looked back. Meanwhile, her husband died. Last year, Hart began a search for her son. And she bequeathed most of her estate to the missing boy. She even bankrolled a trust to fund a continued search for him in case of her death. And Dr. Aurora Hart wasn't *her* given name either. She was born Ann Smith and married a man named Brown. Her attorney thought the son might have been adopted by someone. They had investigators looking for him when she died."

"Five years old," I muttered. "Dr. Hart was in her fifties, so the kid would be—"

"Thirty-six years old," Kapp finished for me.

I thought of the men in the group. Taj? Thirty-six? A possibility. But he'd said his mother was Pakistani. And Quinn? I thought he was in his late twenties, but what if I was wrong?

"The other heirs are Quinn Vogel and Sara Oshima," Kapp added. "A little here, a little there." Would she leave a little money to Quinn if she already knew he was her main heir? But what if she didn't know? I shook my head. Quinn was sleeping with her, wasn't he?

Another man flashed into my mind. Raleigh? I thought he was in his forties, but—

"Has anyone asked the race of the boy's father?" I asked.

"Good question, Lazar," Kapp conceded. "Everyone said they thought he was white, but he was dark-skinned. He was a mystery man."

"Wow," I murmured. "You are good."

Kapp preened for a minute and began talking again.

"You think you're impressed now, Lazar?" he asked rhetorically. "There are two legal suits pending against Dr. Hart for medical malpractice, fraud, and everything else under the sun. It seems that not all her clients did well with her therapy."

I jerked my mind away from the question of Aurora Hart's son.

"Dr. Hart has been sued twice because her clients committed suicide after her intensive workshops," Kapp announced and paused dramatically.

I swallowed involuntarily before asking, "What happened?"

"Huh!" Kapp spouted. "The woman was a menace. Hart

used her psychic skills to figure out some poor sucker was gay and announced it at a *public* seminar. She thought her insight would help him. He shot himself that night. Then she mucked out some poor woman's subconscious, 'helping' her remember supposed foul events from her childhood. That woman lasted a week before taking all of her medications and dying. How's that for a healer?" Kapp sounded angry. My friend was an intensely ethical man in his own weird way. Sometimes I forgot that. "And Hart didn't even drive her own car. Too many busts for driving under the influence. Sara chauffeured her, but people couldn't see through the tinted windows."

My eyes drifted across the street where Dr. Hart's car was still parked. I thought I saw Kim Welch there. I blinked my eyes. And I saw the two policemen. They stood on each side of Kim, holding her arms. They weren't sharing an experience. It looked like they might be arresting her.

"Kapp, look!" I shouted. "They have Kim."

It was lucky we'd already paid for our sandwiches because Kapp and I ran through the deli's doors without another word.

When we got across the street, Kim was crying.

"What seems to be the problem here, officers?" Kapp demanded.

The two men looked at Kapp angrily, then one of them seemed to recognize him and shrink. Officer Jones. Again.

"This woman was near the crime scene," Jones answered.

"I was just walking," Kim sobbed. "I needed to walk."

"You're detaining this woman because she took a walk?" Kapp asked, his voice rising as if he couldn't believe it.

"She's a suspect," Jones replied defensively.

"Have you ever heard the term 'unlawful arrest'?" Kapp prodded.

"We're not arresting her," the other officer whined. Both men let go of Kim's arms simultaneously. "We were . . ."

". . . escorting her," Officer Jones finished for his buddy. "Just escorting her, that's all."

"Humph!" Kapp snorted. "We'll let Ms. Welch be the judge of that."

"I'm sorry," Kim cried, and I reached out for her. Her tiny body felt strange in my arms. She was so small.

"Oh, Cally!" she whimpered. I held her more tightly.

Kapp was the one who noticed the hour. It was almost one o'clock, time for us to go back to our afternoon session.

"I'll take care of these officers," Kapp told us, the word "officers" filled with eighty years worth of contempt. He made shooing motions with his hands. "You two are free to go."

We went. I looked over my shoulder as I walked back to the lodge with my arm around Kim. Kapp was shaking his finger at the officers, and they were cringing like bad dogs.

When we entered the meeting room, Kim was still teary, her shoulders trembling with emotion.

Dotty ran up and took charge of holding her.

"That's all right, sweetie," she cooed. "You're all right."

Taj walked over with a look of concern on his face.

"What happened?" he asked. He laid his hand on Kim's shoulder.

Dotty turned around and slapped Taj across the face.

FOURTEEN

Taj's head snapped back from the force of Dotty's slap. It hadn't been a light, ladylike slap. It had been more of an open-handed two-by-four to the face.

There was a short silence in the room.

Taj screamed. "What's wrong with you?!" He jumped back holding his cheek. His voice wasn't deep anymore. Like a hurt child, he said, "I didn't do anything."

"I'm so sorry," Kim murmured, as if Taj had screamed at her. But Dotty took over again.

"Can't you see this woman's been manhandled?" Dotty demanded of Taj. Her face was as red as her hair. Then she looked into Taj's eyes.

"No, I guess you don't see it," she finally conceded softly. "Sorry."

And with that, she turned back to Kim; Kim who seemed to Dotty to need her ministrations more than Taj did.

"Taj, are you all right?" I asked, wondering how Dotty had known about the manhandling. Or maybe she just believed that a crying woman was always the result of manhandling. My mouth felt dry. I hadn't seen very many people strike out like that in my life. I was afraid of Dotty.

Taj rolled his head around, massaging his neck. "I guess

so," he muttered. He tentatively touched his face with his finger. His cheek was blotched with red. "Jeez, Cally, what did I do?"

"I'm . . . I'm not sure," I admitted. "But you didn't deserve to be slapped."

"Sometimes, I think I have a 'kick me' sign on my back," he sniffed. "People get mad at me for no reason. Like in this restaurant one day, I was just laughing and—"

"Taj?" Kim broke in, her voice quiet. "It wasn't fair that you took the brunt of Dotty's concern for me. If I can do anything for you, just ask, okay?"

Taj nodded cautiously, but he didn't look like he was going to be taking Kim up on her offer any time soon. I could see the wet rings on the armpits of his black T-shirt. If I was afraid of Dotty, he had to be more afraid.

"I'm really sorry, too," Dotty put in, looking down at her feet. From where I stood I could smell the mixed scents of something that might have been spearmint and nervous perspiration coming from the aromatherapist. Anger, guilt? "I got too involved here. See, I really care about people. I just thought Kim needed protection."

"Sure," Taj muttered. What else could he say?

Dotty abruptly stuck out her hand.

Taj flinched, jumping back again. My own hand tightened on my cane.

"Shake?" Dotty offered.

"Oh," Taj answered. He stepped forward to shake the older woman's hand carefully. Very carefully.

I'd find a time to tell him how good he was to forgive Dotty, I told myself. Poor Taj. Maybe he did have an energetic "kick me" sign on him. I'd thought he was a trickster when I'd first met him. Something about him was easy to dislike. Easy to distrust—

"Listen, people," Quinn broke in. "We need some control here. You're all under a strain. I realize that. But you are healers. You work to help people, not to hurt them." His large, expressive eyes sought out both Dotty's and Craig's. I followed his gaze and saw Craig looking at his own feet as he stood by the side wall next to Raleigh.

"You tell 'em, Quinn," Sara put in. And she giggled.

The giggle seemed to jar the whole room. I could almost see its jagged edges. What was wrong with her?

I wondered why Quinn put up with Sara. For the dead doctor's sake? And I wondered what authority Quinn actually had to run this intensive. But before I could wonder anymore, Quinn was speaking again.

"I suggest we all take our seats and discuss this morning's sessions," Quinn ordered, his voice strained. I could even see the effort he was putting into his words, not just in his face, but in the stiffness of his whole body. Still, he was taking charge.

And so we all sat, as if no one had been slapped or squeezed or angered. Once we were seated, Quinn continued.

"What did you learn in this morning's sessions?" he asked quietly. "What did you learn about your own work, about yourself, about your partners' work?"

"Listen, buddy boy," Judd Nyman started off. His strong features were serious, his brows lowered. "I think you're asking the wrong questions. What we should be asking is who murdered Dr. Hart."

Quinn's long face seemed to get longer.

"The police are asking those questions," he said finally, his voice trembling. "If anyone has any information, they should take it to the police. We aren't here to solve murders."

Sara giggled again. I imagined shaking Sara by her shoulders before I could censor it. I slumped in my chair. I didn't want to be angry. There was enough anger in the air. I felt anger, guilt, and fear emanating all around me.

"Okay, I've got a 'sensitive' question for you," Judd barreled along. And I saw fear flash in him. Fear? Judd Nyman? "Is it true? Were you sleeping with the doc?"

If Quinn's face pinched any tighter, it was going to look like a baguette. He took a breath and opened his mouth. But Judd wasn't finished with him.

"Because lovers argue," Judd went on. "That's a known fact. Hey, I'm not asking anything out of line here. We gotta know the facts to solve this thing."

"Mr. Nyman," Quinn began, his voice barely audible.

"Judd," corrected Mr. Nyman nonchalantly. "Just call me Judd."

"Judd, this isn't the time or the place—"

"Hey, that's where you're wrong!" Judd argued. He hit the arm of his chair with his fist. "This is exactly the time and the place. What if we can figure this out ourselves? I'll bet if everyone laid what they knew on the table, we'd be able to put it together. Let's face it. Everyone had a motive."

If Judd had wanted a reaction, he got one. I could swear that everyone in the room stopped breathing for a second. Even I did. I knew a lot. And I wasn't about to share it publicly.

"Like you, buddy boy," Judd accused, pointing at Quinn. "Lovers fall out. Especially when they're in business together—"

"Judd," Ed Lau interjected mildly. His serenity was in place today, his round face relaxed. "I believe Quinn is right. This is neither the time nor the place. Quinn is exercising his responsibility as he should." He turned to Quinn. "And he is doing this in his own time of distress. He is to be commended—"

"Listen, Ed," Judd cut back in. "Maybe you just don't want anyone investigating. You didn't like the doctor. She made fun of your precious Hawaii. And I've seen you mad." Judd held the arms of his chair and leaned toward Ed. "Hey, we've all seen you mad. Did you get mad at Dr. Hart and kill her. Huh?"

Ed shook his head sadly. "I'm not going to engage with you, Mr. Nyman."

"Of course Ed didn't kill her," Dotty blurted out. She turned and glared at Judd. She was a formidable woman, even without slapping anyone. Dotty had seemed grandmotherly before. Abruptly, her plump body looked tough, strong. "You oughtta be ashamed of yourself, trying to upset people. Didn't they teach you any sensitivity along with your reflexology and massage? Don't you even care who you're hurting with your words?"

"That's a laugh!" Judd responded. He grinned. "You just punched a guy out for nothing, and you're lecturing *me* about sensitivity? Hah!"

Dotty rose from her seat, skin inflamed. Judd's grin vanished. His own skin paled. Yes, Dotty was formidable, standing with her legs spread apart in a boxer's crouch, her eyes narrowing in on her prey.

Would Dotty slap him like she'd slapped Taj? Somehow, I didn't feel responsible for stopping her. I almost felt like encouraging her. I put aside the thought.

"Dotty?" Kim whispered from Dotty's side. She reached out a small hand and patted Dotty's strong arm. "He's just baiting you. Please, don't let him do this to you."

"Right," Dotty muttered, reaching in her pocket for a tissue and blowing her nose loudly. "Right."

Once Dotty was seated again, Judd muttered, "Maybe someone needs a class in anger management."

Dotty jumped up again, scattering tissue shreds on the carpet and cushy chair.

"You testosterone-poisoned bag of scum!" she shouted, pointing at Judd. "Where do you get off talking about me like that? Huh? I may be overly emotional, but that's a lot better than having no feelings at all. And you seem to be running a little low on human feelings, mister. Don't you even care who you hurt?"

And Judd, for once, was quiet. But his son wasn't.

Orson stood up from his own seat awkwardly, wrapping one of his long legs around the other. "Dad's just trying to find out who killed Dr. Hart, that's all. That'd be cool, wouldn't it? Why are you so upset? You wouldn't believe what your metabolic cascades look like."

"Thanks, kid," Judd muttered. He reached for his son and patted Orson's standing leg. Orson wobbled and came back into balance.

"I don't know why you guys are even bothering," Sara put in. Her voice was too high. "This is way, way boring. It's *so* obvious who killed her." She gestured with her head toward Craig. "The crazy guy. What else does he have to do before you notice that he's gonzo? He attacked Cally in front of everyone."

"Sara!" Quinn reprimanded.

"What, I can't talk?" she shot back.

"Take my advice, kiddo," Fran spoke up. "You haven't lived long enough to make a judgment like that. Lots of folks are crazy, but it doesn't mean they're killers. Do you really think that Craig has the focus to have rigged the doctor's aura maker?"

"Fine," Sara sniffed. She took a lock of her straight, black hair and curled it around her finger. "Don't listen to what I say. I don't care."

Craig looked up with a confused expression. Was he confused by Fran's defense or her implied agreement that he was crazy? Or was he feigning confusion to reinforce her argument? I remembered what Kapp had told me about Craig's doing electrical wiring for a living. Maybe it wouldn't have required that much focus to kill Dr. Hart.

"I don't want any part of a lynch mob." Raleigh spoke up. "Fran's right. Craig's far too confused to have planned anything so complicated—"

"But is he just confused now that it's over?" Judd questioned aloud. "Maybe his mind was working better before. You guys remember."

Raleigh crossed his arms over his chest. "Oh come on,

man," he chided. "Why would Craig want to kill the doctor? He was one of the few people here who actually liked her, even maybe loved her—"

"As if love *stops* people from killing each other," Sara put in. "Don't you guys read the papers? All those murderers going 'boo-hoo, but I loved her.' Could even be Quinn here." She smiled malignantly at her current boss.

"Sara," I said before I could stop myself. "Why are you so angry at Quinn?"

"Quinn hates me!" Sara put her face in her hands. "All I wanna do is have a little fun, but Quinn is so anal. The doctor gave me a little space, but now that she's gone, what am I going to do? Huh? Do you think Quinn cares?"

"Sara," Quinn answered cautiously. "I do care about you. I know you're hurting. But you're hurting me, too. Can't you understand that?"

"Her brain is too fried to understand," Raleigh murmured.

"What?" Sara objected, her head popping out of her hands.

"Come on, Sara," Raleigh said, more loudly than before. "We can all see you're taking drugs. You're not going to think clearly until you stop."

"I hate you!" Sara screamed, rising from her seat and leaving the room.

"Whoa," Judd put in. "Now there's a woman who is definitely out of control. She just made the top five on my list of contenders for murderer."

"Maybe it was just an accident, not murder," Taj proposed uncertainly. "Maybe we're all chasing a murderer who doesn't exist."

"You'd like that, wouldn't you?" Judd accused. "You had something against the doctor. I don't know what, but something." Judd pointed at his nose. "I'm a hound dog now, on the chase. No one's gonna manipulate me."

I was almost glad Judd had taken on the investigator's

mantel. It let me off the hook. And for all his insensitivity, he was asking questions, questions I didn't have the nerve to ask.

"Listen," Raleigh tried, his calm voice a little worn at the edges. He didn't look handsome at that instant, just tired. "Most of us had problems with Dr. Hart. I'll admit mine. She didn't respect my work. She laughed at it. But there are plenty of people who don't respect my work. I didn't kill her for it."

And then, everyone was with Raleigh, voicing their own objections to the doctor.

"She thought aromatherapy was silly," Dotty put in. "I don't know why she even invited me."

"She made fun of my energy wand," Fran admitted sullenly. "But she kept trying to get me to tell her all the working details."

"She didn't understand chi gung," Ed stated without emotion, at least obvious emotion. "I wondered why she asked me here when she didn't understand the importance of my work."

"I'll go for that," Judd added unexpectedly. He seemed to be arguing against himself. "She thought my work was superficial. And she wouldn't let Orson into the class. He's smarter than a lot of adults, and he's studied metabolic cascades. She just flipped him off, called his study, Biochem 101,"

"But I could see cool stuff right away when I came here," Orson piped up. "See, everyone has a normal system of metabolic cascades. But most of you are all messed up."

Orson swiveled his head to look at Quinn. "Your cascades are barely functioning," he pointed out.

"Shock," Kim explained in a whisper. "Poor Quinn has had an awful shock." A little projection from the psychiatrist?

"And yours are even worse, lady," Orson pronounced,

looking at Kim. "It's really interesting. Your neurotransmitters are like completely shut down. It's like you're not really here. How can you even stand up?"

"She's not standing up," Ed told the boy. Was that a joke?

"Yeah, but—" Orson tried.

"Dr. Hart told me that it was silly to worry about my cat dying," Dotty broke in. She was stranded on the why-we-didn't-like-the-doctor track. "How could she say that?"

We all turned to Quinn. It *was* odd about Dr. Hart. She'd asked plenty of questions about my practice, too. But she'd never offered me any positive feedback. She'd spent more time making fun of me. And all she'd taught us was how to give a great presentation. *No*, I thought. She'd demonstrated an incredible skill at diagnosis. She'd just never gotten to the point of healing the conditions she diagnosed. And she hadn't told us the secret of her diagnostic ability. I knew no more of what Dr. Hart's method had involved at that moment than when I'd arrived, too many days ago.

"Dr. Hart liked to tease," Quinn admitted, his voice tentative.

We all turned to him. We were all curious about the doctor. She was an enigma, even beyond the manner of her death.

Quinn rolled his shoulders, breathed in, and went on.

"Dr. Hart felt that it was good for people to be teased. It stirred up their deepest issues. She thought it was good for them in the long run."

"How about the ones who couldn't deal with their issues?" Kim asked, her quiet voice sharp.

Quinn took another breath. "I know, I know. It was hard on some people. But others, well, they learned from her. They learned what pushed their buttons. They learned where they were stuck."

Raleigh and Ed just shook their heads.

"And she was intuitive," Quinn insisted. "Really intuitive. She could tell people things that they'd forgotten about themselves. She could really see into people."

I nodded, remembering her comments on my bum leg.

"But what then?" Kim objected. "A person remembers their pain, realizes their falsehoods to themselves, gets out from under denial. What then? Who cares for them in their agony?"

"You guys do," Quinn answered. "Dr. Hart was a true sensitive, but she . . . well, she didn't really know where to go from there. Maybe it was her medical training. She worried about it all the time. She said doctors were trained to diagnose and send people to surgeons. She was afraid she couldn't shake that approach. That's one reason she did these intensives. She wanted to teach, but she wanted to learn, too."

"Wait a minute," Dotty ordered, holding out her hand, palm forward. "Are you saying she invited us here to find out what *we* knew?"

"No, no." Quinn shook his head vigorously. "She had a lot to teach, too. But she cared about all of your work. She thought it was important—"

"Like wanting to steal my energy wand," Fran cut in, her tone dry. She didn't have to say, "I told you so." It was in her voice.

"She kept asking me how I did the past-life stuff," Taj added his two-cents worth, "like she could extract it from me or something."

"For all her put-downs, she was real interested in resonance work," Raleigh offered thoughtfully.

"She was running a number on us?" Judd squawked.

Quinn was shaking his head so hard, it looked like it might fall off. "You don't understand. She wanted to heal. She believed in studying every modality to see if it could be helpful in her work—"

"In *her* work," Ed Lau clarified.

"And we had to pay for this?" a chorus of voices demanded as one.

Quinn sank to the floor in one fluid motion and curled up like a wounded caterpillar.

FIFTEEN

Before anyone even had a chance to rise from their chairs, Sara Oshima came rushing back into the meeting room. I had a feeling she'd never been very far away. It couldn't have been more than seconds since Quinn had gone down. She ran up to the front of the room where he lay, curled on the floor.

"Quinn?" she asked softly, a frown squeezing her face for an instant. Was that concern?

A soft sob issued from Quinn's mouth.

Sara smiled. "Quinn, sweetie," she trilled. "Are you waiting for Aurora to come back? Why don't you just have Mr. Zweig conjure her up?"

A collective gasp filled the room.

"Hey—" Judd began. But Sara was on a roll.

"Can't handle the kiddies without Aurora?" she taunted. "What *can* you do without her?"

Quinn's body seemed to convulse.

"Huh, Quinn, sweetie pie?" she kept at him. "Little mama's boy with nasty old Aurora."

"Sara," he whimpered.

Dotty rose and started forward, but Fran held her back. "Wait," she whispered. "Maybe this will bring him out of it."

"Is little Quinnie-poo all afraid without the big bad doctor to back him up?"

"Sara!" Quinn yelped. His body uncurled.

"The big, bad, mean, *fraudulent* Dr. Hart?" she chirped.

Quinn sat up, his tear-streaked face tight with anger.

"Why do you have to talk about her that way?" he demanded. "She was wonderful. She was good to you. She could see things no one else could see—"

"Got you up off of the floor, didn't I?" Sara said cheerfully. "And anyway, it's all true."

"Dr. Hart wasn't fraudulent," Quinn insisted.

"Big deal," Sara commented. "You say honest, I say a scammer. Who cares?"

"I care," he announced. "I care. Dr. Aurora Hart deserves respect."

"And if she was here, she'd give you tough love," Sara fired back. "So deal with it."

She turned to the rest of us.

"That was Dr. Hart, right?" she asked, her words tumbling out faster and faster. "Tough love. She didn't even want me to have a friggin' boyfriend. She thought she could control my life. Well, she couldn't. Ira and I went out the night of her big-deal speech."

"The night she died," Raleigh put in.

"Yeah," Sara replied, her eyes pinched with confusion. "That was so weird. It was like she wanted to punish me or something."

"No, no," Quinn admonished. "Don't think like that, Sara. It'll just drive you crazy . . ." He faltered.

There was a silence around the room. Was Sara already crazy? Were we all? I closed my eyes and found my center. Dr. Hart's death was just making everyone act out. That was all. No one was crazy. Well, except for Craig maybe. And whoever had killed the doctor.

Quinn stood up and stepped in front of Sara. "I'm very sorry for my loss of control," he apologized. "I truly understand how many feelings must be coming up now for all of us. But I still believe we can learn from one another. I would ask that we work together now and try to regain some of what we've lost. Aurora Hart had ideals, I can assure you. I can only hope that I can lead you to achieve some of those ideals without her guiding hand."

"Hey, what healing modality are you trained in, Quinn?" Judd demanded.

Quinn flushed. "I'm certified in Dr. Hart's chakra work, though I can never hope to replace her. She was the actual intuitive. I'm really a facilitator, nothing more."

"You're a very good facilitator, Quinn," I piped up. I couldn't help it. Quinn was trying so hard to finish the doctor's work. What would he do now that she was gone?

"And you, Sara," Ed put in. "What are you trained in?"

"Nothing." She giggled. "I'm a nursing school dropout. I'm just a glorified gofer. Dr. Hart tried to teach me some of the stuff she did, but she kept saying my chakras were all messed up by my relationship with Ira. Still, I'm good at errands, at setting things up. It's a gig."

"And she was like a mother to you?" I probed softly.

"Maybe," she agreed, her eyes losing focus. "Maybe not." Her eyes hardened. "Whatever. But she wasn't my real mother."

Quinn looked at her, opened his mouth, and shut it again. What had he wanted to say?

I never got to ask.

"So, are all you folks ready to go on the garden tour?" a voice boomed from the doorway.

We all looked at the man who stood there. My brain tried to remember who he was. Balding guy, great moustache, big mouth. Monty, Monty English! I was losing it. In all of the angst, I'd not only forgotten all about the garden tour, I'd lost my ability to recognize any face that wasn't in the intensive group.

"I didn't see you out at the van, so I tracked you down," Monty explained cheerfully. "You can call me Sherlock."

"Right, the garden tour," Quinn said, his voice shaky but clear. He was visibly pulling himself up by his energy bootstraps. "I'm sure we're all looking forward to it."

"Whoa, we've got some great gardens here in Swanton!" Monty assured us. He bowed and swept his hand toward the door. "So, folks, let's go look at them," he ordered.

We followed Monty out the door, down the hall, and out the main doors to his stretch van. I had a feeling most of us were going for Quinn's sake. Or maybe people just felt safer in groups. Or maybe we were all in shock. Even Sara climbed into the van, making her way to the back. I sat up front. Quinn took the seat next to me.

Once we were all on board, the van skidded out of the parking lot, and we were moving. I turned to Quinn, trying to think of something to say. His long face was ravaged, his large brown eyes reddened. I swiveled my head forward again.

"The first one we're going to visit is the bulb garden at the Macrae's," Monty announced. "The Macraes own a little winery, but their pride and joy is their garden. And it being spring, what can I tell you? Whooee, wait until you see!"

"Cally?" Quinn whispered from beside me.

I turned cautiously toward him. "Yes?" I said and tuned Monty out.

"Can I talk to you?" he asked.

I nodded, hoping he wasn't going to confess to murder.

"Aurora's gone," he began. His eyes filled with tears. He took a big breath and tightened his fists in an effort to control himself. "Aurora's gone, but I'm still here. I'd like to carry on her work. But I'm . . . I'm not a healer. I'm . . ."

"You're a facilitator," I helped him.

"Yeah. And I think I'm a good one. I'm sensitive to the healing community. I'm sensitive to the needs of clients and other healers. Aurora wasn't always so good with those parts. It wasn't that she was all those things that Sara said. She was just insecure."

He looked into my face as if to see if I believed him. I nodded.

"Aurora knew she was an intuitive from a young age, but she didn't always want to be. In fact, she hated it. It made her different. So she would act brusque. But she had so much love in her." I heard the grief in Quinn's voice. "She was so complex. Name a personality trait she had, and I can tell you she had the opposite, too. She was angry, she was loving. She was confident, she was insecure. She was sad, she had a greater capacity for joy than anyone I've ever known. She could peek into people's souls and find the most intimate things, and yet she was unable to talk to anyone at length without stepping on their toes. She was arrogant, she was ashamed. Do you understand?"

I nodded because I did understand. It made a lot of sense of who Aurora had been, an insensitive sensitive. Insensitive because sensitivity was too painful.

"You *do* understand, don't you?" Quinn paused. "I loved Aurora, and now she's gone. I never thought of life without her. I've been with her since I went to one of her lectures when I was getting my Ph.D. in philosophy. I never finished my Ph.D. But I became very good at managing Dr. Hart's events. And now?" He shook his head.

"So what will you do?" I asked.

"Cally, I have an idea. Just an idea. I want to lay it out for you completely when I'm more coherent, but basically, I'd like to work with you. You're gifted. I can see that. Aurora saw that—"

"Quinn," I cut him off. "I'm not Dr. Aurora Hart. I don't have her charisma. All I want to do is heal people."

"I know, I know," he told me. But he didn't. "Just think

of the possibilities if you could teach what you do to others. Can you imagine? You could help others to do what you do. You could start a movement."

My skin went cold. I wanted to help Quinn. But I didn't want to be Aurora Hart. I wanted to tell him absolutely no, but the words weren't coming out of my mouth. Because Quinn needed a dream to hold on to.

"You have it, like Aurora had it," he went on, his eyes glistening with something other than tears. "The real thing. And Aurora was right about learning from other healers. Exchanging approaches, modalities. The healing community needs a real community—"

"We're here, folks!" Monty yelled over his shoulder.

Quinn jumped in his seat. And I practically leaped out of mine.

My brain was churning when I stepped from the van. Quinn was a stray puppy. But I couldn't take him in, could I?

My nose twitched. What was that sweet smell? My eyes were the next to come alive. I saw that we were at the beginning of a stone pathway, bordered by crocuses and white narcissi. And beyond these flowers, rows and rows of yellow daffodils spreading out to the sides. It was literally stunning. How many daffodils? Hundreds? A thousand? The air was cool and buzzing with insects.

"This is just the start, folks," Monty told us. "Ain't it something?"

"Wow," and "Oh, my," and "Totally cool," joined the murmurs and coos of the group.

A middle-aged couple came down the stone pathway to greet us, both stout and muscular. Had they planted all those bulbs themselves?"

"Greg Macrae," the man greeted us with an all-embracing wave. "And my wife, Yolanda."

Yolanda just smiled. She didn't seem to be the talker in the family.

"We planted all these with a special tiller," Greg told us. "Made just for bulbs. Isn't that right, Yolanda?"

Yolanda smiled and nodded, turning her eyes to the display of flowers dreamily.

"We had to plan it all just right," Greg went on. "The ones that want to bloom too early, we put in extra deep to slow 'em down. The late bloomers not so deep. There're all kinds of tricks to make them come up at once."

He turned and began to walk up the path. I could see a mass of blue beyond the yellow.

"Cally!" a voice hissed in my ear. I turned and saw Sara Oshima's glassy eyes looking into mine. I would have to ask Raleigh exactly what drugs she was on. She wasn't just high, she was gone. "I gotta talk to you, okay?"

"This isn't the best time," I told her. I just wanted to forget the group and enjoy the flowers. "See the daffodils?" I tried.

Sara shrugged her shoulders. Helen Keller would have seen the flowers more clearly, at least in her mind's eye.

"Can I talk to you later?" Sara asked.

"Sure," I answered, hoping I wouldn't regret it.

The blue was getting closer, and it was more than blue.

"Early-blooming irises," Greg told us. "In a couple of months, it'll be late-blooming irises, cyclamen, and lilies.

We walked on the stone path into the field of blue irises, bordered by a brightly colored mixture of anemones. The irises varied, from velvety blue to lilac and every shade in between, with some white mixed in. I had to remind myself to breathe. I just stood for a moment and let my eyes absorb the beauty. Heaven.

"Better than drugs," I told Sara who'd caught up with me again.

"Huh?" she asked.

"Never mind," I murmured and let my eyes wander through the colors—absorbing, feeling.

The group was moving again. I tore my eyes away from

the clouds of irises and moved with them. I heard "oohs" and "ahs" in front of me. Then I saw the tulips. There literally must have been a thousand of them. Maybe more. I couldn't help but think of Aurora when I saw the color groupings, straight from the chakras. There were no pastels here, but masses of red, giving way to orange, yellow, even green-edged blooms and turquoise, then blue, violet, and magenta. And beyond those, stands of multicolored hyacinths.

Yes, definitely better than drugs. I felt myself moving with the flowers as a breeze rippled through them. It was an ocean of flowers and we were in the middle, floating. My body swayed in harmony.

"Hey, so how do you water them all?" Judd asked.

Greg answered, but I let their conversation slip away from my mind. This was too good.

We must have spent at least an hour there. I sat down on the path and just let myself internalize the colors. The group was strangely silent, blessedly silent, as we all communed with flowers, sky, and insects. And finally, our hour was up.

"Time to go, folks," Monty told us, and I wanted to protest.

But I followed the group out, thanking Greg and Yolanda on the way.

"We like to show off," Greg said.

"I like to live in flowers," Yolanda amended.

"You are so lucky," I told her.

"I know," she agreed and clasped my hand with her rough one.

I was still entranced when I got back on the van. What could be more healing than flowers? I sneezed. And what could be more allergenic? But I didn't care. I would see those flowers in my mind for weeks, months, maybe years.

I sat near the front again in the van. I guiltily scanned the seats for Quinn and spotted him near the back with

Raleigh. I wondered if he was making Raleigh the same pitch he'd made me.

I closed my eyes for a moment, seeing the masses of flowers. I opened them again. Taj was sitting next to me. Taj. My mind searched. There was something I wanted to say to Taj. I remembered what it was.

"That was really generous of you to forgive Dotty," I told him.

"Who says I forgave her?" he whispered. He fingered his face. I couldn't see any trace of the slap lingering. "I just don't want her to slap me again." He grinned.

"Scared of a girl?" I teased.

"Very," he conceded readily. "And I wouldn't call her a girl unless you want to get slapped yourself."

"Hee!" I snorted. "Thanks for straightening me out."

"God, those flowers were something," he breathed. "I was wondering if people could be healed just by their presence."

"Yeah," I agreed. I looked at Taj and smiled. Suddenly, I felt a bond with this man. And it felt good. Maybe it was the flowers.

"You know, Cally, I really do understand why Dotty slapped me. While I was looking at the flowers, I thought about it. And I chilled out. See, Dotty was protecting Kim. That's cool. And I came bumbling up, being a guy. I'll bet a guy hassled Kim. So Dotty thinks Kim's bound to get upset if I touch her. It makes sense. Dotty did what seemed right at the time."

"You're a good man, Taj," I told him.

Taj blushed. "On the plus side, Dotty didn't hit me all that hard. It surprised me more than anything."

Before I could reply, Monty yelled over his shoulder. "Okay, folks, listen up!" He had an empty pickle jar in his hand. "The Macraes aren't raising flowers for the money, but they sure make a lot of people happy. If you want to contribute to the bulb fund, put something in the jar."

Monty handed the jar over his shoulder to me. I found a ten dollar bill and put it in before passing it to Taj. I averted my eyes as Taj went through his pockets. It wasn't any of my business what he put in the jar. When he'd passed the jar on, he turned back to me.

"I've been thinking about something else, too," Taj whispered, looking behind us. "You know when Dr. Hart put the moves on me?"

I nodded.

"I'm not so sure she was serious. I think maybe she was just trying to tweak Quinn."

"Yeah," I said slowly, rolling the thought around in my mind. "It would fit."

"Do you think someone really killed her?" Taj asked, his voiced tight with anxiety. Although Taj was a good man, panic always seemed to override any other emotion in him.

"I *think* so," I answered. What else could I say?

Taj considered my opinion for a while.

"I just worry that Quinn—" he began.

Monty pulled his van up in front of an old house and stopped. Or maybe it would be better described as an old mansion, three stories of red brick with a two-story covered stoop flanked by white columns and topped by a balcony.

"This is the Carlton's place," he told us. "They're selling it soon, but Mrs. Carlton put in her spring garden as usual. So enjoy, folks!"

As magnificent as the place was, I didn't see much of a garden in front. There was a clipped lawn bordered by well-trimmed hedges. Shasta daisies fronted the house, with smaller annuals in between.

Monty led us through the back gate. Whoa! There were flowers everywhere back here, a riot of colors, shapes, and sizes, but a controlled riot. The borders were dominated by sweet alyssum and violas. And there were pansies and primroses, poppies, and clumps of nasturtium. And finally lupine, snapdragons, and foxglove. How could Mrs. Carlton bear to part with her garden? And it smelled as good as it looked. Maybe the alyssum? A bumblebee landed on a foxglove as gently as a lover.

"You and I should go into business together," Sara whispered in my ear. At least this time I knew it was Sara. I was beginning to recognize her scent, a floral cologne that was sweet with hospital antiseptic undertones, not to mention her own odor. It couldn't compete with the flowers.

"I helped the doctor a lot," she added when I didn't respond.

"Sara," I finally enunciated. "You're in trouble emotionally. I can see that. You have a drug problem. I can see that, too. You need help. I would give you that help for free. But I don't need a business partner."

"You mean *healing*?" She sneered. "Do you think *healing* would help? How do you think I got this way?"

She turned on her heel and walked off. I tried to focus on the garden. It was beautiful here. And it was quiet. The only sounds were muted voices and the hum of nature. The sun was warm on my face with a light breeze cooling its rays perfectly. But my mind was overloaded. The flowers were not healing Sara. And I wondered if Dr. Hart had somehow harmed her. Though I doubted it. I'd known many Saras in my life, people who always blamed others for their problems. They were the worst clients. Because a healer can't help a client change the multitudes of abusers in their lives. They can only help the client change themselves. And these are the very clients who don't want to change themselves.

Still, by the time Monty told us we had to leave, the garden had worked its magic on me. I was calm again, serene even.

We all climbed back in the van once more, and I sat down in my usual spot. Dotty took the seat next to me this time.

"I'm losing it, Cally," she began. And she kept on talking until we reached the Swanton Hills Lodge. At least she wasn't Sara. Dotty was earnest in her desire to return to normalcy. She swore she'd never hit anyone before in her life. She was scared. She was angry. But she wasn't a murderer. She swore that, too. And I believed her. Still, I believed everyone. I patted her hand and kept my sighs to myself.

When Monty came to a stop in the lodge's parking lot, I was glad to be leaving both the van and its passengers. All I wanted was the solitude of my own room.

I walked into my private room thinking of tulips. But my private room wasn't private. I don't know why I'd imagined it otherwise. Just because I'd paid for it. Just because I held the card key in my hand.

My sister Geneva sat on my bed next to my brother York. And Kapp was plunked down in the easy chair.

I opened my mouth to object. But Geneva was already talking.

"Well, maybe so, but the Dalai Lama never went through menopause," she commented.

I closed my mouth again.

Nearly an hour later, Geneva finally suggested that we go to dinner. I couldn't tell you what she'd been talking about in that hour. I'd been trying to figure out the bit about the Dalai Lama.

Her invitation apparently didn't include Kapp. Kapp rose with the rest of us, but parted company with the Lazars at the lobby. Abruptly, it hit me. Kapp had been quiet the whole time we'd been in my room.

"What's wrong with Kapp?" I asked once we were seated in the Best Fortune Chinese Restaurant where I had last eaten with Dr. Aurora Hart and the gang.

Geneva steepled her hands and looked me in the eye.

"What do you think?" she returned my question.

"I don't know," I tried again in frustration. "I don't have a clue."

"Oh, Cally," she said sadly and shook her head.

I looked to York, but he was searching for vegetarian entrees in the menu. I opened my own menu in resignation.

"So, I've been looking into your Aurora Hart," Geneva announced once we'd ordered. "My friend Tillie took her full seminar. Five thousand dollars and zilch. The Chakra Commitment, hah! The Money in Hart's Pocket Commitment!"

I felt ridiculously compelled to defend the dead doctor. But before I could, I saw the two diners across the room. Fran and Judd? Judd laughed loudly. It was them all right.

"What?" Geneva asked.

"Two of the people from the class," I whispered.

"Ah," she replied, a Mona Lisa smile on her face. She was in spy mode. I could tell. I grinned. She and Kapp really were made for each other.

I spent the rest of the evening enjoying my moo shu prawns and telling my big sister and brother all about the garden tour. I was tired of murder. I was tired of Dr. Hart. I was tired of the intensive. And I made it out of the Best Fortune practically unscathed, marred only by a spot of plum sauce on my blouse.

I opened the door to my room at the lodge carefully. All my tense muscles loosened. I smiled. I was alone. Alone! I even checked the bathroom. Yes, finally alone.

The phone rang. I stared at it. It kept ringing.

I picked it up as if it had fangs.

"Hello?" I murmured.

"Cally, darlin'," Roy's voice came flooding over the line with all its attached memories and longings. "I'm coming back to California!"

"But—"

"No buts, darlin'. Don't you fret. I'm coming home to take care of you." He paused and whispered, "I love you."

Then he hung up.

SIXTEEN

I put on my pajamas slowly, and lay in bed, thinking of Roy. And finally, I dreamed of Roy in a bed of tulips, swaying. We swayed with the tulips in perfect synchronicity. I wanted to stay there forever.

Even as my alarm rang the next morning, I let it be part of my dream, swaying, swaying. But the alarm didn't have the right rhythm. I opened my eyes, reached for my glasses, and slapped the alarm button angrily. If the alarm had been a bug, it would have been dead.

I suppressed a sigh and looked around the room. It was still in earth tones: rust, olive green, copper. I groaned and put my hands over my eyes. A healer gone bad is a sad thing. A chirpy little voice in my head informed me that someone needed a long meditation. But I didn't have time for a long meditation. It was Tuesday. And the last time I'd looked, the Chakra Commitment Intensive was still marching on with all the joy of a masterless zombie. Could I abandon Quinn? I pursed my lips and squinted my eyes, considering. No, I couldn't.

Still, there was Roy. I wondered how long it would take

him to get to the Swanton Hills Lodge from the hills of Kentucky. My longing to see Roy was equalled only by my concern for him. The last time Roy had tried to protect me, he'd ended up in the hospital. He didn't have a cane like I did to wave at people. And for all his accusations of my naïveté, Roy didn't have the sense of danger that I did. He was a trusting man . . . except when it came to the darkness he saw . . . or to trusting himself. I sighed again. Whoa. Talk about self-pity! I did need some meditation time.

I climbed out of bed, struggled out of my pajamas, and propelled myself into the shower. A while later, I was dressed and sitting with my legs crossed on the end of my bed. I imagined the "all" of the universe, going deeper and deeper until I could sense the neutrality that I believed to be at its core. I allowed myself the perspective of neutrality, the acceptance of the human condition, the serenity, the clarity—

Three loud bangs on my door popped me right out of neutral.

I hopped off the end of my bed and grabbed my cane, demanding, "Who's there?"

"Kapp!" a voice shouted back. He pounded on the door some more. "Come on, Lazar. Let me in. I've got muffins."

I paused for a moment. "What kind of muffins?" I asked.

"Peanut butter–carob chip, pineapple-coconut-banana, blueberry-pumpkin—"

I opened the door, cane still in my hand. Kapp stood in front of me, a grin on his bulldog face, a sack of muffins in one hand, and a large brown paper cup complete with plastic lid and red straw in the other.

"And I brought you a strawberry smoothie," Kapp finished up.

"All right," I conceded ungraciously. "Come on in. I can't stop you anyway." I didn't add that I could smell the muffins, too.

"Holy Mary, Lazar," he growled. "It's your brother York who does the magnetic card trick to get in your room."

At least that was one mystery solved. York. I should have guessed.

"What's up with you and Geneva?" I asked as Kapp lowered himself into the easy chair.

"Want a muffin?" he replied, flushing.

"You don't want to talk about it?"

"She's your sister," he declared in a voice filled with righteous indignation.

"Oh, just give me the muffins and the smoothie," I said irritably. I'd never get anything out of him. Kapp was great at prying out secrets, and even better at not revealing them.

"Which flavor do you want?" he asked.

"All of them," I answered. I held out my hands. "It's a bad thing to interrupt a person during meditation."

Kapp rifled the muffin bag and reserved one, handing me the bag and the cup once he'd finished.

"Is that where you learned the cane trick, during meditation?" he tried.

"What cane trick?" I replied nonchalantly as I sat down on the end of the bed again.

"The one where you always know I'm behind you!" he boomed.

"Oh, that one." I bit into a muffin and tasted a rush of coconut and pineapple. "Naah."

"Lazar!" he hissed.

"What?" I said and kept on munching.

"I got some more ideas on the murder," Kapp announced and paused.

I was supposed to beg him to tell me his ideas. I didn't. I took a long slurp from my smoothie instead. It was sweet and cool. I was actually beginning to feel better despite meditation interruptus.

"Craig Zweig spent time in a mental institution after his daughter died," Kapp threw out.

The smoothie didn't taste so sweet anymore. Poor Craig.

"Raleigh Hutchinson did his time in a loony bin, too," Kapp added.

"Really?"

"Yeah, but in his case, it was voluntary. He was trying to get off drugs."

"And did he?" I asked.

"With a vengeance," Kapp answered, smiling, happy to have me hooked. "There's nothing like a reformed whatever-it-is. Hooboy, that man is his own antidrug foundation."

"Hmmm." I took another bite of muffin. My brain clicked. "Did Craig Zweig's daughter ever go to one of Dr. Hart's seminars?"

"No, and believe me, I checked it out." Kapp frowned. "I was sure that was the answer, but it didn't pan out." Great minds and all that. Still . . ." He paused.

"Give," I ordered.

"I got to wondering if Dr. Hart took drugs . . . or gave them," Kapp whispered as if we were in a public square. He leaned forward and squinted at me conspiratorially.

I stopped mid-munch. "Sara Oshima is taking drugs," I mumbled through my muffin. "But I thought Dr. Hart was trying to stop her."

"What if she wasn't?"

I rolled the thought around in my mind. "I don't think so," I said finally. I looked at Kapp. "Is this just an idea, or do you have some kind of tip on this?"

"Mother of God, it's just a hunch, Lazar!" Kapp snapped. "Do I have to present evidence?"

"No," I told him, tired of teasing. The muffins and smoothie were good. I probably wouldn't have had time for breakfast if it hadn't been for Kapp. "Any other hunches?"

Kapp settled back in his chair. "Well, if you follow the money, you get to the missing heir, Quinn, and Sara."

"Got any leads on the missing heir?"

"No, but one of the investigators that the trust hired to find the heir wants to talk to me. He thinks I can help." Kapp tapped his balding head. "*He* trusts my hunches."

I swallowed the last of the pineapple-coconut-banana muffin and stuck my hand back in the bag.

"You know, actually, I think Quinn loses financially with Dr. Hart's death—" I began.

"Loses? He inherits nearly half a million dollars!"

"He does?" I looked at the muffin in my hand, no longer seeing it. Quinn didn't act like a man who'd inherited a fortune. But he had lost someone he'd loved . . . I assumed. "I thought you said he got 'a little.' "

"Hooboy, Lazar! That *is* a little for Dr. Hart. Her estate's worth over twenty million, not counting her business."

"How'd she make that much money?" The muffin in my hand was the blueberry one. I should have known Kapp would have kept the carob chip for himself.

"Her seminar business. People who were serious students put out five thousand for a two-week seminar, and they returned like swallows to Capistrano year after year. She ran these things back to back when she wasn't touring. And she took up to thirty people at a time. You do the math. Thirty times five thousand every two weeks over how many years? That's a few million a year right there. And her books were best-sellers. Hell, I'm surprised she didn't end up with more money."

"What does Sara inherit?" I asked, getting interested.

"A hundred thousand," Kapp answered. "I guess Quinn got bonus pay for snuggling up to the doctor at night."

"Kapp!" I objected.

"Hell, that's what my sources are saying," he defended himself.

"That's what everyone is saying," I agreed. "But it doesn't mean it's true. And even if it is, Quinn is hurting emotionally."

"See if I buy you any more muffins, Lazar," Kapp muttered, settling into a studied sulk.

"Buy?" I shot back. "Weren't these free downstairs?"

Then we heard a new banging on the door.

"What the hell?" asked Kapp. "Are you expecting company?"

"Not rude company," I said, thinking of Roy.

"Open up in there!" a voice shouted. There was something about it. Chief Phlug?

I opened the door cautiously. It *was* Chief Phlug. His short, muscular body was vibrating with anger. His little-boy-never-grown-up features were twisted into something between a sulk and a sneer.

"Hah!" he barked, pointing at Kapp. "The both of you!"

"The both of us, what?" Kapp enquired reasonably.

"You two, both in the same room!"

"And . . ." Kapp kept on, widening his eyes.

"Never mind," the chief said. "Don't try and jerk me around. I know you're some bigshot lawyer, but I'm the law around here."

You and your wife, I thought, but I didn't say it aloud.

"Well, are you going to invite me in?" the chief asked finally.

"Sure, find yourself a seat," I told him, knowing the only seat left was on the writing table.

But Phlug marched in anyway, standing at attention.

"What do you two know about Craig Zweig?"

"Why?" I asked. My heart tightened. Despite Craig's attack, there was something about the man that needed protection. I think most of us in the group felt that.

"You didn't report his assault on you yesterday," the chief accused.

"How did you know about the alleged assault?" I coun-

tered, something of the attorney I'd once been taking over.
Maybe it was Kapp's presence infecting me.

The chief look nonplussed for a moment. He leaned forward. "I don't have to tell you that. You have to answer my questions. I'm the police."

"Is Ms. Lazar a suspect, Chief Phlug?" Kapp asked, his voice as sweet as a strawberry smoothie.

"Whaddaya mean, a suspect?" Phlug stopped and took stock. "She's a witness. She's gotta answer me."

"Ms. Lazar was gracious enough to invite you into her *private* room, Chief Phlug. Maybe you might try a little more respect. Citizens are suing police all the time these days for harassment, you know."

"I'm not harassing her," Phlug objected, his voice rising in pitch. I could even smell an unwholesome sweat of anxiety emanating from him. "I just want to ask some questions. This Craig Zweig is a certified nutcase. And he assaulted Ms. Lazar. He might have killed Dr. Hart."

"A lot of people might have killed Dr. Hart," I pointed out, sitting back down on the end of the bed.

"What's that supposed to mean?" Phlug demanded. "Do you know something you're not telling?"

"I'm sure I don't know anything you don't," I answered. "But mental illness isn't enough to convict Craig Zweig. He may have embraced me in a moment of confusion, but I don't think he has it together enough to carry out the kind of murder that killed Dr. Hart."

"What do you know about the method of Dr. Hart's murder?" the Chief challenged.

"I know she was electrocuted. I know someone probably arranged that electrocution."

"That's not public knowledge," the chief argued.

"Actually, I think it is," I corrected him. I didn't dare look at Kapp, the one who'd made the knowledge public, at least as far as I was concerned.

"Okay, okay," the chief tried, squirming like a caged

bear. "It's public knowledge. Do you know who killed her."

I shook my head.

"Do you have any idea?"

I shook my head again. "But I promise I'll let you know if I find out."

The chief crossed his arms as he glared at me.

"So tell me about your brother," he ordered finally.

"York?" I asked, my pulse speeding up. What about York?

"Yes, York," he answered. "Do you have another one?"

"Uh-huh, I've got a brother named Arnot, too. He does custom cabinetry, really nice work—"

"York Lazar," The chief interrupted. "I wanna know about York Lazar. I hear he's some kinda martial artist, a killing machine."

"York is not a killing machine," I said through tight lips. "He teaches martial arts, mostly to the disabled. He's my brother. What are you asking?"

"I'm asking what the hell he's doing here. He's staying at the lodge. He isn't any more a part of Dr. Hart's class than your friend Kapp is. Why is he here?"

"He's protecting me," I whispered.

"Protecting you?"

"He thinks I need protection since there's a murderer loose."

The chief frowned and thought for a minute.

"I don't understand this whole setup." he concluded.

"Me neither," I told him.

"Okay." He shook his finger at me. "You're in the clear now, but don't try anything. And don't leave town."

Then he turned around and marched out of the room, slamming the door behind him hard enough to shake the artwork on the walls.

"Keerups, and I thought you could be a bully," I said to Kapp after the room stopped shaking.

"Moi?" he put in innocently.

"Toi, tu, whatever" I answered. French wasn't my forte.

"So, who do you think it is, Lazar?" Kapp asked softly.

I paused. "I don't know. Sometimes, I think Sara. Sometimes, Dotty. Sometimes, Quinn. Just about everyone has been a question mark for me. I just don't know yet."

Kapp shook his head.

"It's time for you to go to your morning session," he announced, tapping his watch.

He was right. I jumped up off my bed.

"Thanks Kapp," I said and bussed the older man on his cheek. He blushed and led the way out of my room, mumbling and grumbling. I saluted him with my cane and headed to the intensive.

I got to the meeting room on time for once. Quinn was there in the front of the room, looking better than he had the day before. Half a million dollars better? Raleigh and Ed sat in the first row of seats. Craig stood near a wall, looking up at the ceiling . . . or something. And Kim was in the back row. I didn't sit down, but watched as the others drifted in.

Orson came through the door, chatting with Dotty, animation flavoring his voice.

"So do you think aromas could change metabolic cascades?" Orson was asking. "That'd be awesome to see."

"Let's try," Dotty suggested, matching his enthusiasm. She had what looked like genuine interest on her face and smelled of something like lavender. She didn't look like a slapper today, that was for sure.

Fran and Judd were the next through the door, speaking in hushed whispers that I couldn't make out. Were they a couple? Then Taj arrived, followed closely by Sara. Her step was certain in intent, but wobbly in execution. I thought of what Kapp had said about drugs.

Quinn stretched his mouth into a shape that almost passed for a smile, at least if you ignored the pain in his eyes. We all took seats, all but Sara who stood to one side of the door and Craig who stayed at the wall.

"I thought we could dedicate our work today to Dr. Hart's memory," Quinn began.

No one said amen. Though Craig did look down from the ceiling when Quinn mentioned the doctor's name.

"We'll do our usual one-on-one work, but keeping Dr. Hart's methods in mind."

I nodded and tried to smile back, wondering what methods he meant. Illusion, ruthlessness?

"So choose a partner, someone you haven't worked with before, and do your stuff," he ordered.

I should have done my morning meditation. Because something in me was rebelling against this whole thing. Two more days, I reminded myself. I can make it two more days. And maybe I'd find out who killed Dr. Hart.

I rose from my seat just in time for Judd Nyman to walk up to me. He grinned, looking like he was all teeth.

"Hey, Cally, we haven't worked together," he announced. "You've really been missing something."

I kept my screams internal.

"So what'll it be?" he went on. "Thai massage or reflexology?"

I thought for a moment. The less Judd touched me, the better. I chided myself for the thought. I was sure there was good in Judd. There was good in everyone.

"Reflexology," I answered finally.

"Excellent choice," he commended me. "So, sit down and take off your shoes and socks. I'll sit across from you and do your feet. Usually I have a massage table, but this'll be just fine."

I did as I was told. Judd whipped a hand towel and a jar of cream from his pocket. He toweled my feet first and began massaging the cream onto my right foot.

"This stuff is really great, you know," he told me as he worked, thumbs on the top of my foot and fingers underneath. He didn't have a light touch. "Cures everything, believe me."

"Uh-huh," I muttered.

"Like this," he went on, digging his thumb into my big toe. "You got eye problems, right? I see the glasses. This helps the eyes."

"How about eating a carrot instead?" my mouth asked.

Judd leaned back his head and laughed.

"You're a real kidder, Cally." He lifted my toes with one hand and dug his thumb in on the bottom of my foot. "That's great. This one will relax you."

It didn't. Nor did any of the rest of his foot pummeling. Vaguely, I remembered enjoying a reflexology session at one time in my life, but that practitioner had been more gentle. And she hadn't talked the whole time.

When Quinn yelled, "Switch," I slipped my feet out of Judd's hands as fast as I could without getting friction burns.

"So, was that great or what?" Judd demanded.

I bit back the obvious answer.

"Great," I murmured and put my socks and shoes back on. The cream had a pleasant baby-powder kind of smell. That was a plus. "My feet thank you," I added.

"So do your thing on me, Cally," Judd ordered once I'd finished.

"Is there any specific issue you'd like to work on?" I asked him.

"Naah, unless we can figure out who killed Dr. Hart."

Judd leaned toward me. Actually, his aura felt less intrusive than his physical body language. His aura actually felt, well, healing. That was a surprise. The overblown quality I'd sensed before was gone. Judd's body was surrounded with a hyacinth blue that I associated with physical well-being. That made sense. Judd looked like he was in good health. There were other colors, too, a brown kind of earth energy and a glimmer of yellow. Fear yellow. It looked like

Judd was okay in general, but afraid at this moment. But why? Afraid of being killed or afraid of being exposed as a killer?

"You look very healthy, Judd," I began.

"Damn right!" he agreed. "I do my own feet every night."

"You have a little fear right now—"

"No, not me," he cut in. He leaned his head back and shook it ruefully. "Okay, I'll be straight with you. I wanna solve this murder thing, ya know. I wanna impress my kid. But I'm not so sure I can."

"And that makes you afraid?" The yellow flared.

I sent my mind to the color. Unless Judd was capable of lying energetically, he wasn't kidding me. At least I didn't think so. I sensed he wasn't afraid of being exposed as a killer or of being killed. He was afraid his son, Orson, wouldn't love him.

"Orson adores you, Judd," I assured him.

"You think so?" Judd murmured. "I try and all, but the kid's so smart, a lot smarter than his old man."

"And you love him and validate his intelligence," I reminded him. There wasn't enough time for real energy work. I'd have to try talking. "I've seen it. Orson knows you for who you are."

"That isn't much," Judd muttered. "Yeah, I know I can sling the bullshit, but damn, I love that kid. I just hope he doesn't see an old man when he looks at me. I just . . ."

Finally, I did do some energy work. As Judd talked, I encouraged the yellow to surround itself in a translucent field of acceptance, showing Judd's body the field in my own energy. The translucent field appeared, and the yellow absorbed it without the slightest energetic prod. And finally, where there had been yellow light, there was only translucent light remaining. And Judd was still talking.

". . . but you're right, Cally," he concluded. "I love that kid so much. He knows it."

"You don't have to prove anything,"

"No." Judd smiled. "I guess I don't."

"Next!" Quinn shouted.

"Thanks, Cally," Judd whispered, and he was gone.

I looked around. I hadn't worked with Fran before.

"Fran?" I murmured, walking toward her.

Fran was holding her energy wand in her hand. It was attached to something that plugged into the wall, something electrical with a lot of dials and a screen that was sitting on a spare chair.

"Cally," Fran greeted me brusquely.

"So this is your machine," I said. I bent over and reached out my hand to touch the screen.

"Don't you *ever* touch my stuff!" Fran shouted.

At least she didn't slap me.

SEVENTEEN

I jumped back, raising my cane just in case. This was one angry woman. The adrenaline surging in my veins seemed to light up the scene like a flare. Fran stood, unmoving in her blue denim jacket, adobe-colored skin reddened to copper beneath black hair, turquoise and silver glinting at her wrists and throat.

Then Fran really looked at me, her raisin-black eyes rounding in concern.

"Oh, God. I'm sorry, Cally," she apologized. Her skin lost its copper flush. She sounded sincere. Or maybe it was the cane in my hand.

"No, I'm sorry," I tried, lowering my hand slowly. "I realize how important your invention is to you. I should have thought before trying to touch it."

"No, it's not your fault," she insisted, returning the apology to my side of the net. She reached up to brush a dark wing of hair from her face, jingling bracelets as she did. "I'm just so stressed out. I'm jumpy, I guess."

"How would you like a little energy work?" I offered. I wanted out of the apology upwomanship.

"I suppose I need it, huh?" she said ruefully. Her smile was surprising in its benevolence.

"We all do," I muttered.

She laughed as if I was joking and looked down, her dark hair falling across her face again. "Ain't that the truth? We are an intensive that needs the intensive care unit."

I stared at her. My leftover adrenaline was just beginning to make me queasy. And my brain was on break.

"A little nursing joke," she explained.

"Oh, right." I worked up a chuckle. Actually, the joke *was* pretty funny. I laughed for real an instant later.

Fran flashed me another kind smile. "Glad to see you laughing."

I sat her down a few mutual compliments later and checked her out. I found everything I'd expected to find: anger, sadness, betrayal, frustration . . . and of course, goodness. I helped her release some of the feelings that were howling the loudest, guiding the energy through her toes and fingertips evenly and easily. As I continued to work, she bent forward and whispered.

"Do you think Judd is cute?"

That stopped my concentration cold. Judd Nyman? Judd of the loud mouth and ungentle hands? I was glad I didn't voice my reaction aloud. Because Fran was staring at me with her head cocked like an interested bird.

I turned to look at Judd where he was trying to talk Ed into some reflexology work. Judd wasn't bad looking really. Still, he had to be at least ten years older than Fran. Of course, Kapp was thirty years older than Geneva. But I didn't even want to think about Kapp and Geneva. I tried to see Judd through Fran's eyes. He had a strong face and his own hair, even if that hair was graying.

"He's got a nice smile," I offered.

"Yeah, doesn't he?" Fran leaned even closer. "I think he likes me."

"Were you two friends before the intensive?" I asked.

"No, I just met him. But you know, something clicked.

We're both fighters. And he's a really good father. I've got two boys, so that's important to me."

I nodded.

"We both work out at the gym," she went on. "He looks damn good. Nice butt."

"Right," I murmured. I didn't know if I wanted to be having this conversation.

"And we believe in the same things," Fran added. Her dark eyes were soft, unfocused. "It's like I've known him forever. Do you believe in soul mates?"

"Well . . ." I temporized. There were times when I wondered if Roy and I were soul mates. My friend Dee-Dee was sure of it. "Maybe—"

"Where's Craig Zweig?" Quinn's voice broke in before I had to commit myself further.

"Craig?" a number of voices echoed.

Orson piped up helpfully, "He's gone, dude."

I turned to look at Quinn. I could tell he was having an internal meltdown. At least he was keeping it internal for the moment. Had Chief Phlug made him promise to keep an eye on us? Or to keep track of Craig Zweig?

"Maybe he's in the rest room," Ed suggested reasonably.

"I'll go look!" Orson offered and shot out of the meeting room before anyone could stop him.

Judd followed his son almost as quickly, unsmiling.

"Who was working with Craig last?" Quinn asked.

"I guess I was supposed to," Sara admitted, drawing out her words. "Everyone else had paired up. But he's *so* crazy. I kept my distance."

"Did he say anything?"

"How should I know?" she answered. "I kept away from him. I just told you that. He's not just crazy, he's boring."

Quinn opened his mouth to say something and shut it again. Maybe he'd been thinking of appealing to Sara's better instincts. I'm sure Sara had better instincts, but she kept them well hidden.

"He was quiet today," Raleigh put in. "Preoccupied, I think."

Orson burst back into the room, with Judd right behind him.

"He's not in the men's room in the lobby," he told us. "Maybe he's hiding or something. Do you think he's in his own room? Or—"

"I think we need to break up into teams and find him," Ed Lau suggested ponderously.

I turned to Ed. Worry had sharpened his round face.

"Teams," Quinn agreed weakly. "Thank you, Ed."

"Teams?" I asked. Hadn't we had enough of teams? I certainly had. It took me a moment to realize. Teams, so no one was alone. Teams, so no one got murdered.

"Raleigh," Quinn began hesitantly. "How about you and Taj?"

The two men nodded.

"Judd—"

Fran looked expectant, but Orson beat her to Judd.

"I'll go with Dad," he announced.

Judd nodded. He was a good father. I didn't think he'd let Orson search alone.

"Kim and Cally," Quinn assigned quickly.

I let out a held breath. Kim wasn't the happiest camper on the block, but at least she wasn't prone to shouting, smothering embraces, or slapping. As far as I knew.

Once Quinn had sorted us into teams, he gave us our assignments. Raleigh and Taj would look for Craig in the obvious place, his room. Quinn and Sara would talk to the Jinnahs. Judd and Orson would prowl the halls. Ed, Fran, and Dotty would check the parking lot and sidewalks. And Kim and I would take the rest of the outdoors. We would all meet again, half an hour later in the lobby.

As Quinn was giving us our assignments, I got a queasy feeling once more. Could Craig be dead, murdered? Or had he fled the scene, a more cunning murderer than anyone had realized? I closed my eyes for a moment and tried to feel Craig's presence. Nothing.

"Cally?" Kim murmured by my side.

My eyes popped open.

"Shouldn't we get going?" Kim suggested softly. "Craig could be despondent, even suicidal."

"Right," I agreed, not really ready to consider Craig's mental state. I took a quick glance at my search partner. She wasn't crying then, but her eyes had that look of a person who could cry at any moment. Or maybe she always looked that way. She was such a small woman, and her moon-shaped face and large eyes gave her a childlike look. It was hard to believe she was a practicing psychiatrist.

"Are you comfortable with the idea of searching for Craig?" she asked. Maybe she was a psychiatrist after all.

"Oh, I'm fine," I told her and began walking behind the others to the doorway.

"How are *you* doing?" I asked as we walked down the hall.

"Me?" Kim answered, her eyes getting even bigger. "Oh, I'm fine, too." She paused in her speech for a moment, but kept her feet moving. "Well, a little depressed. Dr. Hart's death was, I don't know, not right. I . . . I . . ."

"Yeah, I know what you mean," I muttered as if I did. What I really knew was that I didn't want her crying again.

We didn't say much more until we got through the lobby doors.

"Death is difficult, of course," Kim went on after we'd stepped outside.

"My parents died when I was a teenager," I confessed. I wondered if psychiatrists magically made their patients say things like that. I hadn't been planning on it.

"I remember," Kim told me gently.

"I'm sorry," I said, stopping in my tracks, remembering, too. I'd already told her about my parents when we'd worked together. "It's your psychiatrist persona, I suppose," I joked. "Does everyone go on and on about the same things?"

"No," she answered seriously. "It's important, Cally. Death isn't trivial. My only brother died. I know what it's like. It's not something you can forget when someone you love dies." Tears formed in her eyes.

Dack. I'd done it. I'd made the psychiatrist cry.

"Let's go look at the trees!" I chirped, pretending not to notice.

We walked over to my favorite oak tree first. But I could still hear Kim sniffling as our feet made squishing noises in the wet grass. Someone must have watered recently. Or maybe it was Kim's tears flooding. And I called myself a healer, ignoring someone in that much pain?

"Kim?" I finally whispered. "Is there anything I can do—"

A figure jumped out from behind the oak tree. I raised my cane without thinking, ready to strike.

"It's that policeman," Kim warned me.

It was that policeman, Officer Jones, last seen being chewed out by my friend Kapp.

"Yikes!" Officer Jones bleated, raising his hands in a pretence of surrender. He grinned. "You'd better put that cane down. You could hurt someone with that thing."

I was just glad that Officer Jones seemed to think that my cane was a joke. I lowered it carefully.

"You startled me, officer," I apologized. "I didn't mean to scare you."

Officer Jones laughed aloud. "Scare me with that thing? Bang, bang, the cane went off!"

I smiled. Kim didn't. I wanted to nudge her, but Officer Jones didn't need a receptive audience. He was his own audience.

After he'd stopped laughing, he asked us what we were doing outside.

"Craig Zweig is missing," I told him.

His grin disappeared.

"Uh-oh," he whispered. "The chief'll have a conniption."

"Not if we find Craig before the chief knows he's missing," I tried.

So we added Officer Jones to our team. For all of his jokes about my cane, Jones was with the plan.

"Anyone tried the parking lot?" he asked.

"Yup," I told him. "Someone's there. They're checking the sidewalks, too. Someone's checking his room. And someone's checking the hotel. We've got outdoor duty."

"Lots of trees," he offered. "If I wanted to hide, I'd just climb a tree."

We looked up into the limbs of the oak we'd been talking under. But we didn't spot Craig Zweig.

"I'll show you the best climbing tree around," Jones went on. "I used to play here as a kid. I know all the best trees."

So Kim and I marched up the green hill, following Officer Jones in the clean spring air. Kim wasn't sniffling anymore. And we were both having a hard time keeping up with the officer's loping gait.

"See, here it is," he announced finally. We were in front of an ancient oak whose branches spread wide enough to shelter an army, or at least a few intensive groups. I looked up and couldn't see the top of the tree. I did see notches in the tree's trunk and a carved heart with initials. "TJ & KA," it read.

"I love the heart," I put in.

Officer Jones blushed. No. Could it be?

"Did you carve that heart—"

"I was just a kid," he whined. "Don't tell Phlug—"

And someone above us laughed.

The three of us jumped simultaneously. Because the shrill sound above us was the laugh of a loon, Craig Zweig's laugh.

"Craig?" I asked tentatively.

He laughed again.

"Craig," Kim cajoled. "Wouldn't it be nice to come down from the tree now?"

"No," the answer came from above.

I walked farther under the leafage and stared up at where the sound had come from. I could just see the tip of a running shoe, way too many branches up.

"Craig, are you upset?" Kim tried again, moving closer under the tree with me.

Craig laughed some more.

Gooseflesh stretched across my arms.

And Officer Jones started climbing. Expertly, he grabbed branches and found footholds, probably the same ones he'd used as a boy. Leaves rained down as he disappeared into the foliage.

Kim and I looked at each other as we waited uselessly. As expertly as Officer Jones was able to climb the tree, could he get Craig down without hurting him?

"Craig, Officer Jones is going to help you down from the tree," I spoke to the branches above me.

"Don't wanna go down," Craig announced.

"I got him!" Officer Jones shouted.

The branches began to shake, more leaves raining down.

"No, don't wanna go!" Craig cried out.

"Look, do I have to push you outta this tree or what?" Officer Jones demanded.

"What," Craig answered.

"How about a net?" I shouted up into the greenery.

"A net?" Officer Jones repeated.

"What if Craig falls—"

And with the word, a body came flopping down branch by branch from the tree. Craig's body. Kim and I grasped our hands together to form a support for his final fall in that instant, as if we'd planned it all along. And all of a sudden, Craig landed, two yards to our side in a fetal ball. Dust flew up around him.

"Ow," he muttered.

"Are you hurt?" I demanded.

"Nah," he answered and stood, brushing off leaves and debris. "I do this all the time at home."

Jones' descent was more dignified. He climbed down much as he'd gone up. Once he was on the ground, he eyed Craig with disgust.

"You're crazy, you know—"

"I know," Craig agreed. He grinned, revealing his snaggly teeth yet again.

Officer Jones turned to Kim and me, his face asking us for the next move.

"Let's all go to the lobby," I suggested.

And amazingly, Craig didn't object. All he said on the walk back was that he was sleepy. I hoped he didn't have a concussion.

Officer Jones, however, had plenty to say. He must have been taking lessons from Chief Phlug.

He berated the intensive group, insane people, and Craig, mostly in that order, over and over again. Loudly.

Kim and I kept our silence. The berating seemed to be a guy thing.

When we finally made it through the lobby doors, most of our group were already assembled inside. I looked at my watch. We were five minutes after the half-hour mark. But *we* had Craig.

I handed our lost lamb over to Fran.

"He took a fall from a tree," I told her. "He says he's okay. He didn't pass out or anything."

Fran took over like the good nurse she was.

"Do you hurt anywhere?" she asked him.

"Nah."

"Did you hit your head?"

"Nah."

She took his pulse and looked into his eyes. She patted down his body. He giggled.

"You're a screwy one," she said affectionately. "Looking for birds in the tree?"

"Tweet?" he tried.

I smiled. I couldn't help it. And finally, I collapsed onto a couch. We'd found Craig. And he didn't seem in any worse shape than when we'd lost him. Kim waved my way and walked off, down the hallway. The rest of the group began making good-bye noises.

"Might as well break early for lunch," Quinn ordered belatedly. "The Jinnahs will have it going in a minute. And we'll have our afternoon discussion as usual."

"No tour?" Sara asked, smirking.

"No tour today," Quinn answered without expression.

Group members milled around as the Jinnahs put food out on the buffet table. Good smells floated my way. I was hungry. I may not have climbed a tree, but I'd climbed a hill. That was enough.

I was about to get up from the couch when Quinn sat down next to me.

"I wanted to thank you for finding Craig," he offered.

"Oh, Officer Jones really found him," I answered truthfully.

"Well, I appreciate your efforts in any case."

I started to get up again and let myself flop back onto the couch.

"Quinn, can I ask you a question?" I tried.

"Of course," he answered. But something in him shrank away.

"Why us?" I asked. "Why did Dr. Hart invite us to this intensive? I know she didn't charge us anywhere near what she charged for her two week seminars—"

I looked more closely at Quinn. His skin was turning a coral shade.

"Are you okay?" I interrupted myself.

"It's kind of a sensitive subject," he commented, not really answering my question. "I'm not sure . . ."

"Listen, Quinn. I got an invitation to attend this thing. Did Dr. Hart just get my name from the phone book?"

"No, from *The Healing Stone*," he blurted out.

"You're kidding!" I hissed. But I knew he wasn't. *The Healing Stone* was a quarterly directory of everything New Age in the area. Mind, body, and spirit were all represented. Nutrition, martial arts, psychic arts, intuitive training, vegetarian restaurants, herbs. Everything under the sun was listed, everything under the stars in fact. Astrology, UFO's, bodywork, spiritual practice. You name it, *The Healing Stone* listed it. I'd paid to post a small ad there for years. And last spring, I'd been interviewed along with some other local healers.

"Did Dr. Hart read my interview?" I asked, suddenly realizing.

Quinn just nodded.

"And the rest?" I asked.

"Other directories, mostly on the Internet."

"But why?"

Quinn leaned back into the cushions on the couch as if he was very tired. He probably was.

"Every year, Dr. Hart toured. And every year, she went to new areas. She gave speeches, and she hosted intensives. She wanted to teach, and she wanted to learn—"

"But—" I began.

"Cally, please, just hear me out." Quinn swiveled his head around, his eyes searching. No one was near enough to hear. He whispered, "I told you she was good at diagnoses, but not as good at healing. She knew alternative healing worked. She'd been chronically ill for years when she was a medical doctor. After that, she worked with a clairvoyant who changed her life. And finally, she realized she was clairvoyant herself—"

"I know this part," I told him. "I read her books."

"Okay, so you know she investigated all kinds of alternative healing. She interviewed healers herself. She studied . . ."

"But she couldn't heal anyone," I finished for him.

Quinn's eyes were moistening. "Aurora was a good person," he told me. "She wanted to be Deepak Chopra or Caroline Myss or Barbara Brennen. Aurora was insecure. It's hard to believe, I know, but she was. She used to cry. She wanted the magic bullet of healing, something she could use that would never fail."

"There isn't any such thing," I argued. "What I do doesn't work for everyone. Any healer will tell you that."

"But she was so good at seeing, Cally. And she really felt that pushing people's hot buttons made them deal with their issues. She . . . she . . ." Quinn put his head in his hands. "Oh God, someone must have killed her for it!" he cried.

"Oh, Quinn," I sighed and wrapped my arm around him. What would he do without the doctor?

"Part of me feels be . . . betrayed, Cally," he stammered through his tears. "Aurora is dead and *I* feel betrayed. How can I be so . . . so selfish?"

"It's not selfish, Quinn," I told him. "It's human. It's grief. It's—"

"Woo, woo, woo, will you look at that?" I heard from above us. I recognized Sara's voice before I even looked up. I could even smell her.

As I brought my eyes up, Sara licked her bottom lip slowly and sensually and thrusted her pelvis our way. Then she followed up verbally.

"Quinnie-poo's found another new love!" she sang out.

"And who would that be?" Chief Phlug demanded from across the room.

EIGHTEEN

I yanked my arm back out from around Quinn's shoulders and tried to stand up. But I wasn't fast enough. Chief Phlug was clearly watching my disentanglement process as he strode toward us, squinting so hard that his actual eyeballs were just a supposition.

"What's going on around here, huh?" the chief demanded once I was standing.

"Quinn and Cally are fooling around, right in front of everyone," Sara answered from the chief's side. And she giggled, the shrill notes of the sound robbing it of any real fun. I tried to swallow, but my mouth was too dry.

"Sara!" Quinn objected. His face was still ravaged by tears and emotion. "Feel free to tear me to shreds, but leave the others alone. Cally was comforting me. Can't you see that? Can't you see that I need some support?"

"Oh, sure." Sara sneered. "You and Dr. Hart were always on me about my morals. I wish she could see you now."

Quinn's face went white.

"If Dr. Hart was here now, she would recognize compassion," I spit out angrily. Finally, I could swallow. But I was shaking both with anger and with the wish not to be subject to such an uncontrollable emotion. "Dr. Hart was a healer. *She* knew what compassion was."

"Thank you, Cally," Quinn murmured. Color was coming back to his face.

Sara stopped sneering and glared my way.

"You think you're better than me, too, don't you?" she snapped. She stepped forward and pushed her face into mine. "Well, you're not. I'm sick of this. You are all too boring. I'm outta here."

She turned and looked at Chief Phlug. "Can't you see what a couple of phonies they are? They probably killed her together."

I heard more than one person gasp. And one of them was me. Did Sara really believe that?

"You wanna make a serious accusation, Ms. Oshima?" Phlug asked slowly.

Sara didn't respond. Her forehead was slick with sweat though.

"Sounds like you've got a big problem, young lady." Chief Phlug lifted his finger and shook it in Sara's moist face. "Sometimes, people need comforting. Laura . . . the sergeant spends half of her time at the station comforting people. Women do that. And Mr. Vogel looks like he needs a little help here. Aren't you supposed to be his friend or something?"

"So arrest me!" Sara ordered dramatically. She put her arms into the air. "I'm not *compassionate*. I'm not a good friend. Oooh, am I in trouble?"

"Listen, Ms. Oshima," Chief Phlug hissed. "All I'd have to do is find your stash, and I could arrest you today and put you away. But I've got a murderer to find. So don't jerk me around, okay?"

"But—"

"I don't know what your problem is," Phlug plowed on. "But I'd say that you owe these two folks an apology."

Sara's eyes narrowed. "Fine," she muttered. "I *owe* them

an apology. Put it on my tab, you . . . you . . ." Sara hesitated. I was sure her hesitation wasn't for lack of exple-
tives. But somewhere in her limbic brain, the fact that she
could be in trouble was sinking in. She lifted her hand to
swipe at the sweat on her forehead. "Fine," she repeated,
swung around, and left the room.

I let the anger leave my body with Sara's exit. It wasn't
easy. Part of me wanted to wallow in self-righteousness.
But another part of me felt pity for Sara, a woman whose
only current happiness seemed derived from the pain of
others. What had warped Sara Oshima so thoroughly?

"Ms. Lazar," Chief Phlug barked into the silence.

My shoulders twitched involuntarily. I'd actually forgotten Chief Phlug while thinking about Sara.

"Yes," I answered carefully, turning my head to face him.

"I understand you brought in Mr. Zweig along with Officer Jones and Kim Welch," he told me. "I wanted to thank
you. Jones is a good officer, loyal and all, but . . ."

"He's a little naïve," I tried.

"Yeah, that," the chief agreed gruffly. "I thought you
could tell me more about the incident from your point of
view."

"Me?" I asked. I couldn't seemed to follow his words. I
was just too tired.

"That's why I'm here," Phlug explained. I heard exasperation in his tone. He shoved his head forward. "Can we
go someplace to talk?"

My eyes drifted longingly to the food on the buffet. I
was hungry as well as tired.

Chief Phlug noticed more than I gave him credit for.
"Get something on a plate first," he suggested. "We can go
outside and you can eat. We'll sit in the car."

I wondered how long our talk was going to last. Too
long, I was sure. So I filled a paper plate with potato-
cheese bake, marinated vegetables, cream cheese wontons,
and almond-apricot cookies. Lots of cookies. If the chief

took me to jail, at least I wouldn't have to eat for a while. I grabbed a bottle of water and stuck it under my arm.

The chief led me outside to his unmarked car as I balanced the overflowing plate carefully in my hands.

When we got to his car, I stood for a moment in the cool breeze, uncertain. Would he want me to sit in the back like a prisoner?

Phlug squinted his eyes again, watching me watch the car. He seemed to come to a decision.

"You can sit up front with me," he offered. I opened my mouth to thank him. "Just don't mess up the seats," he added.

I climbed into the passenger's seat of his car feeling about as comfortable as a teenager on her first date. I closed my door as the chief got in on the driver's side. The car looked pretty much like any other car, except for a lot of gear that might have been for communications and a stray, red bubble light that must have been meant for the roof.

The chief jangled as he got comfortable in his seat. I wondered if he *could* get comfortable with all the stuff he had strapped to his belt. A gun for one thing. I tried not to think about the gun and shoved a wonton into my mouth.

"So, Ms. Lazar—"

"Cally," I mumbled through the wonton.

"Cally," he corrected himself politely. This was a side of the chief I hadn't seen before. "Listen, Cally, I'm gonna put my cards on the table. We don't know who killed Dr. Hart. It would easy to pick any one of a number of people and build a case against them, but that's not how I do business. I wanna know who the real perp is. I just hate building a case against someone if I'm not sure, you know what I mean?"

I nodded. When Monty had talked about the chief, he hadn't bothered to mention that he might be a fair man. But it sounded as if he was. *Goodness is in everyone*, I reminded myself.

"Okay, then," he moved on, his eyes peering through the windshield as if he were driving. "I want you to tell me more about Craig Zweig. I know you don't think he's our killer. I want you to tell me why."

I stopped the spoonful of marinated vegetables on the way to my mouth.

"He doesn't feel like a killer," I explained, or tried to explain. "Craig Zweig might be delusional, but I don't feel anger coming from him. And for all of his electrical knowledge—"

"How'd you know Zweig had electrical knowledge?" Chief Phlug interrupted sharply.

I cursed Kapp as I tried to protect him. "Craig worked for the phone company," I explained blandly. "He did electrical wiring."

"Yeah, I know that, but how do *you* know that?" the chief demanded. He was looking straight at me, not out the windshield.

"People talked about their former professions," I offered. It wasn't exactly a lie. People had talked about their former professions the day Dr. Hart had died. Craig had said he worked for the phone company, stringing line. I just hadn't made the electrical connection, so to speak, until Kapp had mentioned it.

"All right," the chief conceded grudgingly. "But your friend Kapp has a big mouth."

"Yeah, the biggest mouth in ten counties!" I agreed fervently.

The chief reared back his head. "What, does he pull stuff on you, too?"

"You betcha," I said. I tried a wry smile on my tired face. "What are friends for, anyway?"

The chief smiled back for a moment. Then the smile was gone.

"Okay, so you were saying that you knew Zweig had electrical knowledge," he prodded.

"Oh, right," I said, remembering. "But for all of that, Craig isn't very organized. I just can't imagine him organized enough to have planned a murder ahead of time. I mean, can you?"

"Nah," the chief admitted. "That's the one thing that's keeping him outta my jail. He's just too crazy, you know. Unless it's just an act." He paused and zeroed in on me with his eyes again. "Could it be an act?"

I shook my head. "I don't think so. One look at his aura and you know he's—I don't know exactly—but all messed up. His aura is as disorganized as his hair."

"You really see that stuff?" Phlug asked, eyes widening.

"Yeah," I told him. "If I look for it."

"Ya see any murder type stuff on anyone?"

"No," I said uncertainly.

"But you're not sure," the chief accused.

"I'm not sure," I admitted. "I'm not a mind reader. I've seen anger coming from a lot of people, but I don't have enough experience to know if the anger is just everyday anger or murderous anger."

"Yeah, I can understand that," the chief muttered. "It's like those guys who lie, you know. They lie so good, they look innocent, and the innocent ones look guilty. It's not as easy as it looks to know what's what."

"Thanks," I murmured.

"Sara Oshima is another one I'm interested in," the chief announced, ignoring my thank you. "First off, she's a nasty piece of work if I ever saw one. She had motive. And she had access to the doctor's contraption. Whaddaya see on her?"

"Sara." I closed my eyes for a moment. For all that Sara had done, I didn't think she'd murdered the doctor. But how to explain? I opened my eyes again. "I think Dr. Hart mothered Sara. Sara misses her. Sara's nasty, but she wasn't *as* nasty before the doctor died. I think she really misses Dr. Hart. That's why she's acting out. She was desperate for love, and Dr. Hart was kind to her in her own way. Sara might mouth off a lot, but I don't think she killed Dr. Hart."

"How about Quinn Vogel?" the chief pressed.

I shook my head. "I know he had motive of a kind—" I began.

I saw the chief open his mouth to ask how I knew about Quinn's motive.

"Don't ask," I cut him off. "Everyone is hearing everything. I heard Quinn inherits a lot of money. But he's also losing his business. He's completely panicked. And unless he's an awfully good actor, I think he misses Dr. Hart even more than Sara does. I'm not sure about their relationship, but he seems to have truly loved the doctor. He's still defending her even when she's dead. And he's freaking out about what he's going to do next. Without Dr. Hart, Quinn Vogel is unemployed with no references." I paused, and added, "I think he's heartbroken."

"But you're not sure," Phlug challenged.

"Yeah," I murmured. "I'm not sure."

Phlug sighed and tapped the steering wheel in front of him. I took a surreptitious bite of potato-cheese bake. Phlug didn't follow up. I tasted the marinated vegetables. I took a long drink of water. I hoped I wasn't spilling anything on the seats.

"Anything about the rest of these jokers that you're not telling me?" the chief demanded.

I managed to swallow without choking. "Do you know about Dr. Hart's missing son?" I tried.

Phlug glared at me before answering. "I hope I know more about him than you do. But your friend Kapp has probably filled you in."

I shook my head. "Do you mean you've found him?" I asked.

"No, we haven't found him."

"Oh." I took another swallow of water. "See I just wondered if he might have something to do with the group. What if he knows he's Doctor Hart's son and followed her somehow?"

"Taj Gemayel, ya mean," he said thoughtfully. "Yeah, I've wondered. But if he is the murderer, he's screwed up any chance of inheriting. He can't come forward now."

"What if it's someone who's not in the group? Maybe a local who recognized Dr. Hart and realized she was his mother—"

"It's not a local," Phlug stated flatly. "That'd be too much coincidence. Real life doesn't work that way. Got any other bright ideas?"

"Well," I began slowly. "Quinn said something earlier. He said that Dr. Hart thought pushing people's hot buttons was therapeutic. He also said he was afraid that her habit of pushing people's hot buttons was what got her killed."

"Yeah?" Chief Phlug's eyes opened with new interest.

"Do you know of any connection between the group members and Dr. Hart?" I probed. "I mean, what if she hurt someone that someone in the group loved?"

The chief didn't answer right away.

I nibbled on a cookie.

"Okay, I suppose you know all about all the suicides that Dr. Hart caused?" Phlug said.

"I'm not sure," I admitted. "I know there're two suits pending—"

"Two suits and a few out-of-court settlements." Phlug shook his head. "That woman may have been some kind of big hoodoo doctor, but she did a lot of harm. Vogel was up front about the suits and settlements. We've got some people contacting the survivors, trying to see if there's a connection to anyone in the group. We got zip so far though. Your friend Kapp found any connection?"

I shook my head.

"Hah, so he *is* your source!" Chief Phlug hit the steering wheel. Catching me seemed to cheer him up. But not much.

"Ya got anything more to tell me?" he demanded.

I shook my head again.

"Ah, heck. I was afraid of that. You don't know any more than we do."

"I don't think so," I whispered.

He glared at me for a moment before withdrawing his eyes.

"Go on, get out of the car," he ordered. He turned his empty gaze out the windshield again. "You might as well eat your meal in peace."

I wanted to say something, maybe "I'm sorry," or "see you later," but I said nothing as I climbed out of the car. Chief Phlug in a snit was something I didn't want to witness.

So I finished up everything on my plate but the cookies, sitting under my favorite oak tree, breathing in the clean air. Phlug eventually speeded away from the Swanton Hills Lodge parking lot, apparently none the wiser for speaking with me.

I walked back into the lobby. There was still food on the buffet, and Quinn, Raleigh, Taj, and Kim sat on the couches.

"Do you think healing is really about acceptance?" Quinn was asking Raleigh eagerly. Quinn looked almost happy.

"There are a lot of levels of acceptance," Raleigh answered. "Self-acceptance, acceptance of others, acceptance of the human condition. If someone can really accept at all those levels, they will be healed." Raleigh laughed. "I sound like I know. I'm not there yet. But the resonance work seems to help."

"But don't you have to forgive before you can accept?" Taj asked diffidently.

"Absolutely, but forgive who?" Raleigh asked. "That's always the question."

Taj's skin pinkened. "I guess maybe forgiving circumstance or God or something. That's what's so hard for me."

Now, this was a conversation. I didn't want to talk about murder anymore. I wrapped my uneaten cookies in a napkin and threw my plate into the garbage.

"Forgiveness," Kim repeated. She closed her eyes and sighed.

"So the modality of healing isn't as important as the intent of acceptance?" Quinn tried.

I took a seat on a chair between the two couches.

"I'm not really sure," Raleigh admitted. "I've heard a lot of folks use different words, like spirit and unity and balance, but I keep coming back to acceptance. That's how it works for me. But I wouldn't disrespect any other form of healing without checking it out. And there are probably more paths to acceptance than I can even imagine."

"It feels right then?" Quinn prodded. "That's the test?"

"Yeah—"

"Where's Sara?" a loud voice interrupted.

Everyone looked up. Sara's boyfriend, Ira, stood in the doorway, his bushy hair haloed by the light. Or maybe he wasn't her boyfriend. It was hard to tell with Sara.

"I'm not sure where Sara is at the moment," Quinn answered finally. There was no acceptance in his eyes, just endurance.

"Well, I wanna talk to her," Ira insisted. "So tell her to get her butt on down here."

"Sara isn't mine to order around," Quinn responded through tight lips. "Perhaps you'd like to leave a message at the desk.

"Yeah, I wanna leave a message," Ira rapped out. "You just tell her I'm leaving. I've had it with her and all of you. I'm tired of waiting. I'm moving down the highway—"

"Got it," Quinn cut him off. "But I'm not the messenger. Write her a note."

Whoa. Quinn was asking for a fight with this man.

"You think I can't write, huh?" Ira accused. "Well, you're wrong. I have a degree in English, you suckface."

Ira stormed up to the reception desk and pounded on the bell. Its cheery ring seemed incongruous under his heavy fist.

Bob Jinnah approached Sara's soon-to-be-gone significant other with a smile on his dreamy face.

"May I be of help?" he asked.

"I wanna write a letter to Sara Oshima," Ira snapped. "You got any paper? Maybe a pen? And an envelope?"

"Certainly," Bob agreed, unperturbed. He fumbled under the desk and brought out the paper, pen, and envelope.

The room was silent as Ira wrote, scratching his pen so hard, I could hear the sound of tearing paper. He stuffed the paper in the envelope and handed it to Bob.

"Give this to Sara," he ordered. He pocketed the pen and strode out the lobby doors.

Bob Jinnah smiled again, saluted us, and went back into the room behind the reception desk.

"Angry dude," Taj commented absently.

"Now Ira challenges acceptance," Raleigh added, his deep voice resonant with compassion and laughter. At least it sounded that way to me. I felt myself blush. There was just something about the man's voice.

"Forgiveness probably *is* the most important thing of all," Kim chimed in. She looked around the group, her big eyes wide as if in sudden realization.

I nodded my head earnestly and thought of my earlier interaction with Sara. And I couldn't help asking, "So why is it so easy to forget to forgive?"

NINETEEN

Kim put her head into her hands and began to sob softly.

"Now, now," Raleigh crooned. "We all forget to forgive sometimes."

"But . . . but . . ." Kim sniffled.

I got up from my chair to put my arm around her. But before I even got to Kim, a new thought entered my brain like an SUV in overdrive.

"Ira!" I cried out.

"Ira, what?" Quinn asked.

I could feel the blood rushing to my face. I hadn't meant to shout Ira's name aloud.

Kim continued to weep.

"Um," I muttered. But Quinn's eyes were on me. And Raleigh's and Taj's were on Kim. "Quinn, you know the son?" I whispered urgently. "The one who inherits? The one they're looking for?"

Quinn nodded.

"What if he's Ira?"

Quinn paled. "Oh, damn," he whispered. "I never thought of that."

"Did Dr. Hart ever talk about him?"

"Only her memories," he answered quietly. "If Ira was related to her, she never knew it."

"Related to her?" Raleigh questioned. Taj stared at us. Even Kim looked up through her tears.

"It's not important," Quinn pronounced, standing. "It was a private thing about Dr. Hart."

"Right," I agreed and lowered my eyes. It *was* private. And Quinn was still protecting the doctor's memory.

Quinn looked at his watch. "It's just about time for our afternoon session," he informed us with a thin smile.

We left the lobby and all of its good buffet smells to travel down the lodge's hallways to the meeting room. I asked myself if I could handle another afternoon session. But Quinn's straight back in front of me gave me strength. If he could do it, I could do it.

The meeting room was empty except for the five of us when we got there. It smelled of anxiety. Or maybe we did. But it filled up soon enough with the rest of the intensive members.

Craig was the first to arrive. He looked well rested in a rumpled sort of way. The tree respite must have done him some good. Judd and Fran came in together, followed by Dotty, Ed, and Orson. And finally, Sara walked through the doorway. Her face looked blank. She held a piece of hotel stationary in her hand. Was that Ira's note?

I moved toward her, in forgiveness mode. She saw me coming and shoved the stationary in her pocket.

"Sara, I just wanted to say—" I began. I should have been more concise.

"I don't care what you have to say!" she hissed. "I don't care what anyone has to say. This is a prison sentence, and I'm doing my time. Then I'm outta here."

"Where will you go?" I asked her.

"What do you care?" she snapped back. She turned away from me and strode to the front of the room to stand by Quinn. The rest of us took our seats, except of course for Craig, who stood by the wall as usual.

I was remembering why forgiveness was easy to forget.

"Who would like to discuss the insights they had in this morning's session?" Quinn prompted. I could tell that he was trying for a cheery tone, but he couldn't quite pull it off.

There was a silence.

Sara crossed her arms and smiled. I pushed my memory banks a little harder. I'd worked with Judd, but there was nothing to discuss there. And Fran—

Taj spoke up.

"Well, I worked with Kim this morning," Taj began tentatively. "And I began to realize that Dr. Hart had treated me the same way I tend to treat women. I thought it was cool to flirt and push, you know, but now I realize it might have made women uncomfortable. What was fun for me may not have been fun for them. Dr. Hart made me feel . . ." He threw his head back as he faltered, and wiggled his hands in the air. "She made me feel like she didn't respect me, I guess. So, I'm looking on the bright side. I learned something important—"

"Did you go to bed with her?" Sara demanded.

"No!" Taj yelped, his deep hypnotic voice just a memory. "She was just flirting—"

Sara laughed and threw a sideways glance at Quinn.

Quinn ignored her.

"So you learned something positive," Quinn prompted.

"Yeah," Taj agreed, his deep voice back in place. His dark, handsome face was earnest. "I learned that maybe other people don't realize they're making you feel bad. Just like I wasn't trying to make women feel bad. Maybe I learned to forgive a little."

"And did you learn to be kinder to women, too?" Dotty asked, her tone so mild that it robbed her words of any implied reprimand.

"Yeah, and that, too." Taj chuckled. "Thank you, Dotty. I promise I won't forget."

"I saw the whole thing," Craig announced. "I'll bet you thought I couldn't see from outside the room, but I can."

"And what did you see?" Kim asked him quietly.

"I saw you all, dancing like puppets on strings. You think you're in control, but you're not. And then I saw you searching for me. That was really funny." Craig grinned, revealing his poor dentistry. "See, the entities let me look through their eyes. I see a lot more that way—"

"Right," Quinn put in quickly. "You have your own perceptions, your own intuitions. I understand that. But I'm not sure if Taj was finished speaking. Would it be all right if he finished up?"

Craig laughed and the hair went up on my arms. Was he faking that high-pitched loon's laugh? It sounded inhuman. For a moment, I wondered if that laugh belonged to one of his entities, and I shivered again. Because, for all I knew, maybe Craig was telling the truth. Maybe he did see through the eyes of other-world entities—

"Oh, yeah," Taj answered Quinn belatedly. "I guess the other thing is that I feel like I'm doing real work. I don't have to think I'm scamming. That's really cool, because I wasn't sure before. So now I can really enjoy myself."

"Good," Quinn praised him.

"Good," Craig Zweig repeated and laughed again.

How many more sessions were there? Just a few, I reminded myself. I could do this. I took in a breath and thought of light. I let the breath out again.

"Taj, you done?" Fran asked brusquely.

Taj nodded.

"Okay," she muttered. "I'll tell you what's going on with me. I'm paranoid. Yeah, I finally got it. I've let my energy wand take over my whole life. I freak when anyone gets near it. What started as healing has become obsessive."

"Wow," Taj commented.

Fran smiled gently. "Yeah, 'wow.' It ain't pretty, but it's the truth. I see all this crazy stuff going down, and I turn around and look at myself. I want to apologize, especially to you, Cally. I gotta chill out on the wand. I hope I can still use it without being obsessive."

"Knowing that it's an obsession probably makes it a nonobsession," I tried hopefully. "Don't you think?"

"You're okay, kid," Fran told me. "Yeah, I hope so. But I gotta watch myself. I gotta remember that healing is the important thing. When I get angry—"

"It isn't *you* getting angry," Craig piped up.

Fran turned to Craig, her dark eyes confused.

"Whaddaya mean by that?" she demanded.

"It's because the entities are controlling you," he explained shrilly. "You aren't a really, really angry person. But you've attracted the others. And they make you do things. They make you do things you're sorry for. They got me a long time ago, but I know how to fight them." His eyes were wild. He didn't look well rested anymore. I took another deep breath as he spoke. "I tell them I know they're inside me, and I don't let them control me. I was always having to say I'm sorry, but then I realized I could stop it. You can't let them control you. You can't—"

"Craig," Dotty murmured. "Are you sure the entities don't reflect some of your own feelings?"

"Yeah, yeah!" he agreed eagerly. He wiped spittle from the corner of his mouth with the back of his hand and kept on talking. "See, they know your affinities. They know if you'll accept them. If you have no anger, they can't even get ahold of you. But if you do, they move right in."

"We all have anger," Raleigh put in, his voice like velvet. "It's okay to feel anger. It's just important not to act on it in a harmful way."

Craig frowned. "My anger, that's what worries me," he admitted. "I try real hard never to be angry. But it doesn't always work. And they're all around us—

"Oh, puleeze," Sara interrupted. She slapped her palms on the sides of her cheeks and crunched her eyes closed. "You are *so* weird. Do you see any of the rest of us fighting off entities—"

"Yes," he answered simply.

"Sara," Dotty tried. "This is what Craig believes. It's true for him in some way, metaphorically or actually. We can't judge—"

"I can judge," Sara corrected her. "The man's just a nutcase. He probably killed Dr. Hart, and now he's blaming it on entities."

"Sara!" Quinn barked.

Craig shook his head so violently, I was afraid it would scramble his already addled brain. "No," he said. Then, "No!" even louder. "The entities don't control me. And I remember everything I do. They always ask me that at the hospital. And I can always prove I remember what I do. I wouldn't have killed Dr. Hart. Because if I had, I'd remember."

"I believe you," Dotty pronounced.

"So do I," I added.

"Well, you're all as crazy as he is," Sara snapped. "You probably think I did it. Oh, sure. Blame Sara because she's not Ms. Goody Two-shoes. Don't blame the only really crazy person in the room."

"No one has blamed you, Sara," Raleigh told her, but something in his eyes told me he was considering the idea.

"No, but I see the way you're all ready to jump on me. You all think your boring little practices and realizations and modalities are *so* important. And just because I'm not on your level, you treat me like a servant or something. All I want to do is have fun. But no, everyone is *so* serious. So I get the bad rap—"

"*Did* you kill Dr. Hart, Sara?" Ed Lau asked.

"No, I didn't!" she shot back. "Is that clear enough for you? I'm not the bad guy around here. Quinn rolls around crying, and you all feel sorry for him. Well, what about me? I have feelings, too. But you all hate me. Even Dr. Hart got mad at me. First she'd be really cool and nice, and next thing she'd be all over my case—"

"Dr. Hart tried to help you," Quinn broke in. "Maybe she didn't do it perfectly, but she really did care about you."

"Dr. Hart was like that, Sara," Dotty tried next. "She was rough on all of us. That was her style. Remember how she made fun of my cat dying? I hated her at first for it, but I realized later that she was trying to help me come to terms with it. By not sympathizing, she made me face my own emotions alone. I needed to do that. I'm such a wimp about suffering. She made me see that."

"Do you really think she did that for your own good?" Kim asked. She was asking the question sincerely. I could see it in the frown on her open face. "You don't think she was purposefully cruel?"

"No," Dotty answered. "I don't think she was mean on purpose. I think she leaned on our weak points to help us grow. At least I think that might have been why she did what she did. And it's the best way to look at anyway. If her motivations were mixed, why not accept the best one in memory?"

"Yeah," Taj agreed. "It's like forgiving."

"Aw, come on," Judd put in. "Dr. Hart was pulling each and every one of our little chains. If she wasn't trying to be cruel, she was doing an awfully bad job."

"But she believed she was helping people," Quinn insisted. "And she *really* did help some people. She called people on their issues. She made them look at themselves. A lot of people have no idea what they're doing wrong. And they have no one to tell them. Dr. Hart took a risk in challenging people's deep conflicts, but she did it to help them heal."

"Or did she just take the opportunity as a working

healer to let her cruelty roam free?" Fran muttered. "She sure as hell had me freaked out."

"No!" Quinn shouted.

"It's okay, Quinn," Fran assured him, her hand in the air as if in surrender. "I wasn't really accusing Dr. Hart. I was just wondering aloud. I'm sorry about that. Maybe Dotty and Taj are right. Maybe it's time for forgiveness. All I know is that she got to me and pulled all this mean stuff up from me. I hadn't realized I had such meanness in me. Maybe it was good for me. I don't know, that's all."

"She was real," Quinn muttered. "She was a real intuitive, a real healer."

"She *was* intuitive," I commented. My voice seemed so small in that room. I upped my volume. "She could see things that surprised me. Things she couldn't have known about. That was real."

"But what did she do with it?" Judd demanded irritably. He answered himself. "She used her intuitive hunches to get on people's nerves."

"We can't really answer for her motivations," Dotty said. "None of us really knows what went through her mind. But Quinn knew her the best. Why don't we just accept that all that . . . um, stuff she did was for a good reason?"

"Dr. Hart is the only one who isn't controlled by entities," Craig offered. "All the rest of us are. That's why she can see so clearly. Dr. Hart doesn't let the entities get to her—"

"Stop it!" Sara ordered. "I'm not controlled by entities. I'd know it if I was—"

"No, you wouldn't," Craig told her. "How would you know?"

That was a spooky thought. How *would* I know if my feelings were affected by entities? I reminded myself that this was exactly why conspiracy theories worked so well. They couldn't be absolutely disproved. Still, I had to rub my arms to keep the cold away. Craig's ideas made me uncomfortable.

"I'm sensitive enough to know if I'm controlled by entities!" Sara insisted, her voice high with anger, or maybe fear. "Are you really as crazy as you're acting? Or are you just acting like a nutcase so that the police won't suspect you?"

Craig smiled. "You're only mad 'cause I'm right," he mumbled. He looked at the ceiling.

"I am not!" Sara retorted.

"Are, too," Craig muttered smugly.

"You—" Sara began.

"Mr. Zweig," Orson asked, cheerfully interrupting her. "Have you worked with a lot of solvents?"

Craig frowned and shrugged.

"See, it's really interesting," Orson went on. "Your metabolic cascades are all off. If you're seriously allergic to solvents, it'll make you hallucinate. It messes up your leuenkephelin. Or an allergy to meat or wheat will mess up your metenkephelin. And there's your dopamine. It's like really low. Your copper's too high, see. You should take some zinc to balance it out to help with the paranoia. Just to begin with."

Craig looked back up at the ceiling. I think he liked arguing with Sara more than Orson.

"Listen, Mr. Zweig," Orson went on. "It'd be really cool to help you. I brought some zinc with me. Lots of people need it. I'll get it from my room if you want."

Craig just shrugged again. I swiveled my head around to loosen my stiff muscles.

That's when I noticed that we weren't alone. Sergeant DiMarco was in the meeting room, just inside the door. I wondered how long she'd been there, watching us. She smiled my way in a friendly fashion. Abruptly, I remembered Ira.

Nonchalantly, I rose and made my way out of my seat and down the row past Dotty and Taj. Once at the end of the row, I turned and mimed frantically at the sergeant. I pointed to her, to myself, and to the hallway.

She winked and disappeared through the doorway.

I tiptoed from the room. If anyone asked me, I could say I needed a restroom break.

Sergeant DiMarco was just outside of the room when I got there. I could feel the perspiration on my forehead cooling in the hallway. I hadn't even realized I'd been sweating.

"You rang, Ms. Lazar?" the sergeant asked, her voice the perfect butler's.

"Yeah. Tinkle, tinkle," I hissed. "Listen, I think I might have something."

The smile left her face. She made no more jokes.

"What?" she demanded.

"I know you're looking at all the group members to see if they're Dr. Hart's long-lost son. But have you looked at Ira?"

"Ira?" she asked, her brown eyes confused.

"Sara's boyfriend," I reminded her.

"Oh, that Ira," she answered. "You betcha we've looked at Ira. He's a real stinker. He has a rap sheet the length of my arm. But he isn't Dr. Hart's son. His parole officer met with his parents. It's nice when they're on parole. You get cooperation. Ira wasn't adopted. His parents just wish he was. The officer said Ira looks just like his mom. No question. Middle-class parents with a doozy of a son . . ."

"Oh," I said, the adrenaline leaving my body as the sergeant went on about Ira.

"But keep on trying," she finally finished up. She gave me a little pat on the arm. "Web and I certainly appreciate it."

Web? Web? "The chief?"

"Yep," she replied. "Hail to the chief." She laughed. "I'm married to him, you know."

"I know," I whispered, attempting a smile.

Suddenly, a tall, haggard woman walked up to us.

"I'm Carlotta Zweig," the tall woman announced. "I'm here to take my husband home."

Sergeant DiMarco blinked slowly, taking in the situation. When she spoke, she spoke carefully.

"Now, Ms. Zweig," she began. "It's not that simple—"

But before the sergeant could finish her lecture, someone screamed in the meeting room.

"No!" The word could have cracked glass.

There was short silence as the sergeant ran toward the door, then another scream from the room, even louder and higher than the first, "Tell him to stop!"

TWENTY

Carlotta Zweig ran toward the doorway next. I hot-footed it behind her, a heart-pounding third place into the meeting room.

Sara was still screaming when I got there. Sara. I should have guessed.

"It's not true!" she shrieked. Her hands were balled into fists at her side. Even her face seemed balled into a fist. "Dr. Hart is not in this room! Stop saying that!"

"But I see her," Craig was insisting. He looked at the ceiling of the room right over Quinn's and Sara's heads.

No wonder Carlotta Zweig had run so fast. She heard a scream and figured her husband was the cause. Carlotta was one smart woman.

"He's crazy!" Sara kept on, her voice raw but still louder than most opera singers.

"Can't you see her?" Craig asked quietly. "Can't you see the doctor?"

I shivered in spite of all the danger to us among the living. Because I still wasn't sure if Craig did indeed see Dr. Hart's spirit.

Sara ran at Craig, her hands outstretched, long, red fingernails flashing.

Whoa! Sergeant DiMarco and I both sprinted toward the collision, but Carlotta Zweig got there first. Some reflexes! And then I realized how Carlotta must have developed those reflexes. My heart tightened. It had to be a tough job, defending your husband all the time.

"Stop," she told Sara calmly. "Stop it right now."

Sara skidded to a halt, looking up into Carlotta's haggard face.

"But he says—"

"It's true," Craig countered from behind his wife. "Look, you can all see her—"

"Craig," Carlotta ordered. "You stop it, too. Do as I say."

Craig looked down at his feet sullenly, but he kept quiet.

"I'm sorry if my husband upset you," Carlotta apologized in a deep voice. "But you mustn't take him too seriously—"

"But he said Dr. Hart was in the room. He looked right above my head. He's trying to freak me out—"

"I can assure you that Craig is not trying to freak you out," Carlotta explained slowly. "He is only telling you what he sees."

"But—" Sara tried again.

"Let it go, will you?" Quinn begged, his voice tired. "Please?"

"Fine," Sara muttered. "Fine." She walked toward the doorway, turned on her way out to deliver one more comment. "I hope you all kill each other," she said without apparent emotion and finally, she was gone.

Once Sara had left, Carlotta Zweig turned to her husband. Craig looked into his wife's eyes, shifted his view to something above her head briefly, and tried out a lopsided smile on her.

Carlotta just put her face into her hands, closing her eyes for a moment. Then she brought her head back up and placed her hands lightly on Craig's shoulders.

"Honey, we're going to get you home—"

"Can't I stay a little longer?" Craig cajoled. "I'm learning stuff from Dr. Hart."

"Isn't Dr. Hart the one who died?" Carlotta asked the room at large.

"She sure as shootin' is," Sergeant DiMarco answered for all of us.

"But I can still see her—" Craig started in.

"Shush!" Carlotta commanded and placed her finger ever so softly on Craig's lips.

And in that move, I saw Carlotta Zweig's love for her husband. She would always do whatever she could for him. She wouldn't abandon him to the entities. And I felt both admiration and pity for the woman. I thought of Roy and tried not to make any comparisons.

"Ms. Zweig," Sergeant DiMarco spoke up.

Carlotta turned to the sergeant.

"Your husband needs to stay here in Swanton until we figure out how Dr. Hart died," DiMarco told her, trying out her own smile on the woman.

"Is my husband accused of anything?" Carlotta demanded.

"No," the sergeant admitted. She gave up the smile. "But he was a witness, and this is a serious matter. We've requested everyone who was there on the night that Dr. Hart died to stay for the full amount of time they've already reserved for the intensive. We need to settle this. And we need the witnesses to help us."

"My husband is in some distress—" Carlotta began.

"Ma'am," Sergeant DiMarco said quietly. "Your husband would be in a lot more distress if he was locked up in our local jail. And if the chief wasn't a fair man, Mr. Zweig might be locked up. Do you understand what I mean about this being a serious matter?"

Carlotta seemed to deflate. "Yes," she murmured. "I understand. But please try to understand me. Craig isn't violent to others. He only harms himself. I know he's an easy target for accusation, and I'm glad that your chief is fair. I promise you I'll stay with Craig for the rest of his visit here at the lodge. Will that do?"

"That will do just fine, ma'am," the sergeant whispered. "Thank you." And I knew she meant it. I doubted that the chief really had enough of a case to lock Craig Zweig up, fair man or not. And I thought Sergeant DiMarco would make an excellent poker player.

"Craig," Carlotta suggested, turning back to her husband. "Let's go up to your room. You can show me the view."

"Okay," he agreed cheerfully.

Carlotta took Craig's hand in hers in the manner of people long married, and they walked out together.

I turned back to look at those left in the meeting room. The whole intensive group looked as if they were in suspended animation.

Quinn was the first to come back into focus. "Well," he uttered. His voice got stronger. "That was certainly interesting. Does anyone else have anything to offer?"

"Not a thing," Raleigh put in.

"Amen," Fran added softly.

"Okay, let's adjourn for the day," Quinn suggested quickly. "Tomorrow we'll do some more work together. All right?"

People murmured and muttered. It was hard to tell if they were saying yes or no. Then they skedaddled.

The members of the group were very quiet as they made their way to the door to leave. And very fast. I didn't blame them. Each one was probably going to lock themselves into their room and pull the covers over their heads. Or maybe I was projecting a little. Because that was certainly what I wanted to do.

I headed toward the door at the end of the pack. I was almost out when the sergeant spoke to me.

"Ms. Lazar," she said, holding out her hand. "If you'll please remain behind, we can finish our talk."

Our talk? My brain looked for a file that made sense. Hadn't we settled everything in our earlier talk? Ira wasn't Dr. Hart's son. What else did she want from me? I felt a new rush of perspiration. Sergeant DiMarco had out-manipulated Carlotta Zweig. If she wanted anything from me, she'd have no trouble getting it. But I didn't know anything . . . as far as I knew.

"Okay," I mumbled finally. I stepped aside and watched Quinn exit the room, leaving me alone with the sergeant.

"So, what's up?" I asked. I didn't add *besides my pulse rate*.

"Sara Oshima is up," Sergeant DiMarco answered me. "She's beginning to look a little like a suspect. Not that I'm saying she is, but she bears watching, you know what I mean?"

I nodded carefully.

"So, give me your take on Sara," she ordered.

I took a breath and gave her my opinion. "I already told the chief what I thought. I think Sara really cared for Dr. Hart. I think Dr. Hart was a real mother figure for Sara. I think that's what's behind Sara's weird behavior now. She's expressing grief and betrayal and anger over the doctor's death. In her own way. I know it's's not endearing. But I still don't think she killed Dr. Hart."

"Or maybe she's guilty," the sergeant tossed in casually. "We see it all the time. So-and-so loves their spouse, their father, their dog. But so-and-so also hates the same individual. So they kill them. Happens all the time. Love is no barrier to murder. Sometimes, it's the reason."

"But why would Sara—"

"Why?" The sergeant laughed. "Money, for one. Her love/hate deal for another. Or maybe the good doctor was blackmailing her about her drug habit." She paused for a moment and went on. "If you killed someone, and someone else said they saw their ghost in the room, would you flip out?"

"Maybe."

"Well, that's exactly what Sara did. And I didn't see anyone else flipping out."

"Maybe she's just dealing with her loss," I tried.

"Or maybe she's afraid the ghost of Dr. Hart is gonna tell who killed her," Sergeant DiMarco countered.

I thought about it. I was getting tired of defending Sara. But still . . .

"I came in today to watch her myself," the sergeant went on. "Web said he'd heard she was acting really weird. I'd say he was right. I know we're not supposed to say *crazy* these days, but whatever it's called, Sara looks as screwy as Craig Zweig to me. And she's meaner. They're the one's you gotta watch. The mean ones."

I found myself nodding. I hadn't meant to. But Sara *was* mean. There was no denying it. Still, she had a soft side, too. I'd seen it. She was hurting.

I tried to put those thoughts together and express them, but the sergeant was too fast for me.

"Sara also put Dr. Hart into the aura maker," the sergeant added. "She should have noticed if something was wrong with it. She was the last person to touch it."

"What *was* wrong with it?" I asked, trying to remember what Kapp had said.

"Good try," the sergeant commended me. "But that little fact's gotta be confidential. When we get the murderer, we'll know for sure if they can tell us exactly how they rigged it. So, back to Sara." The sergeant raised a closed hand. Her index finger popped out. "First, we've got opportunity, in spades." Her middle finger shot up. "Second, we've got a ruthless temperament. And motive?" Her whole hand opened. "Just take your pick on motive."

"But—"

"Could we be right?" she asked me, her voice quiet and serious.

I swallowed. I didn't want to be responsible for answering that question.

"Maybe," I mumbled. "But I don't—"

"Would you talk to her for us tomorrow?" she asked next.

"Me!" I yelped. "Why me?"

"Look, Cally, if she's the killer, she's dangerous. To you, to everyone," the sergeant explained. "We'll make sure you're watched when you talk to her. But I think she's ready to break. I want to hear what she says when she does. Because she may confess."

"And if she still says she didn't kill Dr. Hart?" I asked.

The sergeant smiled. "That would mean that we've got less pointing to her. You could be doing her a favor."

It was the last bit that really convinced me.

"Okay, I'll talk to her," I agreed.

"All right!" Sergeant DiMarco held out her hand to be shaken. I shook it and shook my head at the same time. Would I ever learn to say no?

"Did you talk this over with the chief?" I probed, curious.

"Yep," the sergeant answered. She looked into my eyes with her big dark ones. "Cally, I love Web. I know we're the town joke, but I love him. I always have. Oh, he's a man, all right. He gets pushy sometimes. But he's a good man. And he loves me, too." She laughed again. "Anyway, if he didn't have me to keep him civil, he'd just get someone else. Tell you a secret though. He's actually shy."

Shy? Aggressive as a cover up for extreme shyness? Actually, it made some sense to me.

"We'll talk to you tomorrow, okay, set up the details," Sergeant DiMarco told me. And with that, she saluted me, turned, and walked out of the meeting room.

I got to lie in my bed with the covers pulled over my face for a while anyway. It was nice in there, smelling of laundry detergent and something that might have been cedar. And it was dark. And best of all, it was quiet. For a while. The inevitable knock on my door came all too soon. I opened it carefully.

The whole gang was there. Kapp. My sisters, Geneva and Melinda. My brother, York.

"Where's Arnot?" I asked, looking for my other brother.

"His kids," York answered brusquely. "Basketball game."

"We found a fabulous place for dinner," Geneva told me and held out a hand. I took it and was in the back of York's Subaru, sandwiched between my sisters, as he speeded toward Sparky's Diner before I had time to think, much less change my clothes or brush my teeth.

Sparky's might or might not have been fabulous, but its decor certainly sparkled. Bright, classic, cartoon blow-ups graced the walls along with 3-D Mona Lisas, Blue Boys, and Whistler's Mothers. The tables glowed in spray-painted silver and the chairs were artificially golden. And everything smelled of onion and garlic. That was a good sign.

When we were seated and got our menus, I saw why we were there. The food wasn't exclusively vegetarian, but there was plenty for York to choose from. After a lot of wrangling, York chose the vegetarian focaccia, refusing to share with the rest of us. The rest of us decided to split a Caesar salad for four, portabella mushroom and spinach dumplings with the Asian dipping sauce, and a giant five-cheese and garlic pizza with eggplant, shitake mushrooms, basil, and green onions.

We had finally ordered when I saw Quinn Vogel and Sara Oshima walk in together. I felt myself blushing with shame as I looked at my unsuspecting victim. Sara didn't seem to be angry, but her eyes were red. So were Quinn's for that matter.

"What?" Geneva asked quietly. She could always tell when I felt guilty.

I whispered out my tale of Sara's behavior and my promise to talk to her for the sergeant the next day.

"Good job, Lazar," Kapp congratulated me. "You're in the loop."

"Kapp!" Geneva hissed.

"Holy Mother, now what?" Kapp demanded. "Let her do her job."

"My sister is a healer, not an investigator," York threw in.

I looked over at the table that Sara and Quinn had taken. It was sparkling, but they weren't. Sara's head was leaned forward and Quinn's expression was pained. At least they weren't secretly happy. That would have really made me suspicious. Sara shook her finger in Quinn's face and he shrank back.

"How come he puts up with her?" Melinda whispered.

"Quinn's lost," York answered. "I'll bet he needs Sara as much as she needs him. Especially with the doctor gone. He's all alone now."

Bingo. York was right. How could I have missed that?

Kim and Dotty came through the door.

"Ho, ho, ho," Kapp rumbled. "The plot thickens."

Kim and Dotty looked as dour as Sara and Quinn. Especially Kim. I tried to remember if I'd ever seen her smile.

Our portabella and spinach dumplings arrived a minute after Dotty and Kim. Eight steaming morsels on a bright blue plate. I grabbed one and dunked it in the soy-ginger dipping sauce. One bite was enough. This place *was* fabulous.

"We've been discussing your mystery," Geneva announced after she'd finished her first dumpling. "We want to help get you out of this hellhole."

"Except for Kapp, who thinks it's fun for Cally to risk her life," York added.

"Lazar!" Kapp yelped, spitting dumpling. I didn't know if he was addressing me or York, or possibly even Geneva who was treating him to her full-force "explain yourself or you'll be sorry" glare.

"I think someone as powerful as Dr. Hart could really

hurt someone sensitive," Melinda offered, her elfish face somber. "She sounds as mean as a lizard to me. I think someone got her back for it."

"But who?" I asked.

"How about Dotty?" Melinda whispered, gesturing Dotty's way with her bony shoulder. "I heard how the doctor made fun of her cat dying."

"No, it's Ed Lau," Kapp argued.

"Ed Lau?"

"Hooboy, that Lau guy is wound tighter than a digital watch."

"You're not supposed to wind a digital watch, are you?" I asked. "Aren't they on batteries or something—"

"That's the point, Lazar," Kapp grumbled and went on. "See, Lau was a science teacher. He dabbled in tai chi, chi gung, and Hawaiian healing. He really got into the Hawaiian healing. Then his wife got cancer and died. He couldn't do a damn thing to save her. He blamed himself. He's mostly Chinese ancestry, only an eighth Hawaiian. So he got this goofy idea into his head that he was impure or something. His wife had been full-blooded Hawaiian. The guy thought he stepped on sacred ground and messed it all up. He thought he caused her death. So now, he just does the chi gung, because of his Chinese ancestry—"

"How can you possibly know all this?" I couldn't help but asking.

"Easy." Kapp grinned. "Dee-Dee has a friend who knows him. Informants everywhere. Heh, heh."

"How does all of that even hope to make a murder motive for the poor man?" Geneva demanded, her nostrils flaring.

"'Cause the dead doctor made fun of him, of all this stuff he thinks is sacred—"

I didn't hear the rest of what Kapp had to say because Taj and Raleigh walked in. My eyes followed them for a moment.

"That's enough!" Sara shouted from her table with Quinn and flung her napkin on the floor. "I am so outta here!"

She left the restaurant like she'd left the meeting room earlier. Sara may not have been good on entrances, but she knew how to make an exit that no one could miss.

I looked back at Raleigh and Taj. They were both watching Sara in silence. Raleigh turned and met my eyes. He nodded my way.

"Now there's an attractive man," Geneva purred from beside me. She stabbed another dumpling and brought it directly to her mouth. "Roy better come on home soon."

"What the hell are you talking about?" Kapp demanded.

"That divine man over there," Geneva informed him. "The one that does the musical resonance."

"Well, I don't see why you think he's so damned attractive," Kapp sputtered.

"Cally does," Geneva said, smiling smugly.

Dack! How did Geneva always do this to me? I told myself to stay calm.

"Roy's coming back very soon," I assured her. "Roy, remember? The man I love."

"Have you told him the truth?" Geneva asked.

TWENTY-ONE

What truth did Geneva expect me to tell Roy? Was I supposed to tell him about my crush on Raleigh? About Dr. Hart's murder? Or maybe about my agreement to grill a suspect?

I pulled my gaze away from Geneva's and speared another dumpling. I couldn't argue with Geneva. I'd keep my mouth shut this time. Or at least keep it stuffed with food. That was a good thought. The Caesar salad came after the dumplings, and I kept my mouth full and chomping romaine and feather-thin slices of parmesan cheese while Kapp and Geneva wrangled.

"Kapp, Kapp," Geneva lectured him. "Sometimes you can be such a fool. You suspect everyone because of their little secrets, but you don't look at temperament. That young woman who just stomped out of here looks like she's more temperamentally suited for murder than Ed Lau. Ed Lau is a healer—"

"Mother of God, they're all healers!" Kapp defended himself. "There are five of them still in this room. You're looking at their outward personas, not their real selves—"

"Okay," Geneva hissed. She looked around the room, and nodded ever so slightly toward Kim Welch. "Are you trying to tell me that a limp dishrag like her could kill someone?"

"Hooboy, that woman's a psychiatrist," Kapp hissed back. "You think she can't fake a case of depression? Hell, I've seen smiling ten-year-olds who were murderers. You'd probably take them home. The best psychopaths are charming. Look at Ted Bundy—"

"Or the music man," Melinda suggested, giggling, her eyes on Raleigh. "I'll bet he's a charmer."

I coughed, but kept on chewing. That was a nasty thought. Raleigh *was* charming. Could there be such a thing as too charming? Quinn paid his bill and left as the conversation continued on its ugly path.

"Even in a psychopath, I'll bet something shows," Geneva argued, "as long as you're sensitive enough to pick it up." She smiled as if to imply that Kapp lacked the necessary sensitivity to judge psychopathology.

Kapp just smiled back. "Okey-dokey," he said cheerfully. "Why don't you tell me who's a psychopath?" He paused to fork in some more salad. "And once you've figured that out, tell me who the murderer is. And remember this, they might not be the same person. Not all murderers are psychopaths. Hah! Some are crazy. Some are angry. Some are addled by drugs or alcohol. The list goes on and on."

Geneva flared her nostrils, ready to scorch Kapp with her reply, but our pizza came before she could, along with York's focaccia.

I took my last bite of salad and reached for a slice of pizza, sticking to my stuffed-mouth policy.

Everyone ate in silence for a while. It was worth it. The garlic, basil, and green onion were perfect complements to the veggies and the five cheeses of the pizza. And York seemed satisfied with his focaccia. But it was York who finally spoke up as the rest of us crammed dough and toppings into our mouths.

"Taj," he whispered. "I think Taj is a psychopath."

"Okay, you're on," Kapp challenged, his voice thick through the pizza. "What's your evidence?"

York flushed. "He's a phony. You said everyone was a healer, but how does talking about someone's past life heal them? Where's the integrity of his practice?"

"I think he's for real—" I began, and stopped. I wasn't talking; I was eating. I'd almost forgotten. But it was all right. No one noticed me anyway.

"So you think a phony and a psychopath are the same thing?" Kapp demanded of York.

York considered this seriously. "I suppose there are degrees," he pronounced finally.

"You betcha, there are degrees. I, for one, can stand up and polish a jury 'till they think my word is gold, but I've never murdered anyone. I've never bilked anyone out of money. I've never—"

"You've lied," Geneva put in.

"The hell I have!" Kapp shot back. "A good attorney never lies. You just don't use undue pressure on your client to tell you the truth if they've got a pretty good story working. Hey, sometimes they're telling the truth in the first place!"

Melinda giggled. Even Geneva hid a smile behind her napkin. York was not amused. Yep, there were definitely degrees of deception.

As we divided the bill and paid it, Dotty and Kim walked out of Sparky's.

We all stood up together. I had my arm around Melinda, when Raleigh and Taj walked up behind us.

"Is this your family, Cally?" Raleigh asked.

I swiveled around, momentarily caught off guard. "Oh, sure," I sputtered. "My sisters, Geneva and Melinda. My brother York. And my friend Kapp."

"It's good to meet you all," Raleigh murmured, his voice low and slow.

"And it's fabulous to meet you," Geneva offered as she reached out her hand.

Raleigh shook Geneva's hand as slowly and smoothly as he spoke. Kapp's face pinkened. York glared at Taj.

Raleigh finally released Geneva's hand, wished us all a good night, and turned to leave with Taj in his wake.

We, too, exited Sparky's Diner and were in York's Subaru, driving back to the lodge.

I finally opened my mouth to speak. I couldn't even remember what I'd been about to say.

Because it was at that moment that we heard the explosion. There was no doubting the sound. Then we saw the flare of flame at least a block over.

"Was that the Boy Scout Hall?" I asked, trying to calculate our relative position. I thought the word *bomb*, but didn't speak it.

"Let's go and see," Kapp suggested eagerly.

"No," York replied quietly, hands tight on the steering wheel.

We were all silent for the rest of the drive back to the lodge. Even Kapp didn't say a word. Maybe he was remembering that he was in a car with four siblings whose parents had died in an explosion. Or maybe it was just the forbidding look on Geneva's face.

York walked me into the lobby of the Swanton Hills Lodge. Half of the intensive members were gathered there, along with Heidi and Bob Jinnah. The only ones I didn't see were Taj, Raleigh, Craig, and Ed. And Sara.

"Do either of you know what that explosion was?" Quinn demanded as York and I came toward the group. He looked shaken, his short hair dishevelled as he ran his hand through it frantically.

We shook our heads.

"Someone must know," Kim said in a small, trembling voice.

"We could call the police," Judd suggested.

The phone rang at the Jinnah's desk. Heidi picked it up after one ring. Everyone watched her as she spoke.

"Swanton Hills—" she began, and stopped. "Yeah, we heard it." She paused and put her hand on her heart. "Oh, God. I don't know. Where are the police?" She paused again. "Thanks for letting me know, Innis. Love to Lisa."

When Heidi looked up and saw her silent audience, she reached for Bob's hand. His hand joined hers, his face vaguely troubled. I wondered how much he understood of what was happening.

"That was a friend of mine," Heidi explained. "The explosion was Dr. Hart's car. The police are there now."

"Was there anyone in it?" Fran asked quietly.

Heidi paused, then spoke very fast. "My friend said she thinks the police are looking for a body, but she's not sure."

"Maybe the car exploded when someone started it," Judd thought aloud.

"You mean someone else got killed?" Orson asked, his voice a thirteen-year-old's despite all his knowledge, a frightened thirteen-year-old's.

"Oh, no!" Kim cried. She shook her head, her voice fading. "No," she whispered. Her eyes lost focus.

Dotty put her arm around the smaller woman and led her to a couch.

"Sara," Quinn announced. His face was as pale as it was long. "She walked out at dinner tonight. She wanted to go after her boyfriend, Ira. She wanted to use Aurora's car, the Mercedes. I told her she couldn't, but she told me she always drove it anyway. I thought she wouldn't use it, but . . ." He swiveled his head and looked around the lobby as if hoping to see his assistant in the space.

"Call Sara's room," Fran ordered.

Heidi nodded and dialed the phone. After a while, she hung up. "No answer," she reported.

"That doesn't necessarily mean that Sara was in the car," Bob Jinnah spoke up unexpectedly. He *did* understand. "She could be any number of places. And it's probably standard police procedure to search for a body. It doesn't necessarily mean there is one."

"Yeah," Heidi concurred after a moment. "Bob is right. We don't really know anything yet. It's hard to wait, but that's all we can do. I'm sure the police will visit soon."

"But—" Judd began.

"Let it go," Fran whispered, nodding at Quinn whose twitching body looked close to collapse.

"I'm taking Kim to her room," Dotty announced, and the group began to break up.

I looked around for York, but he was gone. And I'd never seen him go.

I walked to my room slowly. For all of Bob Jinnah's positive logic, I felt in my bones that someone was dead in that car. If Craig had been around, I would have asked him to search for a new spirit.

I opened my door and stuck my cane in the room automatically, checking for intruders near the door. I entered carefully.

There were no intruders near the door, but two men stood at the end of my bed. York and another man, small and lean with red hair and intense golden eyes. I blinked. It was Roy!

"Cally, darlin'," he drawled and reached out his hand in my direction.

"Roy," I said softly, reaching out my own hand. I felt a flood of warmth enter my icy body. Roy was here.

"See you tomorrow," York muttered. "I let Roy in your room. I hope that's okay."

"More than okay," I breathed.

"Right," York concluded, and he left the room, closing the door gently behind him.

"Oh, Roy," I whispered, crossing the room and wrapping my arms around him. Then I just held him to me, feeling his familiar form and heat and scent. "You came back."

"I knew you were in trouble, Cally," he told me.

I stepped away from him. Roy usually avoided me when I was in trouble. He thought because he saw darkness near me that he was the *cause* of my troubles. But here he was.

"Why did you—" I began.

"As sad as it is that you've had to face such an awful thing, I am truly glad to know that it wasn't my darkness that brought it to you," he explained slowly. He looked into my eyes. "My mama set me straight on things, Cally. She reminded me that I was in Kentucky when this woman died. I wasn't with you. I still see the darkness swirling from me to you just as clearly as before, but that doesn't change the fact that your troubles started while I was back home. They're not happening because I'm near you. I'm just sorry it's taken me so long to believe you, darlin'."

I put my arms around him again. I didn't tell him that a second death might have just occurred, maybe about the time that he'd arrived in Swanton. I just held him and murmured my thanks and love and . . . I felt his soft kiss on my lips, and I even stopped murmuring.

We were doing a slow, timeless dance with our lips locked in place when a knock on the door interrupted the music we'd imagined.

"This is the police!" a voice shouted. "Open up in there."

I let go of Roy and opened up. Both Chief Phlug and Sergeant DiMarco were at the door. I stared at them, my fantasy self still with Roy, sensuality tingling through my body. And I remembered that these two were married. Chief Phlug glared at me as Sergeant DiMarco smiled. He was shy, I remembered, too.

"You were out earlier this evening," the chief started in. He didn't seem shy as he thrust his face toward mine, his breath strong with mint and garlic. "Did you go to the Boy Scout Hall?"

My fantasy self collided with my real life body, and I wasn't tingling with sensuality anymore. I was heavy with dread.

"No," I replied softly. "I was out with my family. Oh, and with Kapp. We heard the explosion when we were riding back from the restaurant. We even saw the flames. But we weren't on the same block as—"

"Explosion?" Roy interrupted, his golden eyes narrowed in confusion.

Phlug turned on Roy. "Who the heck are you?" he demanded. No, not shy at all.

"This is my boyfriend, Roy Beaumont," I briefly introduced the love of my life.

"Well, what's he doing here?" the chief probed. "Aren't there enough people here already?"

"Now, Web," Sergeant DiMarco put in. She put her hand on her husband's shoulder.

"No, I mean it," the chief kept on angrily, shaking off his wife's hand. "I got suspects. I got her family and her know-it-all lawyer friend. I got dead people—"

"Dead people, plural?" I asked quickly, my heart jumping. "Who was in the car?"

"Never you mind, little lady!" Chief Phlug reprimanded me, shaking his finger in my face. "You're not gonna jerk me around. And how'd you know about the car anyway?"

"I was in the lobby," I told him, keeping my voice as calm as I wasn't. "People were talking. They said it was Dr. Hart's car that exploded. Quinn was afraid Sara might have been in the car. Was she?"

Chief Phlug didn't answer me right away. I could tell he was thinking about it, though.

"Now, Cally," Sergeant DiMarco intervened sweetly. "You know we can't tell you everything we've found out."

I had a very unhealerlike urge to slap the sergeant. Because I'd almost gotten the truth out of the chief.

"What happened here tonight?" Roy asked, his voice grave.

"None of your business, boy!" the chief snapped. "If

we're not telling Cally here, do you really think we're going to tell you?"

"But what if Cally's in danger?" he pressed.

"Do you think Cally *is* in danger, Mr. Beaumont?" Sergeant DiMarco asked. There was an insinuation in her question. But I wasn't sure what she was insinuating. Nor was Roy.

Roy cocked his head as he tried to process the sergeant's question.

"People are dyin'," he finally answered. "Yes, ma'am, I believe Cally might be in danger."

"So when did *you* get into town?" the chief finally thought to ask Roy.

"This evening, sir," he answered politely. "I've been in Kentucky with my family."

The chief just glared at him.

Roy reached in his pocket. "Would you like to see my boarding pass stubs?"

"Naah," the chief refused, waving Roy away with his hand. I'm sure he would have liked to have erased Roy at that point. But he couldn't.

"I'd like a look at them," Sergeant DiMarco piped up and put out her hand.

"Okay, Laura," Chief Phlug spit out, turning his glare on his wife. "You look at this guy's airplane stubs, and I'll question the suspect. That all right with you?"

"Just fine," the sergeant replied with a wink my way that seemed to say, "Isn't he cute?" Only, the chief wasn't cute. Roy fished a couple of paper rectangles out of his pocket and handed them to the sergeant.

Chief Phlug shook his head and turned his glare back on me.

"Okay, Ms. Lazar," he began. "You seem to know a lot more than you should anyway. Have you seen anyone near Dr. Hart's car lately?"

"No," I answered. But then I changed my mind. "Well, I saw Kim Welch that day. She was walking near the car and your officers harassed her—"

"My officers don't harass people, *Ms.* Lazar. They just escorted Ms. Welch away from the crime scene. Anyway, I've asked Officer Jones all about that. He said she never got close enough to the car to even touch it, much less tamper with it. We've had the whole area under guard, off and on, pretty much since the night Dr. Hart died. I just wish there'd been someone there this evening." The chief scowled. "But my officers have to eat like everyone else."

I tried to think if I'd seen anyone else near the car but couldn't think of anyone. I turned to Roy, as if he might have the answers I didn't.

"Don't you look at your boyfriend, Ms. Lazar!" Chief Phlug ordered. "I don't even know what he's doing here in your room. And I'm asking *you* the questions."

"Now, Web," Sergeant DiMarco put in again. "Can't you see that Cally needs a little support. Don't you remember courting?"

The chief blushed to the roots of his cropped hair. He *was* shy. At least about some things. And Sergeant DiMarco liked to tease him. I wondered if she was the passive-aggressive to his full-court aggressive.

"May I ask a question?" Roy put in.

"Sure thing," DiMarco answered him cheerfully.

"Is there any problem with my staying here with Cally? If there's any possibility she's in danger, I want to be with her."

I closed my eyes, savoring the words. Roy wanted to stay with me.

"You can do what you darn well please," Chief Phlug shot back. "It's a free country. If I had my way, I'd put the whole lot of these so-called healers in jail, then you could decide if you wanted to stay with your precious girlfriend—"

"Web," Sergeant DiMarco warned. Her voice was serious. His words weren't cute anymore, even to her. They could get him in trouble. And only Sergeant DiMarco seemed to know it.

"Darn it, Laura," the chief complained. "I put my cards on the table. I work hard. Why can't I have an opinion like anyone else?"

"Everyone here respects you, Web," the sergeant told him. "I think we've asked all we need to of these good people. It's time to leave."

The chief threw his hands up in the air and turned on his cowboy-booted heel, heading toward the door. Sergeant DiMarco followed him. Before they got out the door though, I asked one last question.

"Aren't you going to arrange for me to talk to Sara Oshima tomorrow?"

TWENTY-TWO

When Chief Phlug turned back to me, I was afraid I'd gone too far. Really afraid. His face was red and straining with anger. His hand was on the butt of his gun, clasping and unclasping. And his eyes had disappeared into a squint that was aimed in my direction. I'd hoped to recognize a murderer's aura, and what I was seeing looked like one . . . but it shouldn't have been coming from the investigating police chief. Orange flames rolled off Phlug's tense body, screaming rage, murderous rage.

If he was trying to scare me, it was working. I tried to take a deep breath and found that I couldn't. My lungs didn't seem to be working. I breathed through my nose instead, fast and shallow.

"Are you trying to be funny, Ms. Lazar?" the chief asked, his voice too quiet for his body and his energy.

"No, Sergeant DiMarco and I had discussed my speaking to Sara—"

"I know what you and the sergeant talked about." His voice was growing louder. "I don't have to earn your respect. You have to earn mine, understand? I'm the one that can put you in jail—"

"For what, Web?" Sergeant DiMarco interjected gently. "For having a smart mouth?"

"Shut up, Laura," he ordered without turning away from me. "I mean it. If you know something you're not telling me, I can pop you in jail for obstruction of justice. And your boyfriend here, too. If something happens to you two while you're in there, well hey, we can't be on top of everything. I'm not the fool you think I am. If you know something, you'd better tell me now!" He jutted his head forward with the last "now."

Roy stepped forward in front of me. I felt his hand on mine. Roy. I just hoped the chief wouldn't shoot the both of us. It didn't seem like a frivolous idea at that moment.

"I don't know anything I haven't told you," I replied. I barely had the voice to speak. My words came out in a whisper.

"She's just fishing, that's all," the sergeant cajoled, sounding almost as afraid as I felt.

Suddenly, I realized that for all the kidding, Sergeant DiMarco couldn't control her husband's anger. I sensed this as clearly as if she'd told me in words. And I felt something else, too. She was warning me to do the right thing, to say the right things. I thought about the chief. What *were* the right things to say to him?

"Sir—" Roy began.

No! Not Roy. I squeezed his hand hard.

"Chief Phlug," I began, still breathing desperately through my nose. "I want to do everything I can to help you solve Dr. Hart's murder. I know how difficult a time you must be having. I'm sorry if I've said anything that I shouldn't have. I respect you and the hard work you do. You're doing a good job. I wouldn't interfere. I may have been out of line, but I was just trying to help."

The chief began to relax, his hand dropping away from his gun. And Sergeant DiMarco relaxed next to him. My lungs opened up, and I filled them gratefully. It was good to be alive and breathing.

"Just as long as we understand each other, Ms. Lazar," Phlug stated coldly, "everything will be fine. You keep me informed." He slowly pulled his head back, keeping his eyes on me.

"I'll do that," I promised as he and DiMarco turned to the door for the second time and finally left my room.

Once the door shut behind them, I turned to Roy and grabbed him, pulling him to me, and holding on while my body shook. It was good being in the field of his calm presence.

"Thank you," I finally whispered, to Roy, to whatever goodness had protected me, even to the chief and his sergeant.

"Cally?" Roy questioned softly as I drew back from his embrace. "Are you all right now?"

I nodded, but not very convincingly.

"Is the chief truly insane?" he asked, tilting his head.

"I . . . I don't know. But he was out of control. Did you feel it, too?"

"I surely did." Roy exhaled. "I thought the man was going to shoot us right then and there."

"Oh, Roy!" I put my arms around him again.

"There, there, Cally. I'm so sorry I couldn't help. I simply didn't know what to do."

"Roy, you were just right," I assured him. "Anything you could have done or said would have just angered him more."

"And now he's gone," Roy commented. He squatted a little so that he was looking straight into my eyes. "But the chief's not all that's fretting you, is it darlin'?"

"There was an explosion," I breathed. I felt tears in my eyes. "My parents died in an explosion. And I think someone died in this explosion tonight, too."

"This Sara Oshima, the one you talked about?" Roy

prodded ever so quietly, standing again and holding me tight.

"Maybe. I'm not sure. But someone died."

"And it happened this evening—" Roy began slowly.

I reached up and laid my finger on his lips like I'd seen Craig's wife lay her finger on Craig's lips.

"It had nothing to do with you," I assured him. "Remember what your mama told you. My troubles started while you were in Kentucky."

"But—"

"No, Roy," I cut him off. "There's no going back now. You're here. I need you. Don't leave me."

I pressed my lips to his, and we were dancing again. The music lasted into infinity.

Wednesday morning, I woke up with Roy spooned against my back, and it was as if the earlier night's events hadn't ever happened. I turned over to look at him. The sun filtered in through the curtains and haloed Roy's reddish-brown hair. In his sleep, his thin features were rounded, soft like a child's. I sighed and moved to step from the bed.

Roy murmured words I couldn't make out. He was sound asleep. I wondered how much sleep he'd had lately. He was usually up before me. I decided to let him sleep while I found out what was going on downstairs. By then, someone *had* to have the straight story on who, if anyone, had been hurt or killed in the explosion. I was feeling reasonable, no longer fatalistic. Maybe no one had been hurt.

I took a shower and dressed, and Roy was still asleep.

"Roy?" I whispered.

He didn't move.

I got a piece of Swanton Hills Lodge stationary and wrote him a quick note, telling him I'd be downstairs. I put it on my pillow and started to leave the room. But I turned back and added another paragraph. I didn't want this man to forget how much I loved him.

Finally, I left the room and headed down to the lobby.

On the way, an unsettling thought occurred to me. What if Quinn wanted to hold a morning session as usual? I looked at my watch. It was a little after nine. I straightened my shoulders. No one could make me go to another intensive session. No one.

When I got to the lobby, however, I realized there would be no morning session. Chaos reigned.

"No!" Dotty was screaming. "They can't make us stay. It's too hard!"

"But Ms. Booth," Bob Jinnah tried, standing in the middle of the crowd like a ship's steward in charge of handing out insufficient life preservers. "The chief said just another day or so. Closure, you need closure. Blake would say—"

"I don't care about Blake!" Dotty shouted. "Two deaths! I can't handle this emotionally. I just can't. I take care of people. I make them feel better. I don't watch them die."

"Two deaths?" I demanded. My body began to tremble. So much for reason. Back to fatalism.

"Sara Oshima died," Heidi Jinnah offered softly. She stood by Bob's side, her limp, blonde hair unwashed, her face clear of makeup. "She was in the car last night when it exploded. We . . . we're not sure what we can do. It's a terrible thing."

I looked around the room quickly for Quinn. He was on a sofa across from Kim Welch. They both could have been carved from the same slab of marble. Eyes open and unfocused, features slack. Criminy.

I turned to go to Quinn. Poor Quinn. Melinda had said it. He put up with Sara because she was his only friend left. And now, she was gone, too.

"Cally," a low voice stopped me. Raleigh reached out for my hand. "Don't tell me you want to leave with the rest of them."

"Leave?" I repeated, pulling my hand back with some effort.

"Of course she wants to leave," Dotty put in. She pulled out a tissue and blew her nose. Shreds of sandalwood-scented tissue floated down onto her large bosom. "It was bad enough when the doctor died, but Sara was so young. It isn't fair. I can't stand any more suffering. What if Cally is the next victim? How can you even ask her to stay?"

My mind embraced the idea of leaving Swanton. Going home would be good. But then what? At least I had Roy with me. I looked straight up into Raleigh's face. He was no longer an attractive nuisance. His skin was gray, his eyes circled with worry.

"Are you okay?" I asked. Would this shock drive him back to drugs?

He shook his head. "No, not nearly okay. That young woman shouldn't have died. We have to find out who killed her. I can't help but feeling that we should have done something more—"

"*We?*" Taj interrupted. "The *police* have to find out who killed her. Not us. This isn't fun! This isn't a game. This is scary. I want to go home."

"Well, I *am* going home," Fran put in bluntly. Her usually shiny black hair had lost its sheen today. "They can threaten all they want, but they can't keep us here. Take my advice. Just as long as we let them know where we live, that should be enough. They can always find us at home if they need us."

"In Hawaii?" Ed Lau asked. His voice held resigned humor. And he looked serene. I thought of Kapp's accusations. No, not Ed. With chaos surrounding him, Ed was serene. I snuck a look at his aura. Yes, truly serene, though sad.

"Will you stay?" I asked Ed. I felt that I could trust Ed's answer. He was rooted while others were flailing.

"Yes," Ed replied. "I feel much as Raleigh does. We knew these people. We have some responsibility to help the police. It would be dishonest to pretend otherwise."

"But it's not our responsibility!" Taj insisted, his voice

high with tension. Dark rings of sweat circled the neck and armpits of his black T-shirt. "And we might get killed. Who knows who's next. Do you think Sara thought she was going to die? Huh? Do you think she *knew*? I went out with Sara. She just wanted to have a little fun. And now she's dead. Dotty's right. Who's next?"

Judd and Orson trotted up to enter our tangle of people.

"Are you all abandoning ship?" Judd demanded, his brows low and fierce. He didn't wait for an answer but went on. "Because I'm going to stay and see this thing through. Gotta fight for what's right, you know. Orson's going back with his mom as soon as I can get ahold of her."

"But Dad," Orson objected. "Who's gonna protect you? The two of us are a team—"

"Hey, kid," Judd answered, almost gently. "You're the best partner a man could have, but you're way too valuable to stay here. Whoa! You're the most valuable player, ya know."

"But—" Orson began again. His eyes were glistening with what might have been tears.

"Listen to your dad, kid," Fran cut in. "I'll keep an eye out for him. Don't you worry about your father."

"You said you were leaving!" Taj insisted. "Why are you changing your mind now?"

Fran shrugged her shoulders. "Hey, Judd's got a point about fighting—".

"You're all crazy!" Taj shouted. He slapped his hands over his ears. I winced as he did. That must have hurt, especially with the earring. Then he shook his hands at the rest of us. "What's the matter with you all?"

"Taj is right," Dotty backed him up. "We don't want anyone else to be hurt. We . . . we . . ." Dotty brought her shredded tissue to her face again and cried into it, her words muffled as she continued. "I don't want to leave. I don't want to be a coward. But this isn't a fight. We aren't doing any good here. I . . . I . . ."

"Come on, Dotty," Fran urged quietly. "Find your strength. You're a stronger woman than this."

Fran must have known the magic words, because Dotty did seem to find her strength.

Slowly, she straightened her head and tucked what was left of her tissue back into her pocket. "I apologize. I know I'm too emotional. I just want everyone to be okay."

"Come on, Dotty," Fran suggested. "You don't need to apologize. You need to take a load off." She led Dotty to a chair and sat down next to her to talk quietly.

I let out a little breath and turned back to Raleigh.

But Taj hadn't found his strength yet.

"You guys are all afraid of the police, aren't you?" he accused. "That's why you're afraid to leave."

I saw Chief Phlug and Officer Jones walking toward us before Taj did. I looked over Taj's shoulder pointedly, rolling my eyes, trying to warn him, but Mr. Tall, Dark, and Handsome was on a theatrical roll.

"Are you more afraid of that hick police chief or whoever is murdering everyone?" he went on. "I mean, what can Phlug do to us? I'm done with the rest of you." He threw up his hands. "*Finito!* I tried to get you guys to be reasonable, but I've had it. I'm packing and leaving now!"

Taj turned dramatically, arms still upraised, and walked right into Chief Phlug.

"You!" Phlug ordered, pushing Taj away. "You stay right there. Officer Jones, watch this man."

"Yes, sir!" Officer Jones replied, narrowing his eyes in Taj's direction.

"Listen, Chief," Taj tried, but Phlug wasn't having any of it.

"I wanna talk to you, boy," he growled. "But first I have to ask the group of you if anyone's seen Craig Zweig and his wife."

No one answered him. Most of us looked around the

room, as if maybe we'd just spot Craig on the rug or on an end table or something.

"I'll call his room," Heidi Jinnah offered.

"I just came from his room," the chief told her. "He's not there."

"There's your murderer!" Judd Nyman announced. "Craig Zweig's a full-fledged lunatic, and he's never there when you're looking for him. How come you haven't taken him in for questioning?"

"You trying to tell me how to do my job?" Chief Phlug asked.

Anyone but Judd would have recognized the chief's question as rhetorical and backed down.

"Well, you seem to need some help, right?" Judd bull-dozed along. "You don't know who did it, and you're not doing a damn thing that I can see to find out."

Officer Jones winced. Bob Jinnah scuttled toward the lobby doors. Was he running away? Whatever he was doing, the chief didn't seem to notice. He was too focused on Judd.

"Are you cursing at me, Mr. Nyman?" the chief asked.

Judd looked confused. "Damn" probably didn't register as a curse for him. He probably didn't even know he'd said it.

"What the hell are you talking about?" Judd demanded.

"Obstruction of justice, Mr. Nyman," Chief Phlug answered, producing a pair of handcuffs from his belt. "You want action. I'll give you action. Officer Jones, take him in."

Jones switched his gaze from Taj to Judd.

"Put your hands behind your back, Mr. Nyman," Officer Jones ordered Judd, grabbing the handcuffs from his boss.

"What—" Judd asked, really confused.

"No!" Orson shouted. "Chief Phlug, sir, that's my dad. He's gotta take care of me."

"Well, you'd better tell your father to treat the law with respect," the chief answered, more kindly than I expected.

"Dad, just chill, okay?" Orson whispered to his father.

"But, I don't—"

"Please, Dad," Orson begged. "Chill. For me."

Next to his son, Judd fell silent, his shoulders drooping. Orson had been right. Father and son were a team. Judd needed Orson.

Phlug watched Judd deflate and put his palm out for the handcuffs. Officer Jones was as quick handing them back to the chief as he had been grabbing them. I closed my eyes for a moment of thanks. But only a moment.

"Okay, folks," Phlug began, as if Judd had never spoken. "We are going to find the murderer. If you are the murderer, you might as well confess now. Because the courts will be easier on you if you do. If we have to figure out who you are the hard way, which we will, you'll pay. You understand me? This state still has the death penalty. And we *will* find you. We've got stuff at the lab right now. We'll get a match from one of you. And we're talking to people. If one of you is secretly connected to the doctor or her assistant, we'll know. It's only a matter of time. Come on. Someone make my life easier. Somebody talk to me."

No one answered him, though I could hear more than one person crying. But I was too mesmerized by the chief to look and see who.

"Fine," he hissed. "We're gonna have to do it the hard way. If anyone knows anything at all that pertains to these murders—"

"Sir," Bob Jinnah spoke up from behind him.

Bob, I thought instantaneously. Is Bob the murderer?

"Both cars are in the lot, sir." Bob said.

"What cars?" Phlug demanded irritably.

"Mr. and Mrs. Zweig's," Bob answered. "Neither of them has vacated the premises permanently. They are probably merely taking a walk."

"Right!" Phlug barked. "Well, if either or both of them 'merely' walks back in, you let me know, pronto."

"Absolutely," Bob promised.

Chief Phlug focused his gaze back on Taj Gemayel. "I want to talk to you," he said, his voice cold enough to freeze fire.

My stomach tightened. Was there a reason Phlug wanted to talk to Taj? Did he know something we didn't? Was Taj the one?

"I don't know anything," Taj tried, his dark features ashen.

"Fine," Chief Phlug told him. "You can tell me at the station all about what you *don't* know."

The two of them left together. Chief Phlug didn't even bother with handcuffs for Taj.

Officer Jones looked around at the rest of us and smiled his puppy-dog smile. Then he seemed to remember who he was supposed to be. He walked to the lobby entrance and stood with his arms crossed over his chest, frowning as well as he knew how.

"Is there anything we should be doing?" Raleigh asked quietly.

I looked over at Quinn, still on the couch, marble-white.

"Healing," I answered Raleigh. I reached out for his hand and squeezed it. "Starting with ourselves," I added.

Something like a shadow of Raleigh's former charming smile touched his face. "Yes," he said.

I walked over to the couch where Quinn was huddled. He looked up at me, his red-rimmed eyes widening with recognition.

"Cally," he whispered.

I put my hand on his shoulder. "I'm sorry," I told him. "Can I help you?"

Quinn didn't answer at first. His face was tight, as if he was working out a difficult mathematical analysis.

"Yes," he blurted out abruptly. "Yes, I need to talk to you. But I can't talk to you here. Come upstairs to our . . . my suite."

I thought for a moment. I had my cane in my hand. Was I afraid to be alone with Quinn? I thought of the murders. None of them had been one-on-one attacks. Quinn's suite was probably as safe as anywhere else. I took a breath and nodded my agreement.

But first, I had to clear the visit with Officer Jones.

Officer Jones was easy. After a lot of hemming and hawing and blushing, he finally agreed that Quinn and I could talk in private in his suite as long as we didn't leave the lodge.

"Leaving the lodge would really make Chief Phlug mad," he whispered.

"I promise I won't leave," I whispered back.

Officer Jones smiled.

And Quinn and I went upstairs to the suite that he had shared with Dr. Aurora Hart.

Quinn opened the door and gestured me into an earth-toned space that looked like a small living room. He didn't close the door behind him. I was glad. So, this was a suite. I assumed the other door opened onto the bedroom that Quinn and Dr. Aurora Hart had also shared, but I didn't ask. I looked around instead. A footbath sat conspicuously in front of a moss-colored easy chair. I remembered Dr. Hart talking about the appliance the first day of the intensive. She'd claimed a lot for her footbath, telling us that it not only warmed the water and vibrated, but that it had a special device that released *chi* into the water. She'd claimed it was better than a masseuse.

"Is that the doctor's famous footbath?" I asked Quinn with false cheer.

Quinn nodded. "You want to try it while we talk?" he offered, his voice rasping on the last word.

"That would be great. Thank you."

Quinn plugged the footbath into the wall and set a couple of dials.

"It takes a little while to warm up," he explained. His

voice cleared. "I set it the way Aurora liked. I never use it. Please, have a seat."

I sat down in the moss-colored chair and began to pull off my shoes and socks with one hand. I kept my other hand on my cane.

"Look, Cally," Quinn muttered, his eyes on the rug. He still hadn't taken a seat himself. His words speeded up and got louder, pouring from his mouth as the footbath began to bubble. "Aurora is gone. Even Sara is gone. I need to start over. No one can ever replace Aurora, but I want you to work with me. No, I don't just *want* you to work with me, I insist on it!"

TWENTY-THREE

I held one shoe and sock in my hand, my mouth gaping open.

"Quinn, I know you're hurting, but—"

"No, no. Just let me finish," Quinn broke in. His eyes were focused on something I couldn't see. His hands began to fly as fast as his words. "You're a real healer, Cally. You're sensitive. You're intuitive. You have ideals. And I'm sure you could teach others to do what you do. Wouldn't that be wonderful? Think of how much good you could do if you taught others. Take the amount of good you do by your work and multiply it by hundreds, thousands—"

"Quinn, I don't think I can teach what I do," I put in as mildly as possible. I lay my sock and shoe by the footbath and started on my other foot. "It's individual to me. People all intuit in different ways—"

"See!" he burst out. "That's what I mean! 'People intuit in different ways.' That could be one of your hooks. Everyone likes to think they're special. You're already good at making emotional connections with people. Just imagine connecting with a whole audience of people."

I shuddered. Like most people, audiences didn't excite me, not in a good way.

"I'm not a public speaker," I stated for the record.

"Not yet, Cally," Quinn conceded. "But neither was Aurora at first. I can teach you. That's what I'm good at. Managing special people like you. You're for real, Cally. You could be a star in the healing business."

"No," I objected, shaking my head. "Stars are for the movies. Healing is a deeply personal experience. It can't be mass-marketed."

"See! I love it. 'Healing is a deeply personal experience.' Cally, you need to be writing. You have ideas. You could write. You could teach. You could make yourself a movement."

"I could use the footbath," I told him, changing the subject. "Do you think it's ready?"

"Forget the footbath, Cally," Quinn ordered. "Think about what I'm saying. I have a skill for management, for promotion. But I'm not a healer myself. You are. We'd be a team. I could do the parts you don't want to."

"Oh, Quinn," I whispered sadly. "I know you're alone now. So you think I'm your answer. But I'm not. There are other healers in the field who have charisma. Those are the people you should think of working with. People who'd rather talk to an audience than work one on one, practitioner to client. Taj is like that. Lots of people must be. You could find someone the way Aurora found us."

"Cally, are you sure you don't want to work with me?" Quinn asked, tears in his voice. I couldn't look up into his face. "Won't you think it over?"

"I'll think it over if you'll sit down and let me work on you," I replied reluctantly. "But I'm afraid my answer is always going to be no. You credit me for my intuition. And my intuition tells me your path isn't my path."

"Wait a second," Quinn said, holding up his hand. "I wrote down some notes. They're in the other room. How does *The Aura Commitment* sound to you?"

Before I could tell Quinn that I wanted nothing to do

with anything called "The Aura Commitment," he'd made his way to the adjoining room and opened the door. No wonder Quinn and Aurora had been compatible. For all of his tearful sensitivity, there was a ruthlessness about Quinn I hadn't sensed before. He didn't want a healing. I decided I'd enjoy a footbath, listen a little longer, and leave.

I bent down over the swirling waters of the bath. I raised my foot. I could test it with my toe. I didn't want to think about Quinn anymore. How was I going to convince him that he was going to have to live without Aurora, Sara, *and* me?

"No!" a voice shouted. I pulled my foot back, looking up at the same time, expecting to see Quinn. But I saw Kim Welch instead, standing less than a yard away from me. I hadn't heard her come in.

"The footbath is broken," Kim told me. Her voice was shaking. "The doctor asked me to fix it before she died."

"It isn't broken," Quinn objected, back in the room with his notebook in hand. "What are you talking about? Aurora never said anything about you fixing her footbath."

Kim walked to the wall and unplugged the appliance in question.

"What are you doing here anyway?" Quinn asked her. "Did you want to talk to me?"

"I . . . I thought you both could use some work," Kim tried, walking back my way.

Quinn shook his head. He trotted over and plugged the footbath in again, then turned away from the wall.

"Did the chief ask to see me?" he demanded, his face tightening.

"No, the chief wasn't in the lobby when I came up here," Kim answered. "I was just feeling useless, and I thought maybe giving one of you a session might help. Cally said it was a time for healing."

"Thank you, Kim," I offered. "But I just need to relax. The footbath is fine for me—"

"No, please don't use it, Cally," Kim begged. Her face was pale white again, her large eyes filled to the brim with tears. And I was beginning to wonder—

"But why do you care if Cally uses the footbath?" Quinn wanted to know. His voice rose shrilly. "What business is it of yours? Aurora wouldn't mind. Cally and I are having a conversation."

"Quinn, please unplug the footbath," I requested slowly. I stood up, moving to the far side of the appliance, keeping my eyes on the psychiatrist, my hand on my cane.

I heard Quinn pull the plug, muttering. The sound of swirling water ceased abruptly.

Kim seemed to deflate as the sound ceased, her shoulders collapsing inward. Was that relief? Or defeat?

"Kim?" I whispered.

"I only did it because of my brother's suicide," she whispered back. Tears rolled from her eyes. "Dr. Hart did it."

"You mean Dr. Hart killed herself?" I asked, confused again, just when I thought I understood. "But what about Sara Oshima?"

"Oh, Sara," Kim moaned. "I tried to get back to the car, but the police were there every time I was. I didn't mean for Sara—"

"What *are* you talking about?" Quinn snapped.

"And I couldn't get back to fix the footbath either," Kim went on, undeterred. "I rigged the aura maker, the car, and the footbath. It was easy. I've done electrical repairs since I was a kid at my parents' shop. And Dr. Hart didn't keep anything locked. Not her room, the meeting room, or her car. It was so easy to get in. But after she died, everything was locked. I didn't really know which one would get her, you see? So I rigged them all. But I couldn't get back to the ones that hadn't gone off. I didn't think of other people."

"Wait, are you—" Quinn began, confusion in his voice.

Kim slammed a fist into her palm. "It was like I was in a

dream. I only thought about Dr. Hart and me. I forgot about everyone else. Except for my brother."

Kim's face went blank. It was as if her spirit had left her body. Suddenly, I realized that Kim hadn't been in her body most of the time we'd been together. Every time she came back into her body, she cried.

"Your brother?" I prompted her.

"Dr. Hart announced that he was gay right in front of everyone," Kim began slowly. Her eyes focused and teared up once more. "Gay wasn't okay for my brother. My brother was a minister. He had a wife, children. He was trying to find a way to deal with his sexual preference without letting anyone know, and she just blurted it out in front of everyone. He called me, then shot himself that night. She killed him, don't you see? She killed my brother. It wasn't right. So I decided to make sure she didn't kill anyone else—"

"You?" Quinn yelped, finally understanding her. "You killed Aurora!" he screamed. He ran at Kim, hands outstretched.

"No!" I ordered, clasping my cane for backup. "No, Quinn. No more violence."

Quinn stopped a few feet before he reached Kim. He looked around, his eyes wild.

"Please, Quinn," I said softly. "Sit down. Nothing is going to bring Aurora back. Nothing."

Quinn collapsed into the chair I'd been sitting in and burst into angry sobs. I looked back up. Did Kim see him? I didn't think so. She was still looking at me as if Quinn didn't exist. Maybe he couldn't exist in her universe anymore. There would be too much to face if he did.

"I tried to tell you the truth yesterday when we were searching for Craig," Kim explained. "No one thought it was me because I use my married name from my ex-husband. No one connected me to my brother, the man Dr.

Hart killed. I should have forgiven her, but I didn't. I didn't even think of forgiveness. My way seemed so clear. Especially when a friend of mine was invited to the intensive and couldn't participate. It was easy to get him to suggest that I replace him. It seemed so right. But I didn't think about what came next. I just wanted that woman out of the world so she couldn't hurt people anymore."

"Cally!" I heard my name hissed in the pause. Quinn was still sobbing.

I looked over Kim's head and saw Roy in the doorway. But Kim was starting to speak again.

"And now, I've hurt people, killed them. I can't let anyone else take the blame. I'm just so afraid. I was a victim; now I'm a victimizer. That's worse than anything anyone can do to me, that knowledge."

"Chief Phlug's on his way up," Roy whispered my way. Kim didn't hear him.

"Can you help me, Cally?" she asked. "I was going to kill myself, but I can't. I killed Dr. Hart, and I can't kill myself." Tears flooded her eyes again. "Help me. Please, help me."

In two long strides, I stood directly in front of her.

"I'll do everything I can," I told her honestly. "I think the chief will let me stay when he talks to you. At least for a while. And hold this to your heart. For all the mistakes of the past, you're doing the right thing now."

"Am I?" she asked, her voice as soft as a sigh.

"You saved my life," I reminded her.

I let my cane drop to the floor, put my arms around Kim Welch, and held her close as I listened for Chief Phlug's footsteps.

TWENTY-FOUR

"So Kim saved my life," I was winding up. I took a sip of hot, apple spice tea, trying to warm my chilled bones. "And I'll always be grateful."

"But—" a number of people began.

Those of us left from the Chakra Commitment Intensive were gathered that final Thursday in the cool lobby of the Swanton Hills Lodge. Except for Craig Zweig. He and his wife had gone missing again. Still, Kapp, Geneva, York, Melinda, and Roy had joined the group. And we *weren't* having a morning session. Life was good. We were standing around eating all the tasty offerings of the Jinnahs and rehashing the events of the day before.

"But, she's a murderer!" Taj insisted, looking tall, dark, and handsome again in his tight black jeans. He stomped his foot. "How can you defend her?"

Heidi Jinnah brought out a tray of stuffed mushrooms and disappeared behind the desk again. I hadn't seen Bob since he'd brought in the sparkling grape juice. I bit into a raspberry tartlet. Oh, that was good. Not even all the "buts" could spoil it for me.

"Taj," Dotty reprimanded gently, her round, freckled face earnest. "Kim's not an evil monster. She let her feelings sweep her away. And she had some good reasons. But she didn't let Cally die. She could have, but she didn't."

I felt warmer after Dotty spoke, warmed by the touch of her view of Kim. Her truth was a truth I could share. I moved closer to Roy, leaning into him.

Judd snorted in disgust. "I don't understand how you women can be so softheaded. Kim Welch is a murderer, and she's manipulating you, manipulating the system to get sympathy. It wouldn't work with me. She's responsible for two murders."

"Responsibility is a good word," Ed Lau offered thoughtfully. He improved his already impeccable posture ever so slightly with a deep breath. "In fact, it is an exact description of Kim's attitude. She's taken responsibility for her actions, no matter how terrible. Excuse me Quinn, but Dr. Hart was not as responsible with her own healing. She did harm. Kim did a greater harm. But, in the end, we all have to learn to forgive." He paused and muttered. "We must even forgive ourselves sometimes."

Quinn nodded, pale but composed.

"Kim talked to me about her brother," Dotty put in. "She was in a state of total despair over his death. But she kept shutting herself down." Dotty sighed. "I didn't know about the suit her brother's wife had filed against Dr. Hart. I didn't know there were any suits."

"And I did," I admitted. "I knew about the suicide suits, thanks to my friend, Kapp. But when Kim talked about her brother's death, I never thought to connect the two things up."

I felt a smear of guilt obscure the good day. Ed cleared his throat and spoke again.

"Kim was not grounded," he stated.

"Yeah," Raleigh agreed, his resonant voice making two syllables out of the word. "She was in some kind of fugue state. I felt it. And she never wanted to be touched or healed. She only wanted to work on other people."

I nodded, remembering the aura I'd seen, not of her body but around it. Of course, she didn't want anyone working on her. They might see her state.

"She was really out of it after Sara Oshima died," Orson put in. "Her metabolic cascades were, like, totally messed up."

"But she isn't the right temperament!" Judd burst out. He reached up his hands as if trying to grasp Kim's illusion. "She's a wimp."

"Uh-uh," Fran disagreed, through a mouthful of mushroom. Her black hair was glossy again, and her eyes shone. "She's strong in her beliefs. I'm telling you, I'm that way myself sometimes. There's just right and wrong, and nothing in between. Dr. Hart fell into the 'bad' bin for Kim, and that was it. No, Kim isn't a wimp."

"But how could she actually do it?" Taj pressed.

"Did Cally tell you about Kim's electrical background?" Kapp jumped in.

I hadn't. So Kapp it did for me.

"Kim Welch's parents owned an electrical repair shop. Kim worked there after school until she went to college, then still helped out in the summer. Lazar here, you know, Cally, thought Kim must have been a receptionist. Hah! Lazar was caught by her own sexism."

"Hah, yourself," I retorted. I lifted my cane for emphasis. Kapp stepped back and grabbed Geneva's arm. I offered him a smile. Somehow his criticism had cheered me up. "Kapp's right. I just couldn't imagine Kim doing electrical work, even after the police chased her away from Dr. Hart's car. She seemed so helpless."

"After electrical, I guess ordnance is easy," Orson mused. "She actually figured out how to blow up a car."

"Let me tell you," Kapp offered, "she could have learned about bombs from a book. Or the Internet, for that matter."

"Well, the really weird thing, looking back," Fran declared, "was that Kim was acting like she was in shock *be-fore* the doctor was killed. She was hardly in her body at all from the first day on. And when she was, she was crying. It might have gotten a little worse after the doctor died, but not much. Not until Sara died."

Quinn spoke up.

"Dr. Hart accepted Kim Welch as a substitute for another psychiatrist she'd chosen," he said. His voice was stronger than I'd expected. "And Kim told us she did energy work. It seemed like a good fit."

There was an awkward silence. But Kapp broke it.

"The police really would have figured it out sooner or later," he told us. Geneva nodded beside him, a goofy smile on her face. "They were broadening their search for those affected by the suicides. Let me tell you, those guys have computer databases you wouldn't believe."

The lobby door opened before Kapp could really get into lecture mode, and Craig and Carlotta Zweig appeared. Craig looked like he had at the very start of the intensive: shaved, his hair neatly combed and maybe even trimmed. He peered our way and grinned diffidently.

"Craig and I wanted to say good-bye before we took off," Carlotta informed us.

"Carlotty has a lot of work for me to do," Craig piped up. "I gotta fix some doors, and clear the yard, and move around a bunch of file cabinets." Carlotta reached up to stroke his hair. They looked like newlyweds. I felt the warmth of goodness again. Craig was going to be all right. Carlotta would keep him busy . . . and loved.

"Bye!" they sang out together and exited the lobby before anyone had a chance to respond.

"I thought it was him," Judd complained once the lobby door had swung shut.

"So did I," Raleigh admitted. He smiled his old sweet smile, but my heart didn't melt down this time. "I called the police after he attacked Cally."

"That was you?" I asked.

"Yeah. Dumb, huh? But I was really afraid for you, for all of us."

"Not dumb," Ed Lau whispered. "Responsible."

"I thought it was Sara," Quinn confessed. He looked at the floor. "I was sure of it. And I was wrong. Sara had a discipline problem in nursing school. That's why she dropped out. Dr. Hart tried to guide and support her, but the healing atmosphere didn't seem to help. Sara just got worse. Angry, mean, paranoid. I thought she'd killed Aurora. And when the car blew up, I thought she'd killed herself. Ira had deserted her. I was the only friend she had left. And she hated me." He shrugged. "That's why I was so surprised it was Kim. I actually didn't believe what I was hearing at first. I'd already made up my mind."

"Well, I thought it was you," Taj threw in, looking at Quinn. "I thought you killed the doctor in a fit of jealousy because she made a pass at me."

Quinn actually smiled, his eyes out of focus as he brought his head up. "Aurora did that to tweak me, all that flirting. Then we'd laugh together."

"I figured that out," Taj told him hastily.

I wasn't so sure Taj had figured anything out. He wanted something from Quinn—

"Taj and I are going into business together," Quinn announced, and I knew what it was that Taj wanted. Quinn's eyes refocused. "The Past-Life Commitment. Private work, lectures, seminars, books."

"Is that such a good idea, kid?" Fran challenged him.

Quinn whipped his head around to look at her.

"Why?" he demanded. "What's wrong with it?"

"Hey, I know Taj is good at the past-life stuff," Fran backpedaled. "But what about the emotional issues he raises? Aren't you just doing . . ." Fran faltered.

What Dr. Hart did, I finished mentally, pulling up issues

and then leaving the client dangling with all the baggage those issues entailed.

"No," Quinn explained "I won't make that mistake again. We've got a qualified energetic practitioner who's willing to work with us. I met her on our East Coast tour. But Taj will be the star." He smirked at me as if to say, "This could have been yours."

I smiled back at Quinn, so glad it *wasn't* mine.

"Well, congratulations," Kapp offered. He smiled his own shark's smile. "Hey, did you guys hear that Dr. Hart's missing son has been found?"

"What?" voices muttered, including my own. He hadn't told me!

"Dr. Hart had a son, a son she left most of her estate to. A private eye found the guy. He was living in Michigan, of all unholy places. He was working as a dental hygienist. He had no idea who his mother was. Now, presto, he's a multimillionaire."

I bowed slightly in Kapp's direction. He bowed back. He'd seen the look Quinn had given me and guessed its meaning. He was tweaking Quinn on my behalf. At least he was gentle about it.

"Geneva's forgiven Kapp," my brother York whispered in my ear as I finished my bow. "She was giving him a hard time because he put you in danger, but now they've made up." I had mixed emotions about my sister and my friend, but this was a good day. I'd be happy for them.

"Well, I thought it was Taj," Dotty came clean.

"Me!" Taj yelped.

"You," she told him, smiling to take away the sting. "You or Judd."

Ed Lau laughed deeply.

"I, too, thought it was Judd," he admitted.

"Where'd you get that idea?" Fran objected as Orson simultaneously defended his father. "My dad would never do anything so gross!"

"Oh, I see Judd's innocent nature now," Ed explained. "I saw it by the way he spoke to Chief Phlug. He's not shrewd enough to manipulate anything this complex."

"Hey, hey!" Judd objected. "I could be shrewd if I wanted to."

Ed laughed again. I laughed with him. Judd was too cute.

The lobby doors opened again. And there, as if summoned, was Chief Phlug with Sergeant DiMarco beside him.

Taj and Judd stiffened into statues.

"Hiya, folks," Phlug greeted us, as he walked our way. "Just wanted to let you all know what's going on."

Phlug was a different man than he had been in the lobby the day before. He wasn't angry anymore. I remembered the amazing gentleness with which he'd questioned Kim Welch, allowing me to stay with her until they finally left to go to the station. He had his murderer. He was happy.

"Kim Welch has an attorney," he told us. "She's still telling the truth though." The chief shot a glance at Kapp, who opened his mouth to object to the attorney slur and shut it again, wisely. "She admits to both murders. And I truly believe she was pushed over the edge. I won't block an insanity plea if she enters it. I just thought you folks might want to know."

"Thank you—" I began sincerely.

But Bob Jinnah appeared from the back before I could make a speech out of my words.

"Did you enjoy it?" he asked Chief Phlug.

Phlug's face reddened. "Another time," he hissed.

"But, Chief," Sergeant DiMarco insisted, grinning. "Bob lent you the book. He's got a right to know how you felt about it."

Chief Phlug shot her a look and turned back to Bob.

"Nice poems," he muttered.

"Ah, I knew you would enjoy Blake," Bob said, reaching out to shake the chief's hand. "He was a true visionary. Poet, artist—"

"Yeah, great," Chief Phlug cut in, dropping Bob's hand. "We'll talk later."

The chief and Sergeant DiMarco turned and left the lobby.

Most of us were either giggling or chuckling or downright laughing by the time the doors closed behind them. Bob looked confused though.

"Humor?" he asked.

"Yes, humor," Dotty answered kindly.

"Ah," he murmured, clasping his hands together. "Humor. Delightful." He ambled back behind the front desk.

I knew a good exit line when I heard it.

So I took Roy's hand, and we went to search for that perfect duck-filled lake to host our own private picnic.

The mystery series with great karma
by
Claire Daniels

Body of Intuition

Alternative healer Cally Lazar's sensory skills help her soothe her clients' auras. But once in a while, what she finds will make her jump out of her skin.

0-425-18740-3

Strangled Intuition

When a party ends with one of Cally's massage clients strangled with her own necklace, the police suspect the woman's husband. But one look at his aura and Cally knows he's no killer.

0-425-19463-9

"A HOLISTIC PRESCRIPTION FOR FUN.
ENJOYABLE SIDE EFFECTS INCLUDE LAUGHTER."
—LYNNE MURRAY,
MYSTERY READERS JOURNAL

Available wherever books are sold or at
www.penguin.com